POSSESSION

POSSESSION

A MEMPHIS MAGIC NOVEL

ANDREA HAGAN

Library of Congress Control Number: 2022905614

Digital ISBN: 978-0-9994116-2-9
Tradepaper ISBN: 978-0-9994116-3-6

To anyone who's ever been possessed by a thought and couldn't let it go. This book is for you.

Except my mom. Who's probably rolling over in her grave at the very thought of this book. Sorry Mom.

CHAPTER 1

Most folks don't believe in magic. Lucky for us witches. I've been able to fly under the radar the entire twenty-four years of my life. Not on a broom, though—as far as I know that's a myth.

Magic means something different to each witch. For me, magic is tarot cards and cooking in the kitchen with my grandma.

As for where magic originated, well, that also depends on whom you ask. Some claim fallen angels taught herbal magic and charms to their mortal wives, who then taught their children, and so forth and so on. Others believe that the Goddess Lilith gifted us the craft. The rest say our divine power flows from Mother Earth. Regardless of the origin, the most knowledgeable witch I know is wearing a hot-pink T-shirt that says *Slut for Slots* and a picture of a slot machine with three cherries in a row.

"*Bermuda Love Triangle*, seven tonight!" Grandma announces as I join her in the break room of our metaphysical shop Memphis Magic. The best way to describe our shop would be a mullet hairstyle—business in the front, party in the back. Crystals, herbs, books, charms, candles, and various essential oils in the front. Mediumship and séances, tarot cards, past life regression therapy, spell ingredients, and our personal library in the back.

"It's the finale. I'm rooting for Vince, but I think the producers are really pushing for Zach. Uhh, don't get me started on Zach, that phony. It's obvious he doesn't give a flip about Brittany and is just angling for more camera time." My grandma is a lively sixty-four-year-old with salt-and-pepper hair cut pixie short. She's a few inches shorter than I am at five feet, six inches tall and thin as a rail. She has a natural face and an unnatural obsession with reality television.

"Grandma, why do you love that show?" I ask. "It's beyond disgusting watching those people swap bodily fluids. And of course Zach wants more camera time. They all want more camera time, otherwise they wouldn't be 'dating' on television."

"Sweetie, you know in a past life Mama was a voyeur. Watching reality TV is a socially acceptable way to go about it," Aunt Callie tells me as she pours boiling water over sprigs of freshly cut lemon balm. The citrusy aroma fills the room.

"Listen to the expert," Grandma says. My aunt is the shop's certified past life regression therapist. She helps her clients re-member the details of past lives so they can work through those old issues. Grandma volunteered as Aunt Callie's practice case during her training. Who knows, maybe Grandma really was a voyeur in a past life. Although I don't think she got to the second part of the therapy, the whole "working through those old issues" part. If anything, Grandma just uses her "I'm a past life voyeur" excuse as a license to ignore healthy boundaries in this life.

"She may be the expert, but she's still not poking around in my head," I point to my aunt. "Why go looking for trouble in the past when there's plenty of trouble in the present to go around?"

"Aubry, that's where you're wrong," she says, using a box cutter to open a new shipment of crystals. Aunt Callie's also our crystal expert and is dressed exactly how you'd imagine a crystal expert would be—in a gauzy skirt, flowing blouse, and crystal bracelets and necklaces. In her forties, Aunt Callie is a beautiful woman. She has long strawberry-blonde hair, amber eyes, and a golden skin tone. Men of all ages stop and take a second look when she walks by, and let's just say they aren't looking at all those crystals. "The karma we've accumulated in past lives can influence the choices we make in this one," she tells me for the umpteenth time.

Maybe she's right, but I also let her talk me into joining her on a two-week juice cleanse. I lasted two days. Regardless of the sins I may have committed in a previous life, no one deserves the torture of drinking kale juice for fourteen days. No one. Hangry is an actual thing. "Well, I'm going to influence your choice and remind you that if you unpack those crystals, then you have to inventory them into the system."

She stops unpacking the box. "I'll wait on cleansing these."

I figured as much. Aunt Callie isn't into details. Grandma is into details, just not *financial* details. And that is just one of many reasons why I run the business end of Memphis Magic. "I'll take care of it tomorrow. I'm going to head out a little early this evening."

"Where are you off to, sugar pie?" Grandma asks.

"I'm meeting someone."

"If you tell me you're back with Todd…" Grandma doesn't finish that threat because she knows it's an empty one.

"I'm not back with Todd. I'm meeting a nice guy named Brad Cunningham. He just started working at our accounting firm."

I stopped by the other day to drop off some signed documents, and Brad introduced himself. We hit it off and he asked me out on a date. It's been a few months since my breakup with Todd, and I'm ready to get back out there.

"An accountant? How boring," Grandma announces.

"Thank you. Your opinion has been noted."

"Is that what you're wearing?" She eyes my floral skater dress, rain jacket, and sneakers. "Not a very sexy look."

"We're meeting at a coffee shop. What would you have me wear? A bodycon dress and stripper heels?" I'm not sure why I asked that question, as I already know her answer would be a resounding "yes."

Grandma starts to say something, but Aunt Callie interrupts her. "Have fun, sweetie."

"Thank you. I won't be out late."

"No, I can't imagine you would be," Grandma calls after me.

I make the short drive to the coffee shop and snag a great parking spot right out front. Good thing, because the bottom of the sky falls out. Feeding the meter, I make a mad dash for the door.

I close my umbrella and step inside, spotting Brad. He stands and waves me over. "Aubry, so nice to see you."

"You too." Brad surprises me by coming in for a hug. We haven't reached hugging status yet, so I turn my body to do a half-hug. I take a seat across from him.

"You look great," he tells me.

"Thanks," I say as I take off my rain jacket. "So do you." Brad's a good-looking twenty-six-year-old. He's a few inches taller than I am and has a lean frame, dark brown hair, and brown eyes. His khaki pants and zippered sweater layered over his dress shirt and tie scream accountant.

"Here, let me take that for you," he says, reaching over and taking my jacket, draping it across the empty chair beside him.

"Thank you. You know, I've never been to this coffee shop," I comment.

"I thought it would be a good meeting place. It's close to both my office and your shop."

I nod. "How was work?"

"It's the beginning of tax season, so things will be hectic for me for the next few months. Oh, and really good news—I've been assigned to your account. We need to implement a more aggressive strategy for Memphis Magic." He then eagerly tells me all about write-offs and my eyes glaze over.

"That all sounds promising. Shall we order?" I change the subject. I'm going to keep an open mind and not write off this guy just yet, pun intended.

"After you." We stand and walk to the counter. I take a look at the menu and decide on a Mexican hot chocolate. Brad goes with a decaf coffee.

"You don't like coffee? I should have picked something else," Brad leans in to tell me.

"No, this is perfect. I'm just not a coffee fiend." Although I could probably use the caffeine. I'm starting to get a little headache.

"Me neither," he's quick to answer. He insists on paying, and I thank him as we walk back to our table. Points for him for leaving a nice but not over-the-top, trying-to-impress-me tip in the barista's jar.

"So tell me something about yourself. Are you from Memphis?" I ask, giving my temples a quick rub.

"No, I'm from Knoxville, but I transferred here with my firm about a year ago. It was a better career opportunity for me here."

"How do you like Memphis?" I ask.

"So far so good. How about you? Where are you from?"

"Born and raised here."

A barista delivers our drinks, and I give my hot chocolate a stir and take a sip. The sugar does help somewhat, but I don't know…I'm still feeling out of sorts.

"I have to say, you're the only witch I've ever met," he tells me as he sips his coffee.

"I bet you've met witches before and just didn't know it." It's true that some witches broadcast the fact with their style, but I'm not one of those witches.

"None as beautiful as you," he says as he reaches over the table and touches my hand.

I pull my hand back and take another sip of my hot chocolate. We're likewise not at hand holding status yet. I give my temples another rub. My headache has upgraded from dull to throbbing; suddenly, I feel exhausted. "Brad, I'm so sorry, but I need to go. I think I'm coming down with something."

"I hate to hear that. Do you need me to drive you home?"

"No, I'm okay to drive."

"Hopefully it's not the flu. There's a nasty strain going around my office."

"I hope not, either. Again, I'm really sorry."

"Don't apologize," he says as we stand, handing me my jacket.

I drive home and unlock the apartment door. "That good, huh?" Grandma calls after me as I walk to my room and go straight to bed.

CHAPTER 2

"Sugar pie, you feeling better?" Grandma asks the next morning. My aunt just finished leading me through a healing guided visualization, and now I'm sipping on a disgusting "immunity boosting" smoothie. It wasn't green, so I thought I'd give it a shot. Lesson learned.

"We could cancel our trip if you need us to," my aunt adds.

"There's no need to do that. I'm feeling much better. I think it was some kind of twenty-four-hour bug."

"That, or you were bored to death," Grandma suggests.

"Ignore her," my aunt says. "I've forwarded you our hotel information and schedule for the trade show. If everything goes as planned, we'll be back next Friday." I went with Grandma last year to the annual metaphysical trade show held in Tunica and said never again. That's because she asked the nice massage therapist and Reiki master giving me a chair massage if he ever gets requests for happy endings.

She then proceeded to inquire as to the specifics of happy endings, despite the fact that he told her no. In fact, he had never been asked that question in his twenty years of professional experience, emphasis on *professional*. She then informed him that he was awfully touchy for someone in his line of work, emphasis on *touchy*.

"Will you have time to hit the slots?" I ask Grandma. She unapologetically smokes Pall Malls and likes to head over to Tunica on a regular basis, hence her love of gaudy T-shirts. The one she's wearing today has a picture of a crown and says *Queen of the Slot Machine.*

"Why? Am I throwing off a lucky vibe?" she asks me with excitement. I occasionally receive psychic premonitions. I once told Grandma I thought she was going to have good luck come to her that day, so she hightailed it over to Tunica. By the time she included the gas expense, she might have broken even. But I guess in the gambling world, that's considered a win.

"Sorry." I shake my head.

"Dang it. And I'm rooming with *this* buzzkill, so I won't be getting lucky in another department, if you catch my drift," Grandma dramatically stage whispers while pointing to my aunt.

Aunt Callie sighs and says, "A couple more things before we take off. I already rescheduled the séance that was set for this afternoon. Also, keep an eye out for a FedEx package, and call Amelia when you get it. She's been hounding me for the past week, threatening to hex me if she doesn't get her red candles and ague root to hex her 'neighbor from hell' Florence."

"Wouldn't she have a hard time hexing you if she doesn't have what she needs to hex Florence in the first place?" I point out. Florence Ingram and Amelia Hayes are both witches in our circle. I don't condone or support dark magic. What you put out there in the world always comes back to you. But I'm not too worried about this latest threat, seeing how Amelia and Florence have been threatening to hex each other for years.

"Good point, but still call her. You know how Amelia gets her granny panties in a twist," Grandma adds. Vivian Brooks would never be caught dead in granny panties. I know, as she left her unmentionables in the dryer the other day. I pulled out a pair of boy shorts that said on the backside *The witch is back!* and a thong that said on the front in gold cursive *I cast a spell on you.* Some things can't be unseen.

"Alright, Mama, let's hit the road," Aunt Callie says. A true southern goodbye can take upward of thirty minutes or more, as multiple rounds of hugs and last-minute details must be exchanged.

I flip over the open for business sign. And on this dreary spring day, I don't expect much business. Rain is wonderful for Grandma's rooftop herb garden, but not so wonderful for our bottom line. I shake my head, as that sounded way too much like Brad. He texted me earlier this morning and asked how I was feeling. I told him I was much better and apologized again for having to bail. He asked me out to dinner this weekend and I said yes. It's only fair I give the guy one more chance.

I dust the shelves and neatly line up all the essential oils. Next, I unpack the new shipment of crystals and add them into our system. Aunt Callie would want her crystal babies in the sunshine to give them a proper cleansing, but the weather isn't in a cooperative kind of mood. Instead, I light a sage bundle and give them a quick cleanse.

I'm waving the smoke around a pale yellow-colored citrine pillar when suddenly my line of sight vanishes. For a split second,

I see an image of myself holding a séance and then I'm back to holding a sage bundle.

Okay, that was weird. I am not a medium and I don't lead séances. Sure, I've participated in enough of them with Grandma to know the mechanics, but actually leading one and channeling a spirit is above my magical pay grade. "Universe, I think you sent that message to the wrong clairvoyant."

It's a painfully slow morning. I ring up a grand total of one customer. I think about hanging up the closed sign and walking upstairs to the apartment and binge-watching a show in bed. Instead, I settle for the corner reading nook, plopping down on a well-loved bean bag. Bad idea, as I catch myself nodding off on more than one occasion.

My phone chimes, and I jerk awake. It's Julia Stafford, my friend and the newest member of our circle.

> **JULIA:** I'm gonna grab Thai, want me to bring you back something?

> **ME:** Red chicken curry number 2. You're awesome!

> **JULIA:** I know.

It's not long before the door chimes, and in hurries Julia carrying two takeout bags. "I'm glad you braved this mess. I would have wound up eating a soggy peanut butter sandwich alone in the break room."

She drops her umbrella and takes off her soaked windbreaker and hangs it on a hook behind the counter. "I could do without the rain. I've already had two cancellations and a no-show this morning." Julia owns a salon three buildings down from Memphis Magic and what many would think of when they imagine a modern-day witch. She's in her thirties with jet-black hair cut in an asymmetrical bob that I could never pull off in a million years, black nails, tattoo sleeves, and a nose ring.

She eyes my hair. "You need a trim."

"Are you saying that in your professional opinion, or are you saying that because you need to fill a canceled spot?" It has been a while since my last haircut. I grab a strand of my long golden-brown hair and examine the ends. Okay, so it's been more than a while.

"Both," she replies. I lead her to the break room, and we have a seat at the table. "Did you watch the finale of *Bermuda Love Triangle* last night?" Julia hands me my takeout container and opens her bag of spring rolls, taking a bite.

"Thank you and no. I'm apparently the only sane woman in America that doesn't watch that show," I say between bites of curry. "Although Grandma has informed me that Zach is a camera whore."

"Hey, it's my guilty pleasure. Well, one of my many guilty pleasures." I don't need to hear the details of her other guilty pleasures. Grandma, on the other hand, wouldn't miss an opportunity to hear all about the goings-on in Julia's "hobby room." Julia is a Domme in the BDSM world. That's all I really know about the subject. Honestly, that's more than I ever wanted to know about the subject.

We finish lunch and head back to the front of the shop. "I'm going to grab some peppermint oil," she tells me.

"A trade for lunch and saving me from a rainy day of boredom." I walk over to the shelf and hand her the little bottle, and she puts it in her messenger bag. "Hey, do you think the Universe ever sends a person a message that was meant for someone else?"

"Like a text message sent to the wrong number?"

"Exactly."

She considers a moment. "No. Even if the text is sent to the wrong person, it's still the right person."

"Ugh, that's a very guru non-answer answer."

She shrugs unapologetically and makes me promise to call her shop and set up my hair appointment.

CHAPTER 3

The rain continues throughout the afternoon, and I decide to call time. I'm in the process of flipping over the closed sign when I spot two middle-aged women making a mad dash for the door. I hold it open for them as they enter the shop. "Welcome to Memphis Magic. I'm Aubry. Is there anything I can help you ladies with today?" I ask as they close their umbrellas and wipe their wet shoes on the welcome mat.

"Hello. I'm Debbie Baker," a rather robust woman in her late-forties says. "This is my friend Nancy." She nods to her friend. "We have an appointment with Vivian." Oh no. This was the séance that Aunt Callie said she had rescheduled.

"Ladies, I'm terribly sorry for the mix-up, but did you have a chance to check your voicemail? My grandma had to go out of town, so the séance will unfortunately have to be rescheduled. But I would be happy to give you a tarot card reading since you braved this downpour," I offer. "On the house."

Debbie shakes her head and then bursts into tears. "You don't understand," she says between sobs. "My daughter Charlotte is missing. I don't know what else to do."

Nancy pats Debbie's hand and turns to me. "This isn't like Charlotte. She calls and checks in with her mama every day. We've been to the police and filed a missing person's report, but they didn't seem concerned."

"Why don't we sit down?" I lead them to the reading nook, and the ladies take a seat on the couch. "Can I get you some herbal tea?"

Debbie pulls out a handkerchief from her oversized pocketbook. "No, thank you, dear."

"When was the last time you spoke with your daughter?" I ask.

"Two days ago. Charlotte called me between classes. She's a senior at the University of Memphis. She's in the pre-medicine program and is very serious about her studies. She graduates in May and then starts Harvard medical school in the fall," she says proudly. "I'm the one who tells her to get out of the library and go have a little fun." She tears up again and dabs her eyes. "My daughter listened to me and went out with friends to a bar, and that's the last anyone saw her."

"Have you spoken to her friends?"

"I talked to her roommate, Jen. Charlotte didn't show up to class yesterday, and Jen knew that something was wrong and called me. We've spoken to Charlotte's professors and her friends. They're all worried. Charlotte never misses class. Ever."

"Was your daughter seeing someone?"

"No, Charlotte doesn't have a boyfriend. School always comes first."

"What about someone from the bar? Have you been there yet to see if any of the employees remember Charlotte? Maybe they saw her leave with someone." I hate to be the one to break it to Debbie, but her daughter may have simply hooked up with someone and blew off class.

"I've been to the bar, but no one was helpful."

"I'm so sorry about your daughter, but perhaps it's best to give the police more time to do their investigation," I gently suggest.

"They wouldn't even take my report because it hasn't been seventy-two hours since she's been missing," Debbie says. "There is no investigation!" She looks at me with pain in her eyes. Holding up her phone, she shows me a picture. Charlotte looks around my age, with black hair cut into a short bob, honeyed-colored skin much darker than her mother's, and glasses framing her pretty face. "I want to contact my mother, Opal Baker. She and Charlotte were very close. Maybe she could help me find my daughter."

I can't believe I'm even considering this. I would have already sent them on their way but for that premonition I received this morning. I've never had one turn out to be wrong.

"Okay, we will *try* to contact Charlotte's grandmother. But you must understand that mediumship isn't my gift. And I certainly can't guarantee how this will go, or if we'll even make contact with Opal. And even if we do make contact, she likely doesn't have any knowledge of Charlotte's whereabouts." A big misconception is that the departed hold all the answers. I've attended enough séances to know that simply isn't the case.

"There's no harm in trying," Debbie says hopefully.

"You ladies sit tight while I prepare our room. Do you have a picture of your mother or an object that belonged to her, by chance?" She pulls out a picture from her wallet and hands it to me.

I lock the front door and then walk to the back to prepare our séance room. "Universe, are you sure about this?" No answer, but it was more of a rhetorical question anyway. Giving the room a quick smudging, I grab three blessed candles and set them on the round table, one in front of each of the three chairs we'll be using, forming a triangle.

Intuitively, I grab a piece of chalk and draw a large circle around the table and chairs. That's not what Grandma does, but I'm going with my gut on this. I remove the extra chairs that we won't need and set them to the side.

Escorting the ladies back, they take their seat as I light the candles and place the picture in the center of the table. I say an invocation of protection, and we grasp hands. I don't remember the exact words Grandma uses, but it's close enough. And while holding hands isn't necessary according to Grandma, most people just expect it because they've seen it on television.

"Opal Baker, please join us," I say politely but firmly. "Your daughter Debbie is here and would like to commune with you." We wait. Nothing happens, and I start to get nervous. Crap, maybe I did something wrong?

"Opal Baker, are you here? Rap the table once for yes." Silence. I wait for a minute or so. "Debbie, I don't think this is—"

I stop as the energy of the room shifts and the temperature drops ever so slightly. A soft knock on the table causes Debbie and her friend to gasp. So maybe the Universe didn't lead me astray.

"Opal Baker, do you know of your granddaughter Charlotte's whereabouts?" I ask with more confidence. "Rap the table once for yes, two for no." Two knocks. She doesn't know.

"Debbie, is there anything you'd like to ask your mother? Phrase it as a yes or no question."

Debbie asks some questions, and the spirit answers via knocks. We learn that Opal is with her husband, Charlotte's grandfather, and they are both at peace. When Debbie runs out of questions, I thank Grandmother Opal for joining us.

I'm in the middle of reciting Vivian's invocation of closure when I receive a vision of a man with the most beautiful eyes I've ever seen. I can't quite make out the details of his face, except to say that he's a good-looking guy around my age, maybe a few years older.

But the eyes. The most unusual shade of blue, I'd call them bright aquamarine. I sit there, dumbfounded.

And then it happens. One second I'm staring at this man with the beautiful eyes, and the next second I feel him jump inside me.

CHAPTER 4

"Thank you, ladies," I say, quickly ushering them to the door. Debbie tries to pay, but I insist it's on the house. I have to get them out of here now. "Please keep me updated about Charlotte."

When they're gone and I've locked the door behind them, I turn to address my squatter. "Who are you? Why are you in me? *How* are you in me?" My voice raises several octaves. Okay, I'm in full-on panic mode. I've attended my share of séances, and not once have I ever seen this happen, nor has Grandma ever mentioned the possibility of a beautiful-eyed being materializing out of the thin air and hitching a ride with the channeler. I get mad when I get scared, and right now I am pissed.

I run to the front of the shop, frantically looking for something to help me get rid of this, whatever it is. I grab a bundle of sage and take off behind the counter, looking for a lighter.

You're going to try and smoke me out like a wasp? He asks incredulously in my mind. If I weren't so scared I might admit that this entity has one super sexy voice. It's not a thick southern accent, more of just a pinch of southern. *That stinks, by the way.*

"It's called smudging, but yes, it's the same idea as smoking out a nuisance pest. And I'm sorry if you think it stinks, but you could save me the trouble if you'd just leave!"

Little girl, you summoned me! Trust me, I have better things to do than get stuck in some wannabe Sabrina the Teenage Witch.

"First, I'm twenty-four years old, hardly a teenager. Second, the fact that you even know who Sabrina the Teenage Witch is concerns me. And third, how are you talking in my mind?"

I light the sage bundle and wait until the flame burns out and the bundle is gently smoking before I start waving it around my body. "I release all negative energy," I say out loud to set my intention, moving the bundle from head to toe.

Who said I'm made of negative energy? The only negativity I feel is coming off of you. In droves.

I ignore him and continue speaking out loud. "I release all energy that does not serve me."

Who said I'd never serve you? I could think of a few scenarios that I might be willing to serve you. Naked breakfast, assuming you play your cards right.

"You're trespassing, and now you're hitting on me? Unbelievable! The only cards I touch are tarot cards, and only if hell freezes over would you and I be having naked breakfast together!"

Dang it, I'm getting distracted. I come up with a quick spell and chant:

Trespasser leave from me today.
I banish you from my body, be safely on your way.

Words hold power, and chanting them out loud helps raise energy and add power to a spell. It doesn't necessarily have to rhyme, but I just prefer a rhythmic spell. I chant over and over, envisioning this being leaving my body.

It's quiet. I didn't feel anything magical happen, but I've also never tried to remove a talking entity from my person, either. I take some deep meditative breaths and open my eyes.

Feel better? I'm not into meditation, although I've heard that Tantric sex is amazing.

"Argh! Get out!" I run upstairs to the kitchen. I grab a jar of bay leaves and pick out the largest one I can find.

Is it really the best time to make soup?

Also known as the wishing leaf, a bay leaf is a versatile herb for spell casting. I ignore him, rummaging through the junk drawer. Grabbing a fine-tipped permanent marker, I hold the intention in my mind and then write a banishing spell on the bay leaf:

Entity be gone from my body,
drifting down the river.
Wherever it belongs, safely do deliver.

It's a long spell for this small of a space, but I write in tee-ny-tiny print to make it fit. I hold the bay leaf and visualize it glowing with the power of my intention.

I run back downstairs and out the back door, heading a block over to the Mississippi River. Memphis is known as the Bluff City, and because most of the city sits on higher ground than the river, it's relatively safe from flooding. But that also means I have to navigate down a precarious hill to get close enough to the water to throw in my leaf.

Do not fall into this mud pit. I have no intention of drowning with you today.

I ignore him and reach the bottom of the hill. Thinking of my intention, I release my bay leaf, watching it float away. I quickly lose sight of it and turn around, trudging my way up the hill. It's quiet in my head when I return to the shop. I am hopeful my spell worked.

I see that we've gotten off on the wrong foot. I am Damion. And you are?

Never gonna hear the end of it when Grandma learns that I botched a séance I shouldn't have been hosting solo in the first place.

CHAPTER 5

I hustle over to the crystal section of the shop. Maybe black onyx would help banish this entity. I grab the stone and hold it to my heart chakra:

> With loving energy I send you away.
> Be gone from me entity on this day.

Closing my eyes, I envision this entity transferring into the stone. He makes a throat clearing sound.

I walk behind the counter and pull Aunt Callie's three-ring binder, my cheat sheet for crystals and their healing properties. "What are you?" I stall for time until I can figure out how to get rid of this thing. Let's see, agate to prevent psychic attacks. It's too late to prevent anything—what I need is damage control. I keep flipping.

Why did you summon me?

"I didn't summon you!" I practically shout.

You did.

"I did not!"

You most certainly did. Let's look at the facts, shall we? You're wearing an Ematille stone whilst inside a magic circle with blessed candles forming a triangle. Poof, I'm here. What else would you call it except a summoning?

"Ematille stone?" I ask. "You mean my bloodstone bracelet?" I look down at the dark-green beads with red specks encircling my left wrist. My best friend, Maddie, gave it to me a few months before her death. I wear this bracelet every day.

I assume you found your grimoires for dummies online? He says, not even trying to hide his low opinion of my occult knowledge.

"Look, I didn't summon you. I was trying to help a mother find her missing daughter. We were talking to her grandmother's spirit, and then you crashed the party. And I'd really like for you to explain how it is that you're inside my head, and more importantly why you won't get out!" I pause for a second as his words sink in. "Wait a minute, you're a demon?" Oh shit, I'm in trouble. Maybe I need holy water. Or does that only work on vampires? I don't know; I hate scary movies.

I am the demon known as Damion, at your service, he says smoothly.

"Demon Damion, how alliterative," I say tartly.

I prefer Debonaire Damion. Delicious Damion. Delectable Damion. Debauched Damion. Rolls off the tongue, I agree.

I roll my eyes. "I'm Aubry. I would say that it's a pleasure to meet you, but who are we kidding." I guess there's no harm in telling him my name. Or is that the first step in him stealing my soul? He can speak in my head, but I don't think he has access to everything that's in there. Oh my Goddess, I hope not. *Damion, come out so that we can have sex. I'm so hot for you,* I think in my mind. A pervert demon would definitely respond to that.

Tsk tsk. I thought southern women were known for their hospitality. Yes, I have a pretty thick southern accent, but better to drawl out the vowels than to butcher the entire alphabet like a Yankee.

I think his response was to my verbal comment? I try again to be one hundred percent sure that my thoughts are safe. *Damion, come out and fuck me right here on the counter.* I wait. Nothing. "Damion, let's assume for the sake of argument that I summoned you. If you're a demon, why aren't you offering me a one-sided, soul-stealing deal? And since no deal was even discussed, let alone reached, why are you in my body?"

I. Don't. Know. He spits out the words one by one. *It's never happened before.*

"Really, you've never possessed someone?"

No, he says haughtily. *I'm quite fond of the physical perfection that is my body.*

I snort. "Pride before the fall. What do you consider physical perfection? Horns and forked tail? Maybe a little pitchfork accessory?" I know I probably shouldn't antagonize a demon, but his arrogance is rubbing me the wrong way.

It's his turn to snort. *I'm a Cambion,* he says as if that explains everything. *Do you know nothing of demonology?*

"Not much," I admit.

I am part demon, part human. Possession is not one of my many skills.

"What skill set do you possess?" I can't help it. Curiosity is one of my fatal flaws. I wonder if Eve felt the same way?

I could show instead of tell, had some complete and total moron not summoned and trapped me.

24

Moron? The nerve of this demon. I'm about to lay into him when the doorbell rings. *Listen,* I think to him, *I've got to get rid of whoever is out there. Please be quiet until we're alone and then we can sort this out.*

I am but your humble servant, he says mockingly.

"So you can read my thoughts!"

Elvis chooses this moment to make his way into the shop. *Could you be any more of a stereotype?* Damion snorts.

"Some stereotypes are true, what can I say?" Elvis is a midnight-black Bombay with bright copper-colored eyes. Grandma thinks it's hilarious to announce "Elvis has left the building" anytime the cat wanders out of the room. It was funny the first hundred times. Our cat is seven years old. You do the math.

"Look, can you read my thoughts or not? What am I thinking right now?" I think of what I was going to cook for dinner before things went to pot. Now that Damion mentioned it, soup does sound good on this rainy day.

How sexy of a voice I have and how you'd like to see if the rest of me matches up.

I'm being serious! I mentally shoot him the bird.

I can hear you mentally speak to me. I can't hear your thoughts, unless there's not much going on up there. In that case, yes, I can hear the deafening silence.

Thank the Goddess for small favors. I ignore his rude comment and head to the front of the shop.

"Good evening, Brenda," I sing out as I unlock the door. Brenda's our regular FedEx delivery woman and Grandma's friend. She's in her mid-fifties with short hair and ebony skin. She's one of our biggest buyers of candles and other various herbs for her magic practice. Her other supplier is a butcher shop several blocks away, except the butcher doesn't actually do the butchering. Let's just say that I always want to stay on Brenda's good side.

She stops to look at our new collection of tourist kitsch. Aunt Callie thinks it's in poor taste, but Grandma agrees with me that a tourist section is needed. Our shop is located near the trolley stop, and we get quite a bit of foot traffic. Brenda holds up a strand of Mardi Gras beads. "Folks do know that we ain't New Orleans, yes?"

"As long as they take their beads over to Beale Street to get drunk and pee somewhere other than by my car, I don't care what they think." If you've ever stepped in a puddle of urine while exiting your car during Mardi Gras week, then you'll understand where I'm coming from. "Oh, I sold one of your dolls the other day," I tell her. Brenda makes our voodoo dolls, another hit with the tourists. "A bachelorette party stopped by. One of the bridesmaids wanted to poke pins in her cheating ex-boyfriend."

"In that case, you should have told her how to charge the doll," Brenda says with a wink.

Unless a voodoo doll is properly charged, you can stick pins in one until the cows come home and it won't do a thing. That's why I don't have a problem selling them to tourists. "Sign here," she says.

I walk around the counter and do as instructed. Brenda gives me a penetrating look. Uh-oh. Can she sense my demon problem? "Would you like some coffee for the road?" I politely encourage her to leave.

She shakes her head, her gaze still homed in on me like a laser. I scurry back behind the counter and busy myself opening the package. At least I won't be getting hexed by Amelia, as these are the supplies she requested. I glance back up to find Brenda still watching me intently. The phone rings as I wave and tell her to have a good day.

"Memphis Magic, this is Aubry. How may I help you?" I answer as I watch Brenda out of the corner of my eye to make sure she leaves.

"Aubry, dear."

"Amelia, why's it so loud?" It sounds like she's on an airport runway.

"What's that? Hold on a moment. There. I was under the dryer." Amelia has a standing weekly hair appointment at the beauty parlor, as she calls it. "Has my order arrived?"

"I just received a new shipment of red candles and ague root."

She sighs dramatically. "Finally. I'll be over shortly."

"Amelia, please don't hex Florence." I've played mediator with these two more times than I can count. They are the best of friends until they have a falling-out, and then one threatens the other with magical harm. Eventually, they make up and take a cruise together. It's been this way for as long as I can remember.

"Then you tell that old bitty to cut her magnolia tree. It's encroaching on my property," she tells me with righteous indignation.

"Let me see what I can do."

I hang up and call Florence. "Florence, would you consider trimming your magnolia tree? Amelia is threatening to hex you. Couldn't you humor her? I know how reasonable you are." I'm not above flattery and bald-faced lies.

"Aubry, darling, I'm not going to butcher my one-hundred-year-old majestic tree just because that old crone has nothing better to do than obsess over her property line." I don't point out that she apparently has nothing better to do either, as she recently had her property line surveyed in retaliation to

Amelia commissioning her own survey. "Tell that old witch to be ready to go tomorrow morning at six sharp. And she doesn't need three oversized suitcases for a three-day cruise, for crying out loud!"

I sigh and call Amelia. "I've spoken to Florence. She's agreed to let her landscaper look into the issue while the two of you are on your cruise. I am to remind you to make sure you're ready at six and to pack an extra hat or two." Does a little white lie count against your good karma if it's told with the best of intentions? I don't know. The road to hell is paved with good intentions, or so the old sayin' goes. Maybe I should ask my resident devil?

"Thank you, dear. That reminds me, I need to stop by the boutique to pick up a few last-minute things, maybe a new lightweight jacket and a pair of sandals. I'd rather over pack than be halfway to Haiti and realize I didn't bring enough evening attire."

"I couldn't agree more. Have a wonderful trip!" I say cheerily and hang up. Crisis averted.

I walk to the back of the shop and unlock our private library. It's a small room with four floor-to-ceiling bookshelves and a well-loved oak table in the center. I grab a book on herbal magic and find a protection spell against demonic attack. Not exactly what I'm looking for, but I think I can modify the spell to make it work.

Moving to the break room where we keep jars of our more potent herbs, I mix an abramelin potion of cinnamon, myrrh, and ginger with a mortar and pestle. The book calls for galangal, but I don't have that ingredient, so ginger will just have to work in a pinch. I hurry upstairs to the patio and pour the mixture in a circle around myself and chant:

Sacred abramelin stop this attack.
From whence he came from send
this Cambion safely back.

If you're finished screwing around, pack a bag. We're driving to Mississippi.

"Screwing around?" I snort. "I am trying to banish you! And why would I even consider driving you to Mississippi?"

Because I live in Jackson. I need to contact my friend to see if he knows a way out of this mess you've made.

"You've blamed this on me, but who's to say someone didn't place a curse on you, and I happened to be at the wrong place at the wrong time? I mean, you're part human, so I would assume you are susceptible to magic."

We can discuss your incorrect assumption on the road. Go get ready.

"Why don't you just poof us over there, or however you demons materialize?"

I can't. I already tried and it didn't work.

"So you weren't even going to give me notice; you were just going to kidnap me?" That sounds about right.

Don't be so melodramatic. Let's go.

I pack my overnight bag and catch Elvis up to speed. He really doesn't seem too concerned that I'm possessed by a demon. I set out an extra bowl of food and water for him anyway and tell him to watch over things while I'm gone.

The look he gives me lets me know that he'll think about it, and then he returns to more important things like taking a nap.

CHAPTER 6

Ever been on a three-hour road trip with a backseat driver? Ever been on a three-hour road trip with a backseat driver from hell? *Get over. Exit here. Speed up. Slow down. Pass them. Pass them on the median. Pass them on the shoulder.*

"Enough!" I snap and Fort Knox my mind. I literally imagine a cartoon version of Fort Knox with guard towers, infrared security beams, and a giant steel wall topped with barbed wire around my mind. It must have worked, because for the rest of the trip I enjoy blessed silence.

The GPS guides me to Damion's house. I park on the street and then lower my mental defenses. *Was that necessary?*

"It was, and your home is beautiful." Floodlights illuminate an old, restored Craftsman. I grab my bag and walk up the steps carved into the yard to the front door. Two white rocking chairs sit empty to the left of the door. "How are we going to get in?" I wonder out loud.

Go look under the potted plant by the rocking chair. I do as instructed and find a key hidden beneath.

"That is completely unsafe," I inform him as I unlock the door. *My home is warded, it's plenty safe.*

Speaking of safety, "How do I know I'm not walking into some kind of trap?"

Isn't it a little late now to ask that question?

An excellent point, dang it. I slowly open the door and peek my head inside, expecting to find a creepy dungeon. Instead, I'm met with a warm and inviting home. I feel no nefarious vibes as I pass a sitting room that's been converted to a masculine-looking study with a cozy fireplace. Down the hall, I enter the living room that opens into an impressive chef's kitchen.

I pick up a framed picture situated on a bookcase shelf. The little blond boy in this picture has to be Damion as a child—those unusual bright aquamarine eyes give him away. He's hugged by a smiling woman with green eyes and blonde curly hair. "Your mother?" I ask.

Yes.

"She's lovely," I say, setting the picture down. "Should we do a walk-through and make sure everything seems in order? I don't practice dark magic, but I do know if someone has magically attacked you, they'd probably have taken a personal item."

My feet start walking not of my own accord. "So you can just commandeer my body?"

Yes. I've given you the utmost courtesy and respect thus far. You're welcome. He starts moving my feet toward the kitchen, but I lock down with all my bullheaded might. My body jerks to a stop. Ha! *Let me take over. I know my house, you don't. I'll be much more efficient this way.*

"Fine, but a little warning next time," I grumble. He takes over, and we do a quick walk-through of the house. It's a weird feeling, my body moving without me doing the moving. "Can you tell if anything is out of place?"

It doesn't appear so.

My hands grab his cell phone, and Damion sends a message to a contact named Gabe. I assume this is the friend he mentioned earlier.

> **DAMION:** I need your help. Can you meet me at my house?

> **GABE:** I'm stuck in an arbitration that's gone long. What's up?

> **DAMION:** It can wait. Meet me at my house tomorrow morning.

> **GABE:** Will do.

Damion's still in control as he walks me to his bedroom. "This is not what I expected your bedroom to look like," I admit.

What did you expect? Red walls, framed pentagrams, souls trapped in jars on a shelf?

"I don't know, a little more edge, a little less Martha Stewart?" An inviting king-size bed with a plush gray comforter takes up one wall, and on the other wall is a matching dresser with a huge mounted flat-screen television. In the corner is a very expensive-looking leather chair. Props to him for not using it as a clothes catch-all.

I grab my small toiletry bag from my duffle and make my way to his bathroom. I figured out the first time nature called to ask him for privacy. He claims he can give it to me. I'll take him at his word because the alternative is too horrifying.

"All finished. Thank you," I say as I walk to the bedroom. It failed to occur to me while packing that Damion and I would be sleeping together tonight, or else I would have chosen a more modest sleep ensemble. I'm wearing a skimpy white tank top and sleep shorts. It certainly doesn't help the situation that I'm crawling into Damion's bed, with what I assume is his scent on his sheets. It's an extremely masculine smell—woodsy mixed with some other fragrance I can't put my finger on. Couple that with his sexy voice inside my head, it's an annoyingly erotic combination.

Comfortable? Damion asks as I'm reaching for the lamp to turn off the light. I'm ready to pass out. It's been a heck of a long day.

"Yes."

Too bad. Move to the other side.

"Why?"

Because you're on my side of the bed.

"What kind of logic is that? We're in my body, ergo if I'm sleeping on your side of the bed, then that means you're sleeping on your side of the bed."

Because the next time you sleep with me, I'll be back in my body and you'll be on the other side. Go ahead and get used to it.

"You might be the most conceited demon I've ever met." Granted, he's the only demon I've ever met, but still.

Sleep well. Dream about me tonight.

"Wait, are you teasing me, or can you actually control my dreams?"

"Why?" His sexy voice fills the air. "Would you like me to enter your dreams? Should we have an erotic dream tonight?" He whispers seductively, his voice projecting from my mouth.

"Shall I make you come for me? Make you scream and drench the sheets?" I ignore him *and* the tingling between my thighs. "If so, then scoot over. You're still on my side."

"Ugh, you are such a prick. Good night!" I slam Fort Knox around my mind. I hear faint laughter as I do. Now I'm worried. Could he actually control my dreams? The worst part is I'm aroused by the mere possibility. I begin a deep breathing exercise Aunt Callie taught me that I don't use nearly enough, and eventually I drift off to sleep.

)))�𝄞◐◑(((

I stand on a dirt path in the woods and begin walking. A full moon shines brightly overhead illuminating the way. At least, I think I'm going the right way? A creature makes a screeching noise, and my heart rate increases. I try not to freak out as I pick up my pace and reach a fork in the path. I don't know which way to go. Okay, now is the time to freak out.

I hear the faint whisper of a familiar voice. "Maddie?" I follow the voice and take the path on the left. I see a white figure ahead, but it feels like my feet are stuck in cement. No matter how hard I try, I can't move. "Maddie!"

"Why didn't you see it coming?" she asks. The figure slowly begins to disappear.

"No, Maddie, don't go. Let me help you now. I'm sorry." I sink down to my knees on the cold dirt path and cry.

Aubry! I hear Damion's voice, and I sit up so fast in bed it makes my head spin. *Aubry, it was a dream, lie back down,* Damion says in a calm voice. *It's alright. Lie back down.*

"It was a dream," I repeat to calm myself as tears run down my face. "It felt so real." I dry the tears with the bottom of my tank top and lie back down.

Tell me.

"It was nothing."

Liar.

"Fine, it was something. Something that I'm not going to tell you."

Perhaps I could help you.

"Why would you want to help me? You don't know me." And I certainly don't know him. Oh, I know enough about him to know that I shouldn't trust him. Deals with devils and all that.

You don't trust me.

"Hey, I thought you couldn't read my mind!"

I don't need to. You don't trust me, and that's understandable. So I will endeavor to earn your trust.

"Isn't that exactly what a tricky demon would say?" I glance at the clock. It's almost seven, so I might as well get up. I pull back the covers and stretch. "I need solo bathroom time, please."

I towel dry my hair after a quick shower and start opening drawers, looking for a hair dryer. Well, that's my excuse. Really, I just want to snoop and see if he's given a woman drawer privileges. Nope. Men's razors, aftershave, deodorant. For a creature so vain, I expected more manscaping items.

No hair dryer. That's okay. My hair has some natural waves, and I can get away with letting it air dry. I dust the smattering of freckles on my nose with powder. I used to hate my freckles when I was a teenager, but now I've learned to love what the good Goddess gave me. My big blue eyes are my best feature, and I'll occasionally play them up with heavy eye makeup, but my go-to look is less fussy. I give my eyelashes a quick swipe of mascara and add some lip gloss and I'm good to go.

Knock knock. Can I come out?

"Yes." It's eerie looking in the mirror knowing Damion can look back at me through my eyes. "You know it's considered rude to stare," I tell him. He doesn't respond. "Hellcat got your tongue?"

I break our gaze as I pack up my things, slipping on my ankle boots and sliding on my bloodstone bracelet. It clashes terribly with my blue tunic. Yes, I'm a girly girl. So what? Not all young witches are into the goth look. "What's the plan? We bank on the hope that your friend Gabe can help us get unstuck?" His not taunting me or throwing out sexual innuendoes back in the bathroom is disconcerting. I'm not sure what to make of it.

That's the idea. Let's get you coffee and breakfast before he arrives.

"Sounds good, I'm starving." I don't always drink coffee, but yesterday was a long day. Add in the three-hour road trip with the demonic backseat driver from hell *and* pile on my unsettling dream, it's a miracle I'm upright.

Let me take over and make you breakfast and then I promise to return you to the driver's seat. Let's just pray that your driving skills have magically improved from last night.

You try driving with a control freak barking orders in your head, I retort, and he laughs.

I may be stubborn, but I let him take over. I'm not going to pass up a breakfast offer. *Not naked breakfast, I'm afraid,* he says as we walk to the kitchen and grab a carton of eggs from the fridge.

I mentally snort as we turn on the gas burner and grab a frying pan from the cabinet. *You're picturing me naked right now, aren't you?* he asks as I watch my hand whisk the eggs and expertly pour the mixture into the pan. *Do you understand now why it's so imperative we return me to my body?*

You have a ridiculously high opinion of yourself. And yes, I might be trying to picture what he looks like naked, and no, I will not admit that to him.

We plate an omelet a few minutes later and pour a cup of coffee. *Cream or milk, if you have it please.* He tops off my coffee and we sit down on a leather stool at the island. I'm back in control and make short work of my breakfast. *Thank you, this is delicious.*

You're welcome.

I'm chewing the last bite when the doorbell rings. I take my coffee over to the front door and peer out the glass pane.

I assume this is Gabe?

Yes.

"Good morning, Gabe," I say, opening the door.

"Morning," Gabe says in a strong Mississippi accent. It makes me think of magnolia leaves and sweet tea. I have a southern accent, but this man has a Southern accent with a capital S. "And who might you be?" he asks with a charming smile. I'm tall at five feet eight, but he's several inches taller than me, so I'd guess him at six feet three or so. He's a good-looking man with dark features of indeterminate origin, dark brown eyes, brown hair, and beautiful golden skin. Dressed smartly in a designer suit, he appears to be in his mid-to-late twenties.

Damion takes over and his voice says, "Gabe, it's me. This is Aubry."

Gabe busts out laughing. We close the door and head to the couch.

"Damion, what on earth have you done?" Gabe asks in a bemused tone.

"Not me. Her," Damion practically growls.

I take back over and tell the tale of my first attempted séance. Damion interjects to make sure Gabe knows what a complete and total halfwit I am because I employed demon-summoning items in my circle.

"I've never heard of an unintentional possession. Unintentional on the part of the demon, I should say. And I've never heard of a Cambion executing a successful possession." Gabe pauses to think for a moment. "I'm going to have to do some research. It's probably best if the two of you return to Aubry's shop. What was done there will likely have to be undone there. Aubry, hand me your phone." I comply, and he begins typing. "I've added myself to your contacts." He returns my phone and places a kiss on the top of my hand with dramatic flair.

"Why couldn't I have gotten stuck with a southern gentleman?" I bemoan. Damion snorts.

"Damion, you'd best be a gentleman to our new friend," Gabe says with a smile. I can tell that he's getting way too much enjoyment out of our predicament. He releases my hand and stands. "Should we involve the Arbitrator?"

"Not yet," Damion answers.

"Very well. But you know that I'm going to bill you for this."

Still think he's a gentleman? Damion asks me.

As long as he bills you and not me.

But I thought we were in this together?

"Gabe, how much is your hourly rate, if you don't mind me asking?" He rattles off an obscene number, and I just about fall off the couch. *We're definitely not in this together,* I inform Damion.

We escort Gabe out, and I let Damion take over so that he can get his house in order before we hit the road. He checks his email and returns some phone calls that sound work-related, so I shield my mind to give him privacy. When I remove the mental fortress, I find us going through his mail. I watch my hand slip his phone and wallet into my bag. *Let's go.*

"'Please' is a polite little word us southerners like to use."

Remember that when we're in bed and you're begging me for more.

"Please," I snort.

CHAPTER 7

Damion takes over the wheel on our return trip. I'm delighted to learn it is possible to take a catnap of the mind, but not of the body. I wake to the sound of him laying on the horn. Good grief, he's just as aggressive a driver as he is a backseat driver.

"Is Gabe a demon?"

No.

"So he's human?"

No.

"Then what is he?" I ask in an exasperated tone.

He'd probably try to tell you he's a demigod, but don't listen to that nonsense. He's a Nephilim.

"In English?"

He's half human, half fallen angel.

"But I thought a fallen angel was a demon, so wouldn't he be a Cambion like you?"

Not exactly. His father is a Watcher, a member of a group of angels who procreated with human women and were bound to Earth as punishment, or so the story goes. Completely different from the other group of supposed fallen angels who rebelled against their god.

"I thought angels were light and demons were dark? But Gabe has dark hair and dark eyes and you have light hair and light eyes." I'll never forget Damion's hauntingly beautiful eyes as long as I live, but I'm certainly not going to tell him that.

You watch too much TV.

"How are you friends with him? I thought angels and demons were enemies."

Why on earth would you think that?

Television, I don't answer. Otherwise, I would just prove his last point for him. "How do you know him?"

He's my law partner.

Damion is a lawyer. I should have known. "Could you be any more of a stereotype?" I throw back at him.

He laughs out loud. It's a disturbingly sexy sound. *Yes, I'm a demon and a lawyer. Some stereotypes are true, what can I say?*

"What kind of law do you practice?"

The demonic kind.

"Who's dumb enough to get into a legal dispute with a demon?"

You'd be surprised.

He aggressively tailgates the car in front of us and then whips over into the right lane to pass. "You realize that I'm mortal over here?" I should have stayed asleep. Maybe people with extreme road rage are really just the victims of demonic possession. That's a disturbing thought.

As am I, but that does not excuse this idiot's failure to get over.

"Really, you're mortal? So one day you'll die?"

Are you always this morbid? Yes, one day I'll die.

"Is your body exactly like a human's?"

Why? Are there certain parts that interest you more than others? When I return to my body, you're more than welcome to perform a head-to-toe inspection.

I ignore that little invitation and the thoughts it conjures. "What about superhuman senses, like speed or strength?"

It depends. I'm going to be faster and stronger than a human, but a full-blooded demon is going to be faster and stronger than I am.

"How old are you?"

What are we playing, 21 Questions?

I patiently wait him out. *I'm twenty-five years old, and that concludes 21 Questions.* He lays on the horn because the car in front of us doesn't go the instant the light turns green.

Somehow, someway, we make it back in one piece. I unlock the shop and then check phone messages and fire up the computer. Don't think it hasn't occurred to me to just call Grandma and Aunt Callie and beg for help, but then they'd come back early, and I'd never hear the end of it. I've also thought about driving to Tunica and asking for help in person, but vetoed that as well. I made this magical mess. I'm capable of cleaning it up. At least that's the pep talk I give myself.

My phone chimes, and I look at the text and groan. Crap. I'd completely forgotten about tonight's dinner plans with Brad, and now it'd be beyond rude to cancel this late. I've already bailed on him once.

Problem? Damion asks.

"Listen to me and listen to me good. I'm going out to dinner tonight with a nice, normal man, and you will stay out of it." Honestly, I wouldn't have minded if Brad had texted me saying he needed to cancel. I *want* to like Brad more than I *actually* like Brad.

I'll be happy to accompany you tonight as your chaperone.

"No, no, and no," I say. "I want you to create little soundproof headphones and wear them for the duration of the evening. I don't want commentary. I don't want a play-by-play of your thoughts and feelings concerning my date. I don't want an audience."

Why don't you want an audience? Are you planning on intimacy this evening? Because as your chaperone, I'd be duty bound to intercede.

"No, for your information. My hands are a bit too full at the moment to even consider a relationship."

Oh, you will definitely have your hands full with me. Very full. Overflowing full. Double-fisted full.

"Ugh, you are so *full* of yourself it's disgusting. Keep all references of your package to yourself."

He laughs, and it sends a shiver down my spine, which pisses me off even more.

"I'm going to get ready; I need privacy, please." I walk upstairs to the apartment and go to my bathroom. I'm adding the final touch of red lip gloss when I hear Damion mentally knock. "Come in," I say. "I mean it, Damion. You will stay the fuck out of my personal life."

He makes a *tsk tsk* sound. *And to think such a pretty southern lady has such an ugly mouth.*

I give him a saccharine sweet smile. "I'll take that as a compliment." I have to agree that I do clean up well. I've curled my long golden-brown hair and finger combed it into loose waves. My blue eyes are highlighted with liner and mascara, and I'm wearing a little black dress, my go-to fancy dinner outfit. I forgot lotion, so I bend over and rub some on my legs. I might also be messing with Damion. Maybe just a smidgen.

And will there be fucking tonight? Since you so eloquently brought it up.

"Maybe." I shrug as I turn from the mirror and slip on my heels. "Why, Damion? Would you be scandalized?" I feign shock. Of course there's not going to be, but I'm enjoying fucking with Damion.

Oh my sweet Aubry, I'd dare venture that you've never had a satisfying fuck in your entire life. You've only ever played it safe, and your favorite flavor is vanilla. It feels like a warm finger runs up and down my spine. I try to ignore the resulting goose bumps. *Let me know when you're ready to taste a different flavor,* he says in a voice smooth as silk.

My phone chimes. Saved by the ringtone. I glance at the message, pretending my nipples aren't hard.

> **BRAD:** Running 15 minutes behind.

> **ME:** No problem, I'll just meet you there. See you in a little bit.

> **BRAD:** Can't wait!

I lock up behind me and think about Damion's commentary on my love life. He hit dangerously close to home. As for the rest of it...well, I refuse to even think about the flavor comment. Or the phantom touch. Especially the phantom touch. I didn't even know he could touch me, and now I'm wondering what other ways he could touch me. Okay, so I'm *trying* not to think about it.

Traffic is typical for a Friday evening, meaning Brad and I will probably wind up at the restaurant at the same time. I'm honestly glad for the excuse to drive myself, as it's easier to end the date this way. Damion refuses to let someone over. They honk at us, and then we honk back at them. "Has anyone ever told you that you are an extremely aggressive driver?"

I'll take that as a compliment.

We arrive at the restaurant and Damion parks my car. I take back over and walk inside and spot Brad seated in the lobby. "Hey, Brad."

"Aubry, I'm so glad to see you." He stands, going in for a hug. Still not on hugging status, so I turn my body and we do the half-hug again.

Not a good move to come on that strong right out of the gate.

I do not need your play-by-play, remember?

"Aubry?" Brad asks.

"I'm sorry, what did you say?"

"Are you ready?"

"Ready."

I walk with Brad to the hostess booth and she checks us in. We follow the woman to our table and Brad pulls out my chair for me.

"Thank you. I've never eaten here before," I say.

"One of my favorites," Brad replies with an easy smile, taking a seat across from me.

"What's good?" I ask, looking over the menu.

"I highly recommend the filet."

"Sounds good to me," I announce, closing my menu. "I like your tie. It's a little jazzier than the others I've seen you wear." Brad is everything I *think* I should want in a normal, straitlaced man. Eventually I do want to get married and have a family, be part of a stable two-parent unit. I wouldn't trade Grandma for the world, but there were times growing up I longed for conventional.

"Thank you, casual Friday," he responds.

Damion makes a snoring *zzzzzzzz* sound.

Good, stay asleep for the rest of the date.

The real question is whether you can stay awake for the rest of the date.

"And you look beautiful," Brad returns with a smile.

"Thank you. So you had to work late?"

"Tax season is upon us. I reviewed your account this week. I've got some really exciting ideas I'd love to share with you."

"Oh, I forgot to look at sides. What's good?" I ask, grabbing my menu in a desperate attempt to steer the conversation away from accountant speak.

Nice diversion, but if he breaks out a balance sheet, we're out of here.

I try not to laugh. *Will you butt out?*

Our server appears and Brad and I both order steak, mine cooked medium and Brad's well-done.

Damion makes a gagging sound. *No self-respecting man orders a steak well-done.*

I ignore Damion's commentary as a runner drops off the bread basket. Don't mind if I do. "So Brad, what are some things you're into? Besides work," I quickly amend as I butter my roll.

"I'm a big racquetball player. I get together with a group of guys from the office twice a week to play."

My God, can you imagine that group? Racquetballs and retainers flying everywhere.

Be nice.

"I like to get at least twenty minutes of physical activity a day," Brad continues.

I'm sure he logs his time in a spreadsheet.

"How about you? You look like you take care of your body."

Agreed. Although I could certainly help you in that department.

You are horrible, I inform Damion and will my mouth not to smile. "I practice yoga with my aunt. She's more dedicated than I am, but I try to get to class when I can."

"You really should make it a daily habit. I block out activity time in my calendar to make sure that I follow through."

Need I say more?

No, he really needn't. Dinner is served and we proceed to make small talk. The most boring small talk in the history of small talk.

Our server appears to remove our plates and offers dessert. Brad responds with a yes before I can respond with a no. It's not that I don't love dessert, it's just that I'm ready for this date to end. I'm starting to get a dull headache, not to mention the dullness of this entire evening. I hate to admit it, but Grandma was right.

"I'll have the raspberry sorbet. Thank you." I hand the dessert menu to our server.

"Decaf coffee for me, thank you. I'm a vanilla ice cream man, myself," Brad tells me.

And ladies and gentlemen of the jury, I rest my case, Damion says in a dramatized courtroom voice.

"On second thought, I'd like vanilla ice cream instead of the sorbet. Thank you."

My ice cream is brought out a few minutes later and I take a bite and inwardly moan. I clench my thighs together and wiggle my lower half a little in my seat for dramatic effect. Brad can't see, but this show isn't for him anyway. "Brad, would you like a bite?" I hold out the spoon and I swear I hear a faint growl in my head.

Brad pays the check and we walk to my car. "Sure I can't talk you into coming over to my house?" he asks hopefully.

I shake my head no. "With Grandma and Aunt Callie out of town, I'm running the shop solo and I need to be up and at it early tomorrow morning. Thanks for the lovely dinner."

"You're welcome," he replies and leans forward to kiss me. I turn my head so he kisses my cheek. I'm feeling pretty drained as I get in my car and head back home. It's been a long forty-eight hours.

CHAPTER 8

Back in the apartment, I ask Damion for privacy and get ready for bed. I massage some diffused peppermint oil on my temples and the back of my neck to fend off a full-blown headache. It's time to write off Brad for good, I think with a sigh. I'm just glad Grandma isn't here, else I would never hear the end of it.

I decide to torture Damion by slipping into my sexiest lace camisole and a skimpy pair of matching panties. He got me all hot and bothered in his bed last night, so tonight I'll give him a little taste of his own medicine.

"You can come out," I tell Damion as I step into my bedroom. My room is a fairly large space, with the original hardwood floors, an old exposed-beam ceiling, and brick walls. Candles and other magical odds and ends are positioned on my dresser. On the other side of the room, a repurposed headboard frames a comfy queen bed with a lush white comforter and fluffy white decorative pillows.

This is not what I expected your bedroom to look like.

"What did you expect? Black walls, skulls in the corner, spiders in jars?"

I don't know, a little more edge, a little less Martha Stewart?

"Ha ha."

Why do women love decorative pillows? Damion asks as I remove them one by one and place them on a bench at the foot of the bed.

"I don't know, but it's a universal truth."

What's that smell?

"Peppermint oil. I was getting a little headache."

He takes over, and we have a seat on my bed. It feels like warm hands are massaging my scalp, and I try not to purr like a cat. He moves the touch down to my temples. *There. How's that?*

It feels like heaven and please don't stop, I don't say. "Better, thank you." I climb under the covers. "Comfortable?" I ask Damion.

Yes.

"Good. I'm not going to make a big fuss about you sleeping on my side of the bed. See what a grown-up I am? Sleep well. Dream about me. Would you like me to enter your dreams?" I taunt him. "Should we have an erotic dream tonight?" I whisper. "Shall I make you come for me? Make you scream and drench the sheets?" I parrot back his words from last night. I'm not sure where these brass balls of mine have come from. All I know is that I'm getting a perverse pleasure in taunting him.

He laughs and says from my mouth, "Aubry, you think you can tease me and remain safe because I don't have my body. What you haven't considered is I don't need my body to give you the most intense orgasm of your life." My left leg becomes all warm and tingly, and then the feeling moves over to my right leg. "Now imagine me touching you like that *between* your legs." So much for getting *him* all hot and bothered. "Sweet dreams."

And it's back to meditative breathing.

A warm ocean breeze lightly kisses my exposed skin. I'm lying on my stomach on a lounge chair as I bask in the glorious sunshine. An empty white-sand beach with azure-blue water as calm as a bathtub stretches as far as I can see.

Strong hands begin rubbing coconut-scented sunscreen on my back, and a sigh escapes my lips. I crane my neck, but I have to squint and look away. I can't see Damion because the sun is directly behind us.

He leans down and tickles my ear with his stubble as he whispers, "Are you ready to taste another flavor?" The most delicious masculine smell envelops me—it's that same smell from his sheets, except amplified to the nth degree. My core begins to clench, and my nipples become painfully hard.

I lick my lips as his warm finger runs the length of my spine, and then he begins toying with the strings of my bikini. My skin is tingling now, the nerve endings gone haywire. "I'm perfectly happy with vanilla," I have every intention of replying tartly, but it comes out way too breathy.

Laughter tickles my ear and I try not to shiver. "Liar."

"So what's your plan? Seduce me and then steal my soul?" That thought quickly sobers me up from this little lust trance.

"My sweet Aubry, I'm not going to *steal* anything. But you are going to give me what I want," he says, jerking me up by my ponytail to where I'm on my knees, my back pressed to his muscular chest, my ass snuggled against his very hard cock. From what I can feel, he wasn't exaggerating about it being a double-fisted job. "You will be mine," he whispers seductively, still gripping my ponytail.

I will my hips to remain perfectly still, because dang it, they desperately want to grind against him. "In your dreams. And in the future, stay out of *my* dreams."

He laughs, which pisses me off even more. "Very well. I'll be a good boy and wait until you're ready."

And just like that, he disappears, causing me to lose my support. I tumble off the lounge chair. "You are still a prick," I shout, spitting a mouthful of sand.

CHAPTER 9

I decide the best course of action is to pretend last night's dream never happened. My body, unfortunately, doesn't get the memo. I wake up frustrated and have to ask Damion for solo "bathroom" time so I can take care of business with my vibrator. I've never been more pissed off while getting off.

Today's definitely a coffee kind of day, so I brew a pot while I grab a bowl of cereal. We're out of the good stuff, so I have to settle for a bowl of Aunt Callie's sprouted grains. "Gross," I say after the first bite.

What's wrong? Damion asks.

"This is Aunt Callie's cereal from the health food store. It tastes like cardboard."

For the love of God, please let me take over. If we're going to have to share this vessel of yours, I cannot sit back in good faith and watch you abuse it.

Damion takes control and a few minutes later, I'm eating French toast. Even without maple syrup, which we're out of, it's still delicious. "Thank you, this is good. Who taught you how to cook?" I ask.

My mother. And you might be meeting her soon if we're still stuck together. I join her for a meal once a week. If I don't show up soon, she'll send the hounds out after me.

"Hellhounds?" I joke, but then realize I shouldn't joke because maybe there is such a thing as hellhounds. I decide I'd rather not find out. I'm a cat person, anyway.

What about your mother?

"She passed away when I was a baby."

I'm sorry.

"Thank you."

I wash up the dishes and walk downstairs to our library. I'm not sure what exactly I'm looking for, only that I have to try to fix this mess. Help me out here, Universe. I close my eyes, running my hand along the bookshelf until I intuitively stop on a book spine. I open my eyes and grab *The Divine Magic of the Moon* from the shelf and walk over to the table.

What's next, a divining rod?

I ignore his taunting and flip through the book. The doorbell chimes, and I walk out to the front of the shop. I unlock the door and Gabe steps in, closing his umbrella.

"Aubry, a pleasure to see you again." He gives my hand a kiss. "Damion, I presume you're still enjoying Aubry's company?"

"Enjoying might be a strong word, but we're still stuck together," I offer.

I can think of a few things we could do that would make our time together so much more enjoyable.

I could too, and that concerns me. He takes over my voice. "Gabe, tell me you have good news."

"Yours is a fascinating case. Unprecedented." I don't like the sound of that one bit. It's up there with a doctor telling you, "I've never seen this before." I don't want to be involved with Damion setting any kind of demonic precedent. "There are no recorded cases of Cambion possession. Perhaps your situation is the byproduct of a demon trap gone awry."

"What's a demon trap?" I ask.

"Demons are powerful beings, but they're not infallible. There have been cases of enterprising witches trapping a demon for various reasons. If a possession is involved, it's usually because the witch placed a dead body in the circle in order to reanimate the corpse. But I'm getting ahead of myself. Let's start from the beginning. Show me where the séance took place."

I lead Gabe to the back of the shop and into the séance room and flip on the lights. I walk over to the table. "I'd like to state for the record I did not intend to summon Damion, let alone trap him, or any demon for that matter. Oh, and there was no corpse in my circle."

"So noted," Gabe says.

"I sat here, the ladies sat there," I point. "The candles are right where I left them."

"And the chalk circle on the floor?" Gabe asks.

"I drew it. I've never seen my grandma use one before in a séance. I don't know why; I just had the intuitive feeling that I should draw one before we started."

I jump, startled at the sight of the candles floating toward me. I grab them out of the air as the table floats off to the side and the rug slides out of the way.

"Just making sure there are no drawings or etchings hidden." Gabe floats a piece of chalk over and begins drawing his own circle with a pentagram in the center and elaborate symbols. Smaller circles meet inside the larger one. It takes him about five minutes to complete. If I tried drawing all that, it would take me at least half an hour.

"Step inside and have a seat. We'll try a reverse demon trap. What can trap a demon can also be used to exorcise a demon." I comply, sitting down cross-legged. Gabe begins chanting in a language I don't know. Latin perhaps? My body erupts in goose bumps as the energy level inside the circle elevates. Gabe's dark eyes glow with power as he raises his hands in receiving position. He closes his eyes, and then booms out the last part of his chant. He stands perfectly still for a moment, and then opens his eyes and lowers his arms.

Damion?

Still here. He sounds positively aggrieved.

"We're still bound together," I announce.

Gabe rubs his chin thoughtfully and is silent for a moment. He offers his hand and helps pull me to my feet. With a flourish of his other hand, his circle disappears. "Let's try again, but we'll use your circle this time, Aubry."

"Sure," I shrug. Gabe fills in my circle, and I step inside and we repeat the ritual. Nothing. I step out. "What about holy water?"

"She watches too much TV," Damion informs Gabe.

Gabe nods. "Holy water is just a smoke screen, theater a priest uses during the exorcism so the higher-ups in the Church don't realize the priest is really engaging in sorcery." Gabe thinks for a moment. "That gives me a thought. I'll pay my priest friend a visit and see if he's ever heard of something like this. I can't tell you the last time I visited Nicaragua."

"What about holy water on vampires?"

"See what I mean, too much TV," Damion responds.

"Vampires are a myth," Gabe informs me. "But like all myths, it grew from a kernel of truth. There is a caste of demons who deal exclusively in the blood trade."

"What do you mean, they'll make a deal with a human in exchange for their blood?"

"Like any demon, they employ a number of methods to get what they desire," Damion answers without really answering my question. That's a demon lawyer for you.

"A reverse demon trap should have done the trick. Some other magic must be at play here, either interfering or binding you two together somehow," Gabe muses. "I'm going to check out the ladies who attended the séance," he tells me as I escort him out.

"Alright, but I can't imagine Debbie and her friend were involved." But that does remind me—I wonder if Debbie found her daughter Charlotte? I hope so.

Later that evening, I slip a garnet under my pillow. *What's that?*

"Demonic dream protection."

Damion makes a *tsk tsk* sound. *My wanton witch doesn't want to play with me tonight?*

The scary thing is that a part of me wants to play with him. So instead, I answer, "Not your wanton witch and no, I don't want to play in a rigged game."

He laughs and it feels like warm hands are gently massaging my shoulders. I try not to sigh; it feels so nice. *Not my wanton witch. Yet*, he whispers as I drift off to sleep.

I'm back on the wooded path, wearing the same white billowing dress. "Maddie, where are you?" I call. I hear rustling in the trees and pick up the pace. I keep going until I reach a fork in the path. I follow the faint sound of a voice and turn left. A white figure hovers ahead, but just like the last time, I'm unable to move any closer.

"You gave up on me," Maddie says sadly.

"No, I didn't! I just don't know what to do," I try to explain. "Do you need help crossing over? Do you know who killed you? Tell me how I can help you," I cry, but she's already gone.

CHAPTER 10

My cell phone chimes, and I walk behind the counter and read the message:

> **BRAD:** Had a wonderful time with you the other night. When can I see you again?

Ugh, I really don't feel like fooling with Brad right now. Can I end this non-relationship thing we've got going with a text message, or is that rude?

Will you be sticking with vanilla, pretending that you're vanilla? Because you, my sweet Aubry, are definitely not vanilla.

"The only thing that's sticking is you. In my craw. And so what if I like vanilla? It's a perfectly nice flavor," I say in what I'm sure is an extremely defensive tone.

Bullshit. You've been playing it safe personally, and if I had to guess, I'd say magically as well. Why?

"How about instead of dispensing unsolicited advice, you focus your attention on finding a solution to our little joined at the hip problem." This demon is far too insightful.

My cell chimes again. It's a selfie of Grandma holding a neon-colored cocktail that looks like a hangover waiting to happen.

> **ME:** I hope this is from last night...or is it this morning's hair of the dog?

> **GRANDMA:** Last night...you missed all the fun! Whatcha been up to?

> **ME:** Not much, things are pretty slow around here.

Your grandmother, I presume? Damion asks.

"Yes."

And you're not going to tell her about me?

"I hadn't planned on it."

Ah, so ours is a forbidden romance.

I dramatically roll my eyes and fire off a text to Aunt Callie while I'm thinking about it, letting her know that I talked Amelia down from the whole hexing Florence ledge. They're probably in Haiti by now, and Goddess only hopes that Amelia packed enough evening wear. I smile at the thought of three oversized suitcases.

I grab my cards and return to the back room. I sage the space and light a candle, and I then lay out a beautiful embroidered purple silk cloth that Aunt Callie brought back from her trip to India several years ago. Closing my eyes and centering my energy,

I clear the deck and mentally set my intention to receive guidance on how to exorcise Damion.

All you need is a turban and a crystal ball.

I ignore his taunting as I cut the deck into three piles. A three-card linear spread is what I go with; it just feels right. I flip over the cards. "Oh boy." The Devil. The Moon. Justice.

What? Damion asks.

"These are all major Arcana cards, meaning big life-changing events." I point to the first card. "Devil upright. Stuck in a situation, or it could also signify a strange or unusual experience. Either of those apply to us, wouldn't you say?

"Second, the Moon upright. The card of illusion. Arguably the most mysterious tarot card. Things aren't what they seem, or it could mean pay attention to dreams." Like my dreams about Maddie, I think as a huge wave of guilt washes over me. I quickly shove down those thoughts. "Devil and the Moon together point to some type of dark, shady underworld. Maybe dark magic?

"Third card, Justice upright. Truth. Fairness. Things must be balanced or it could signify an ending. Justice with the Moon? Maybe some type of loophole."

You charge people money for this?

I ignore the insult. "We have more information than when we started. I think law and contracts when I hear the word 'loophole.' What about some kind of demonic law loophole?"

How would I find a loophole in a law that doesn't exist to begin with? Gabe has confirmed that there are no known cases of Cambion possession.

"I don't know, you're the lawyer. Make yourself useful."

I'd be more than happy to demonstrate just how useful I can be, he whispers seductively, a touch running up and down my spine.

"Not that kind of usefulness," I try to chastise, but it comes out too breathy.

Forcing myself to snap out of it, I walk upstairs to the rooftop patio. It's guarded by a tall privacy wall—the perfect place for our circle to meet and perform rituals. Mother Nature has given us a brief respite on the downpour. Now it's just light sprinkles hitting my purple umbrella. Grandma asked me to look after her herb garden while she's gone, but with all the rain, there's no need to water. But I still check it out, touching each plant and sending them a little love. I cut a few sprigs of mint and walk back downstairs before the clouds open up again.

My phone chimes.

> **BRAD:** I'm headed to my office. Tax season is officially upon us. I received an email from our secretary about Memphis Magic's account. We're missing January's receipts. Can you pull those for me? I'll just swing by and pick them up.

Is Brad angling for a visit or is this legit? I could have sworn those receipts were in a file I dropped off at their office last week. I go to our accounting department, otherwise known as my messy desk located in an oversized storage closet. Sure enough, there the paperwork sits under a pile of vendor receipts.

> **ME:** Sorry about that, found them on my desk. Happy to drop them off tomorrow during business hours.

> **BRAD:** Really, it's no trouble. Be there in about 15 minutes.

> **ME:** Sure, thanks. I have a pretty tight schedule today. Text me when you're here and I'll just run them out to your car so you don't have to get out in the rain. Park in our side lot and I'll come out through the back door.

There, surely he'll get the hint.

There's no way he got that hint, Damion informs me. *Subtle is not a language vanilla Brad speaks.*

Damion's probably right, but admitting so is not a language I speak.

Walking to the break room, I turn on the kettle to make some tea with the fresh mint. Mint has a host of magical properties, including inspiration. Here's to hoping I'll be inspired to come up with the answer to our little dilemma.

I'm blowing on my steaming cup of tea when Brad texts me he's here. I grab the manila file folder and my umbrella and walk to our private entrance. When I unlock the back door and step outside, I have to stifle a scream. "Holy shit! You scared me to death!" I did not expect to see Brad by the door. In fact, I specifically instructed him to stay in his car.

"I'm sorry, Aubry. I didn't mean to scare you. I just wanted to see you."

I hand him the file. "Brad, you're a nice guy, but my life is so busy right now, I'm not interested in starting up a relationship." There, nothing subtle about that.

"I'm sorry to hear that. I'll be on my way, then," he says, looking and sounding defeated.

"Take care, Brad." I feel terrible, but there's nothing left to be said.

Turning to walk back inside, I don't make it very far. I feel the most excruciating pain in my head, and all goes black.

CHAPTER 11

"What?" I wake, disoriented. I try to rub my pounding head but soon realize my hands are bound with zip ties. I'm lying on a filthy pallet in what looks like a dilapidated basement.

What happened? I demand.

Brad knocked you out with a baseball bat and then stuffed you in his trunk.

What?

I know. I would have figured a racquetball man such as Brad would have used a racquet.

For fuck's sake, now's not the time to joke! Why didn't you take over and do something?

I tried to intervene, but your body was in such a state of shock that I couldn't make your limbs move.

I'm still in a state of shock, but can you do something now? Can you break the zip ties?

No. I already tried. I'm strong in my body, but not in yours.

I adjust my eyes to the dim lighting and realize I'm not alone. Brad's seated at a folding table with a kerosene lantern on it and a hunting knife in his hand. Beyond him is a rickety staircase. I've got to make a break toward those stairs. No way am I letting this jerk turn me into a *Silence of the Lambs* skin suit. Granted, I've never seen the movie, but I do know that a psycho and a skin suit were involved.

I try to stand, but can't because my ankles are likewise bound in zip ties. "Brad, what do you think you're doing?" I try to keep the hysteria at bay, letting anger be the emotion that wins out.

"Hold that thought. I need to move my car. I had to illegally park in the alley to carry you inside. I'd hate to get towed. What an inconvenience that would be."

"You *illegally* kidnapped me, you freakin' psycho! How about that for an inconvenience," I call after him as he walks up the stairs.

I hear something, almost like a moan. Struggling to sit up-right, Damion helps me by taking over. I spot a pallet of dirty blankets in the corner across from me. I think I see the outline of another person. "Hello? Is someone else here? Brad Cunningham kidnapped me. Did he kidnap you too?"

"Yes," a small voice answers.

"I'm Aubry Brooks. What's your name?"

"Charlotte Patel," the woman says a bit louder.

"Charlotte Patel! Is your mom Debbie and your grandmother Opal?"

"Yes! How do you know that?"

"I met your mom! She's been looking for you!" The Universe typically has a really good sense of humor. Right now I'm not finding that to be the case.

"How do you know my mom?"

"It's a long story. Is there any way out of here besides those stairs?"

"No, I don't think so. There are no windows and I haven't seen another door."

"Hang in there. We're going to get out of here."

I hear the door open and watch Brad descend the stairs with a whistle and a pep in his step. "Aubry, glad to see you're okay. I didn't want to hurt you too badly; I just needed you to cooperate."

"If you think knocking a woman unconscious is her 'cooperating' then you are delusional."

"Has anyone ever told you that you have a smart mouth?"

He does make a valid point.

Either do something useful like save us or hush!

"Brad, what is it that you want? Let's bottom line it."

"Now there's the Aubry I love." I try not to throw up in my mouth. "The moment I met you, I was so enchanted by the feel of your energy. So magical. I had to have more. But you were such a cocktease, never wanting to spread your legs to give me what I deserve, and then you have the nerve to break up with me! No ma'am, that won't do."

"First of all, I never broke up with you because we were never *together*." I want that out there on the record. "Second of all, what do you mean the 'feel' of my energy?" I think for a moment. "Oh my Goddess, you're an energy vampire!" An energy vampire is the equivalent of a human parasite. They're narcissistic leeches who siphon off power and energy from others. I'd felt drained after being around him those few times, but I thought it was just because I was getting sick or I just wasn't into him and we lacked spark. Now I see I was literally drained because this jerk was stealing my life spark!

Damion, tell me you have a plan.

Oh ye of little faith.

I'd have more faith if I saw this plan in action!

Patience.

"Where are we?" I ask Brad.

"We are in one of my personal investments. Real estate losses are an excellent tax write-off. You're really not maximizing your tax avoidance opportunities with Memphis Magic. Too bad you're not going to leave this room, because I really could have helped you with your next quarter."

Damion snorts. *Even playing the role of the villain, he still might be the most vanilla man in the world.*

Brad walks over to Charlotte and picks her up and sits her in an old office chair. "And 'energy vampire' is a derogatory term. I prefer 'energy opportunist.' Those who are either too weak or too dumb to guard their aura get conquered." An aura is an energy field that each person has around his or her body. I obviously need to do some energy healing work if this little twit was able to break into mine so easily and feed from me.

He rolls Charlotte closer to me. From the look of her, she's been slowly drained of her spirit by this sick bastard. She looks like a ghost of the vibrant woman in the picture her mom showed me. She's not wearing any clothes, and her left forearm is covered with a bloody bandage. Her eyes are shut, and it appears she's slipped out of consciousness. "Aubry Brooks, may I introduce you to Charlotte Patel."

"You're going to kill her if you don't get her to a hospital!"

"Nonsense. I can feel her energy. She's fine. Charlotte was my love before you came along." I highly doubt that Charlotte believed she was this lunatic's love, but I don't interrupt him.

"Her energy was good, not as delicious as yours, but enough to take the edge off. But your energy?" Brad says as if he's savoring it right now. "I actually put effort into wooing you. And I expect a return on investment."

"You think talking tax write-offs and mauling an overcooked steak is wooing a woman?" I realize I'm in no position to have so much attitude, but come on!

I told you no self-respecting man orders a well-done steak.

"On second thought, I like that smart mouth," he says, now rubbing himself through his khaki pants.

"You are one sick fuck," I say with disgust. "Where are her clothes and why is her arm bleeding?" I demand.

"Charlotte really didn't raise my energy the way I envisioned," he says in a disappointed tone. "So I took a page from the vampire playbook—I sampled her blood to see if that would give me the power my body deserves." He holds up the wicked-looking knife and cleans the jagged blade with a small cloth. "That didn't work, either," he says, placing the knife down.

"Of course it didn't work, you freak."

"But that's why I have you, Aubry," he says with a smile. "Your energy sings to me in a way hers never did. I'm still mulling over how the two of us should begin, my little siren," he continues. "I'd prefer Charlotte rouse so at least she can make herself useful and watch us. Tasting her fear while fucking you—I'm so turned on just thinking about it."

He stands, unbuttoning his shirt, and begins taking off his belt. His fingers move to the buttons of his khakis. All the bravado swooshes out of me like a deflated balloon and fear takes over.

But then suddenly, it's like I've been hit with a shot of adrenaline on steroids. My temperature rises and I feel an electric energy coursing through my veins. I close my eyes and groan. It's almost too much power for my body to handle. *What's happening to me?*

Damion doesn't answer. Instead, my eyes snap open and his voice booms out, "Brad Cunningham!"

Brad jerks his head around, a startled look of fear in his eyes. "Wh—Wh—What?"

"I am a demon, that's all you need know. Harm this vessel that I currently possess and I will be forced to harm yours. I'd prefer not to play musical chairs with bodies. I am just now breaking this one in." He has control at the moment, and if I weren't in freak-out mode, I'd roll my eyes and flip him off for the "breaking in" comment.

"I have been summoned here. What is it, Brad Cunningham, that you seek? Let us make a deal so that I may be on my way. Power enhancement is my specialty. Are you ready to let me help you unleash the tremendous power inside you?"

I see Brad's chest puff in pride from Damion's flattery. "Yes! I know that I have my own power. I don't need these stupid bitches. You could help me learn how to use it?" I see skepticism in his eyes, but I also see it warring with his lust for power.

"Brad Cunningham, I feel your power. Such a unique man you are, destined for bigger and better things. Many a great man have I helped. Just like yourself, only needing a slight nudge in the right direction. Can't you feel it?" Damion asks, and Brad smiles smugly. "Yes, you can. You are superior, yet unsure how to harness such staggering power. Let me help you unlock your true potential."

A scroll floats above us. "Brad Cunningham, free me so we may finalize our deal and that you may finally live the life of your dreams." I see Brad hesitate, but the greed in his eyes tells me that Damion's almost got him. "You're a man who deserves respect. And my friend, when you unleash your power, women will bow at your feet."

Brad slowly rises and I'm not sure what's going to happen next. To say that it's nerve-racking to watch a psycho yielding a blade walk toward you would be quite an understatement. But Brad is too caught up in his self-aggrandizing delusion, and he makes quick work of the ties on my wrists and ankles.

Damion stands me up, and an old-fashioned quill pen materializes in my left hand and the contract in my right. "Brad Cunningham, sign and step into your greatness."

As Brad reaches for the pen, I poke his finger with the sharp quill, drawing a tiny drop of blood. "Ouch!" Brad whines. He takes the pen and starts looking over the contract. I stand beside him and glance at the document. It's a one-page ancient-looking scroll, the font size starting out large and decreasing in size to nearly microscopic print at the bottom.

The beginning looks like any run-of-the-mill contract. I skip to the bottom and read:

> I acknowledge the entirety of our agreement
> is contained within the four corners of this
> document and that any claims, discussions, or
> promises made during the contract negotiations
> are not part of this contract. This contract is
> irrevocable in this life or any other lifetimes. I
> waive any and all rights of appeal, in any human
> or demonic legal system. I acknowledge that any
> claims made by the Demon do not guarantee a
> particular outcome. I have voluntarily and with

due consideration relinquished all rights to my soul and acknowledge that the Demon can call my soul due at any time, regardless of the outcome of any promises made by the Demon. In addition, the Demon may also call a favor due of me at any time...

That's as much as I can make out without the help of a magnifying glass.

"Brad Cunningham, did I make a mistake in deeming you worthy of my aid?"

"Of course not!" Brad yells and furiously signs. His blood-inked name blazes like fire, and the contract floats back to my hands. A sigil appears in my right hand and I stamp on the signature line. The contract glows red and quickly rolls itself shut, disappearing along with the sigil. If Brad wasn't such a monster, I would almost feel sorry for him. The devil's always in the details, and it's a safe bet that those are some pretty damning details written in that teeny-tiny print.

"Yes! More power!" Brad triumphantly cries. But then his cries of triumph quickly turn into cries of agony, and I have to cover my ears with my hands. This must be what hell sounds like—wailing and gnashing of teeth.

What's happening? I think to Damion.

"He got his wish. I amplified his power." He removes my hands from my ears to make air quotes around power. Thankfully, Brad stops screaming. "But since he has no power, other than the covetous desire to take power from others, he's stuck on a vicious feedback loop of wanting and then taking power from himself. I never agreed to give Brad additional power, nor did I guarantee any outcome. I've performed my end of the agreement."

Yep, definitely a lawyer. I run over and check Charlotte's pulse. She's unconscious, but I feel a faint heartbeat. I walk over to Brad who's lying down in the fetal position on this filthy floor. I see a bulge in his back pocket. I don't want to, but I stick my hand in there. Yes, it's his cell phone!

Rookie villain mistake.

Thank the Goddess for small favors.

Not the Goddess. Your thanks to me can begin at any moment.

This time I do roll my eyes as I call the police.

CHAPTER 12

I'm sitting on the curb outside the warehouse with a cup of terrible coffee and a blanket wrapped around my shoulders. Crime scene tape blocks off the area and police lights flash. Paramedics arrived earlier and whisked Charlotte to the hospital. They checked me out at the scene, but I already knew I had suffered a small concussion and said no thank you to further treatment.

It's taken what feels like forever to give my statement. I tell the detective the truth—Brad seemed like a normal guy, but he turned out to be a sociopath. He knocked me out and I woke up in his warehouse, where I feared for the worst, but then he cut me loose. He had a psychotic break from reality, and I took the opportunity to grab his cell phone to call for help. Sure, a few crucial facts were omitted. But had I given the unabridged version, I'd be the next one hauled outta here on suspicion of a psychotic break.

Charlotte and I were the only two found on the premises, but I'm told that detectives are getting a warrant to search Brad's house and office. I just nod, as I'm too tired to say much else.

Aubry!

What?

The detective is still talking to you.

"I'm sorry, what was that?" I ask with a yawn.

"Is there someone I can call to come get you?" the detective asks.

"No, thank you. I would just like a ride back to my apartment, please."

A police cruiser drops me off, and I numbly unlock the door and climb the stairs to the apartment. I strip and step in the shower before the water has time to heat up. I start shaking violently, and the more I try to make my body stop, the more it shakes. I sink to the floor and tuck my knees to my chest and begin to cry.

Shhh, Damion says. *Don't fight it. Just let it out and let it pass through you. It's okay, I've got you.*

I don't remember getting out of the shower or putting on a long-sleeved T-shirt and leggings or crawling into bed with an ice pack for the lump on the back of my head. But Damion must have done those things for me, because I wake to find myself tucked snugly in bed.

"Good morning. You must be Aubry's grandmother and aunt. It's a pleasure to meet you. My name is Damion. Aubry's had quite a time while you've been away."

I snap my eyes open to see Grandma and Aunt Callie standing by my bed with mouths agape. "Grandma, Aunt Callie, I have a small possession problem," I groan.

We move to the kitchen table and I recount my tale, with Damion interjecting here and there. Honestly, they take the whole "I'm possessed by a demon" news surprisingly well. Elvis, having already heard the story, wasn't interested in hearing it a second time and fell asleep on the couch. Then again, he wasn't interested in hearing it the first time.

After Grandma performs an unsuccessful unbinding spell, she shrugs and informs me, "I had a demon lover once in a past life." Aunt Callie nods in confirmation. "Let's just say I understand why Lilith dumped Adam in the Garden of Eden and took up with that bad boy Lucifer." She winks at me. The legend goes that Lilith was Adam's first wife, not Eve. But there was soon trouble in paradise, as Lilith did not want to submit to Adam—namely they both wanted to be on top during copulation. So Lilith ran off and took up with a demon, Lucifer or Samael, depending on who's telling the story.

Damion laughs. "Grandma, don't say things like that around him. My body's barely big enough to house this demon's ego as is," I groan.

Grandma presses on, completely ignoring my protests. "I've never been with a Cambion, though. Aubry, when we finally figure out how to exorcise Damion, are you calling dibs?"

Now I'm the one who laughs. "Go for it, Grandma."

I'm going to insist that you call dibs and protect me from your grandmother. You owe me.

I don't owe you.

You most certainly do owe me from saving you from the most vanilla man in the world.

You demon lawyers seem awfully fond of something. Let me think, what is it? Ah yes, a contract. Which I did not sign, so I don't owe you. And besides, you saved me because doing so saved your arrogant behind. Don't leave out that little fact.

He laughs in my mind. *Alright, Ally McBeal, you may rest your case.*

The fact that you know who Ally McBeal is concerns me.

"Well, why wouldn't you go for it?" Grandma continues. "All I'm saying is that you might want to try something different and step out of your good-girl comfort zone. What was your high school boyfriend's name? Well, the fact that I can't even remember says it all. And don't get me started on that wannabe wizard, Todd. I guess he was your version of dating a bad boy, but he wasn't a bad boy, he just was bad. There's a big difference. Then you go from bad to bland and pick a milk toast accountant," Grandma says, critiquing my love life.

"One, my high school boyfriend's name was Ryan, who has a lovely wife and two kids and proudly serves our country." Thank you, social media. "Two, Todd was a wannabe chaote, not a wizard." I'm not sure how that helps my cause, but I press on. "And three, Brad was not my boyfriend. But since he turned out to be a psycho, I'm not sure that you can call him milk toast!"

Pointing out the fact that Brad is a psycho doesn't help your case, Damion advises.

"Sugar pie, I'm worried you have your aunt's horrible judgment when it comes to men."

"Mama, you do know that I'm in the room," Aunt Callie says dryly.

Grandma ignores her and presses on. "You bring home a motorcycle-riding deadbeat like Callie's first husband, and I'll have to stage an intervention. Damion, do you ride a motorcycle?"

"He wasn't a deadbeat, he was a con man," Aunt Callie says.

Pointing out the fact that her ex-husband is a con man doesn't help her case, either.

Elvis decides that the conversation has become much more interesting and is now purring and circling my legs. I, on the other hand, have had enough of this conversation, both silent *and* verbal.

I pick up the cat and announce, "If you'll excuse us, Elvis and I have left the building." I dramatically march back to my room, cat in one hand, teacup in the other. Is it immature to storm out of the room when someone holds up a mirror and you don't like what you see? Sure it is. But at least I'm mature enough to acknowledge that it's immature.

Elvis quickly informs me that he'll have no part in this nonsense and begins scratching on my bedroom door. I have to open it to let him out, completely negating my grand exit.

CHAPTER 13

I walk downstairs, ready for things to get back to normal. Well, as normal as they can be considering I'm still possessed by a Cambion.

"Tell me about the trade show," I say as I flip through a backlog of mail I've neglected. Bills, catalogs, and fast food coupons that go in the trash. The fast food coupons, not the bills. Grandma is of the opinion that a bill is only a suggestion to pay, and she'll get around to paying it if and when she feels like it. And that is one of the countless reasons why I run the business end of our shop.

I stop on a flyer for New Life Spiritual Center. "Have you heard of this place?" I read it aloud, "'New Life Spiritual Center, offering wellness classes, spiritual direction, meditation, and yoga. Individual, group, and corporate retreats offered.'"

Grandma looks at the flyer and nods. "Yep, they had a table at the show. The owner or maybe the center's guru, I'm not really sure who he was, but a man was there selling the retreat. And he was one fine-looking man, let me tell you," she informs me with a whistle.

Damion snorts. *Please. Your grandmother will need resuscitation when she sees me.*

You are so vain, it's obscene. And she'll probably be the one to suggest mouth-to-mouth, but don't let her fool you. Her heart is perfectly healthy.

I throw the flyer in the trash. "Well, what else was good this year?" They tell me about the latest and greatest in new age merchandise, and I agree to look into a few items for the shop.

"Oh, I forgot to tell you. We saw Todd," Aunt Callie says.

"You mean you ran into him in the casino?" I ask.

"I mean he was there at the trade show. He's the leader of a group of chaos magicians. Can you believe that?"

"I can," Grandma snorts. "Of course he fancies himself a leader."

"Grandma, I've got it. You never liked Todd and you never will. I broke up with him and we're never getting back together, so can you please drop it?"

Aunt Callie saves me by changing the subject. "I have some appointments this morning, but find me around midday and we'll try a guided meditation to release Damion."

"If it were me, I'd be in no rush to get rid of a seduction demon," Grandma chimes in. "No siree."

"Thank you, Grandma," I say, ignoring her as I busy myself with paperwork.

It's a beautiful sunshine-filled day, and we get quite a few customers. When there's a lull, I pull out *The Divine Magic of the Moon,* the book I "randomly" selected to help with the Damion situation. I flip through it and a folded piece of paper stuck between the pages falls out. I pick up the paper and open it. On it is some kind of sigil drawn with what looks to be a red permanent marker.

What is that? Damion asks. *It looks like a demon sigil, but it's not one I'm familiar with.*

I don't know. The mark that you placed on Brad's contract, that's your sigil?

Yes. Think of it as a magical signature. It holds power, but that power can be turned against a demon under certain circumstances.

Like the demon trap Gabe was talking about?

Yes.

I walk to the break room to find Grandma making herbal tea. Aunt Callie is drinking what looks to be some kind of disgusting kale smoothie. "Before you ask, the answer is no. I do not want to go on a green smoothie challenge with you." Fool me once, shame on you. Fool me twice, shame on me. I haven't forgotten the green juice cleanse. "Do either of you know where this book came from?"

Grandma takes a closer look. "That's mine. It's a good one. You should read it."

"Do you know what this is?" I hold up the paper. "I found it in the book."

"No clue," Grandma says. Aunt Callie shakes her head no.

Lunch rolls around, and Grandma and I order Chinese takeout despite my aunt's condemnation of the MSG content. We ignore her and enjoy our food, and then she leads me on a guided meditation to invite Damion to exit my body. When I'm brought back out of the trance with the count of three, Damion announces that he is still here, but he is definitely more zenned out than when we started, so that was something at least.

You, on the other hand, are wound too tight. You know what would help with that?

81

Later that evening, I ride with Aunt Callie to yoga. *Is this who taught you how to drive? If so, that explains everything.*

If you could hop from my body to hers, you would just so you could take over the steering wheel.

And your point?

Trying to practice yoga with Damion is an exercise in patience, which I guess is the point of yoga in the first place. I'm holding a headstand when I begin to shake.

Want me to take over?

No, I don't. I lose concentration and tumble out of the pose.

I'm holding the side splits when Damion whispers, *I didn't know you were this flexible. Mmmm, this gives me ideas.*

You are a dirty, dirty demon. I try hard not to smile and fail miserably. Aunt Callie looks over at me, and I quickly shut my eyes and ignore her.

"Hey girls and guy, the new season of *House Guest* is about to come on. Who's in?" Grandma asks as soon as we walk through the door.

"How is *House Guest* different from *Bermuda Love Triangle?*" I make the mistake of asking. Grandma explains the finer nuances of a show about people hooking up while competing for prizes versus a show about people hooking up.

"Sugar pie, I worry you have too much of your Aunt Callie's boring sensibility."

"Mama, I'm still in the room," Aunt Callie says. "I'll pass. I'm working on a new hypnosis induction script that I'd like to finish this evening."

"It's a pass for me as well. I've got some reading to do," I say as I head to my room.

"I hope it's at least something steamy. Maybe light a few candles, get Damion to read you some erotica in that sexy voice of his. Do you need to borrow my e-reader? I've got a fairly diverse erotica collection. Damion, what are you into? Any fetishes? What about feet?"

"Gross and good night," I toss over my shoulder.

I climb into bed and pick up *The Divine Magic of the Moon.* Damion takes over my hands, lighting a candle on the nightstand. He opens the book to the first page, and in an erotic whisper, begins reading the introduction. I smile, falling asleep to the sound of his sexy voice and the feel of my feet being lightly massaged by a phantom touch.

CHAPTER 14

The next morning, I run the shop solo. Grandma's gambling in Tunica and Aunt Callie is, well, not here. "I swear, sometimes it feels like I'm the only adult in this family. Elvis, don't you think so?" Elvis responds by ignoring me.

The door chimes and I'm surprised when I see Charlotte and her mama, Debbie.

"Aubry, how can we ever repay you?" Debbie says as she begins to cry and pulls me in for a big bear hug.

"No repayment necessary," I say when she finally lets me go.

"Charlotte, it's nice to see you," I say as we hug. She looks much better than when I saw her tied to the chair in Brad's warehouse. She's shorter than I am and curvier, with a soft face and skin the color of honey. Her short black hair frames her delicate face beautifully. She's wearing glasses that make her look studious yet stylish. I notice some bruising around her wrists and a bandage on her left arm protruding beneath her shirt.

"Aubry, you saved my life," she tells me.

"We caught a lucky break, that's for sure," I vaguely reply.

Charlotte turns to her mama. "Mom, I promise I'm fine. Go on to work."

"Where do you work?" I ask. Debbie reaches into her tote bag and pulls out a box. I open it to find six chocolate croissants. "Now this is the type of repayment I will accept," I say as I grab one and take a bite. "Delicious."

"Mom owns a bakery in Germantown."

"Please tell me you deliver to the metro Memphis area," I say as I finish my croissant. Germantown is a suburb about thirty minutes east of Memphis.

"For you, I'll deliver to Memphis. One more gift," she says and pulls a pink keychain out of her tote bag. I must have a confused look on my face. "Pepper spray," she explains.

"She gave me one too," Charlotte says. Debbie gives her daughter a worried look. "Mom, I'm okay. Go," she says kindly but firmly.

"Alright, baby girl. I'm going. You call me as soon as you get home from class."

"Yes, ma'am," Charlotte says with a hug. Debbie turns to me and pulls me in for another hug. Reluctantly, she leaves.

"How are you feeling?" I delicately ask Charlotte when we're alone. I offer her a croissant, but she shakes her head no.

"My mom has been feeding me round the clock. Her way of trying to help," she trails off.

"If you ever want to talk about it, I'm here for you." I realize we don't know each other, but I get the feeling Charlotte is a kindred spirit.

"Thank you," she says, rubbing her bandaged arm. I'm about to change the subject when she says quietly, "I'm seeing a trauma therapist. That's the only way my mom would even consider not dragging me back home with her." She looks at me intently. "I know it wasn't luck that got us out of Brad's basement alive."

"Whatever you want to call it, the guy had a break with reality and I was able to talk him into cutting me loose. Luckily, he had a cell phone," I retell the official police version of events.

"Bullshit," she says, startling me. "I was drifting in and out, but I was awake when your demon tricked Brad. I heard the whole thing." She pauses. "So you're possessed?"

"Yes." I suppose there's no use denying it.

"Why aren't you climbing on the ceiling or puking green slime?"

"*The Exorcist?*" I take a guess.

"Well, yes, that's really the extent of my demonic knowledge. That movie was terrifying."

"That's why I didn't watch it."

"But you want this demon to leave?"

"My name is Damion," he interjects.

Charlotte's eyes go wide, but she composes herself. "And Damion, I also owe you a thank you."

"Charlotte, to answer your question, I'm ready for Damion to leave," I take back over. "He's worn out his welcome." If I'm being completely honest, I've gotten used to having him around. In fact, I might actually miss him once he's gone. Is this the demonic possession version of Stockholm Syndrome?

So much for southern hospitality.

Southern hospitably is for invited guests.

You invited me with your demon-summoning tools.

I'm still not convinced that's true, but invitation rescinded.

Luckily for you, my invitation of naked breakfast remains unrescinded.

Is unrescinded even a word?

"I'm a healer," Charlotte says, and I snap my attention back to her. "May I see if I can help?"

"I'm game." I lock the front door, and Charlotte instructs me to lie down on the couch in the reading nook. She begins moving her hands about an inch from my body, starting at my head and moving down to my feet, and then back up.

"That's surprising. I assumed your energy centers would be completely turned upside down. You did have some unusual energy around your head, but maybe that's just because you've got someone else in there with you. But overall, I got the feeling that your energy and Damion's energy fit nicely together."

I can think of another way that we would fit nicely together.

"Thanks for giving it a shot," I tell Charlotte and ignore Damion.

"How did you come to be possessed?"

"It's a long story." I don't want to tell her it happened during the séance I held on behalf of her mama, as I get the feeling that Charlotte's got enough trauma to process. I don't know the details of her captivity, but I can take a guess. I certainly don't want her to think it's her fault that a bossy Cambion possessed me and won't leave.

"Hey, our circle is meeting in a few days to try and help release Damion. Would you like to join us? It's a full moon, and my aunt, grandma, and the three other witches in our circle are going to perform a ritual."

"I'm not a witch," Charlotte says, but I see the curiosity in her eyes.

"You just used some pretty nifty magic on me. Why don't you come and just hang out? And then if you want to participate with us, you're more than welcome to."

"I'll think about it," Charlotte hesitantly says. "Well, I've got to get back to class."

"I'm so glad you stopped by. Hopefully, I'll see you soon."

Charlotte leaves and I place the pepper spray behind the counter and wonder what it would be like to have a caring, albeit slightly overprotective mama. I wouldn't know.

You alright?

"Yes," I fib and then get back to work.

CHAPTER 15

The days pass quickly with me running the shop and searching for a spell to exorcise Damion. Gabe informs us we can safely rule out Charlotte's mama and her friend as having a hand in our situation. I could have saved Gabe the billable hours and told him that.

Damion and I alternate between fussing and flirting. I'm not sure which one I enjoy more, and I'm not sure what that says about me.

Grandma wears us down—we're in the living room watching *House Guest*. She gives us a rundown of what happened on the premiere episode; otherwise, we would have been unable to follow along. Dramatic eye roll.

"Brant and Gia are this season's showmance. They're a strong power couple, but when it comes to a puzzle challenge, neither one of them could find their way out of a wet paper bag. Hey, if Damion's still stuck with you, the two of you should audition for the show!"

"Not happening."

"I bet the producers would love it—an instant showmance!" she continues, ignoring me. "There's a casting call in Nashville in two months. Aubry, that'll give you time to work on your pitch and get some headshots taken. I'd also suggest some bikini pics."

"Definitely not happening."

"Don't be such a prude. You have a hot bod, might as well use it to team Daubry's advantage. That can be your showmance nickname." She pauses for a second and continues, "On second thought, let Damion do the pitch; Aubry, you be the eye candy."

"Vivian, we'll certainly keep our options open," Damion says.

You're an enabler.

I'm team Daubry all the way. And I'd be happy to help you with your bikini pics. I'm an excellent photographer. They'd be tasteful, of course.

Uh-huh. Sure they'd be.

We proceed to watch grown men and women dress up in clown costumes and navigate an obstacle course with pies being flung at them from mechanical arms. I can't make this stuff up.

Back in my room, I attempt an uncrossing spell. Grandma made me a sachet of sage, dragon blood powder, and lemon oil. I cast a protection circle, light my sachet and chant:

> Power of dragon, purifying lemon and salt.
> I uncross Damion the binding halt.
> Freed from my body Damion
> rise and do me no harm.
> Thus be so with the aid of this charm.

Damion informs me that even with the lemon, sage is stinky.

The next morning, a thousand-piece jigsaw puzzle is spread out on the kitchen table. "What's with this?" I ask. Grandma and I haven't put together a puzzle since I was a kid.

"Your training for *House Guest*," she announces.

"You are delusional, you know that, right?"

"I don't want you two repeating a Brant and Gia mistake."

After eating breakfast at the island, as eating at the kitchen table is no longer an option, I work on the puzzle. Well, Damion does. I was intent on ignoring it until Grandma admits defeat and shoves it back in whatever closet it came from. The picture on the box shows a completed puzzle of the twelve zodiac signs.

What's your sign? I ask Damion.

Leo. Figures he's the lion. Arrogant. Stubborn. Likes being in charge. *How about you?*

Aquarius. Independent. Stubborn. Likes being right.

He puts down a puzzle piece and grabs my phone, and a minute later he reads to me, *The attraction between the king,* he pauses dramatically, *that would be me,* and then continues, *and Aquarius is off the charts. If these two ever move off their personal battlefield, expect them to set the sheets on fire.*

I assume you got your astrological knowledge from zodiac dating for dummies online. What he just said about Leo and Aquarius compatibility is true, but that doesn't mean I have to acknowledge it. I am a stubborn Aquarius, after all.

We close the shop early to give us time to prepare for tonight's full moon circle. I gather the supplies we'll need and carve my intention *Release* into the candle. I slip on my gauzy black dress, for no reason other than this is my moon ritual dress. When I put it on, it helps me get in the right frame of mind. *All you need is a pointy black hat and a broom.*

"Good idea, no one's ever thought of that," I reply smartly, and Damion laughs.

Amelia and Florence are the first to arrive. They rode together, so they must have had a good time on their cruise. That, or Amelia's been so busy unpacking all those extra suitcases, she forgot to measure the offending magnolia branch. "Aubry, dear, how is demonic possession treating you?" Amelia asks. Several years older than Grandma, although Amelia won't admit her age, she has short raven-black hair she meticulously keeps colored and coiffed, dark brown eyes, and makeup expertly applied to her timeless face.

"Vivian told us *all* about your predicament," Florence adds. Like Amelia, Florence refuses to reveal her age. Also like Amelia, Florence is always dressed to the nines and perfectly put together. She has short blonde hair that she keeps religiously colored and styled, and is always wearing an obscene number of diamonds.

I look over at Grandma. "Of course you did." She gives me an unapologetic shrug.

Julia is the next to arrive, looking badass as usual in a leather biker jacket and black leather pants. "Julia, dear, tell us what's new?" Amelia asks.

"Busy with work, which is a good thing." Julia goes on to talk about her salon.

"She means what's new in the *boudoir*," Grandma interjects.

"That is *not* what I mean. Vivian, don't be so tacky," Amelia scoffs.

"Speaking of what's new in the boudoir, guess who made a new gentleman friend on our cruise?" Florence dramatically announces. She loves being the bearer of juicy gossip almost as much as Vivian.

"He's a perfectly nice man from Mobile who happens to enjoy playing bridge. And a decent bridge partner is hard to find," Amelia retorts.

"He's a younger man, fifteen years her junior," Florence stage whispers. "And I dare you to find a better bridge partner than me. I'm the one who has to carry your dead weight."

"Oh for goodness' sake, can we talk about more pressing matters, like Aubry being possessed by a demon?" Amelia exclaims.

"Since when?" Julia demands.

"I was waiting to tell you at my next hair appointment, as a text message doesn't do this story justice," Grandma announces and then proceeds to tell the story, in all its embellished glory. "And he sounds like one sexy demon," she concludes.

"Vivian, you are too kind," Damion says, playing to the audience.

The doorbell chimes. "Alright, ladies, that's Charlotte. Please don't scare her off tonight." I point at Grandma.

"Don't know why you're singling me out," she huffs.

"Really? You don't know why?" I toss over my shoulder. I escort Charlotte inside and make the rounds of introductions.

"Charlotte, dear, wonderful to have you join us," Amelia says.

"Boy, you and Aubry have been through the wringer with that piece of work Brad." I cut Grandma a look that she ignores. Two words that don't go together—Grandma and tact.

"Very true. So tonight your group will try to help Aubry release Damion?" Charlotte demonstrates how to tactfully change the subject.

"Yes," Aunt Callie says. "We're going to perform a modified letting go ritual, but instead of asking the Goddess to help us let

93

go of some kind of emotional baggage, we're all going to focus on Aubry letting go of Damion and releasing him from her body."

"This is the first time one of us has ever been possessed by a demon. It's all very exciting," Florence adds.

"Charlotte, if you want to join us, we'll go upstairs, join hands, and Vivian will guide us. Just keep an open mind and your energy positive," Aunt Callie explains.

"I'm in," Charlotte tells us. I hand her a pen and show her our intention statement and ask her to write on a thin sheet of paper—*Release Damion from Aubry's body and safely return him to his own.*

We walk upstairs to the outdoor patio, gathering in a circle around the moon candle, an empty ashtray, and a bowl of water. Grasping hands, Grandma begins with an invocation of the Goddess and our petition:

> Fire purify from Aubry's body Damion,
> return him safely to his own.
> Lead him out of Aubry, may the way be shown.

> Water cleanse from Aubry's body
> Damion, return him safely to his own.
> Lead him out of Aubry, may the way be shown.

One by one we burn our intention statement and drop it into the bowl. I then pick up the bowl of blessed moon water and drink. I feel the magic crackling in the air as Grandma thanks the Moon and we close our circle.

Back downstairs, Grandma turns to me. "Well?"

Damion answers for me. "That was a nice ceremony."

CHAPTER 16

Back on the wooded path, I come to the same fork in the road. This time, I know to turn left. A familiar figure hovers up ahead. "Maddie, wait!" I yell, willing my feet to move toward her.

She holds up a Tower tarot card and disappears.

"Maddie!" I cry. "What does the Tower card mean? Please come back!"

Aubry! I wake to the sound of Damion's voice inside my head. *It's alright.*

"No, it's really not." I sit up and tuck my knees to my chest, calming my breathing and focusing on decreasing my heart rate. I take in a deep belly breath through my nose and hold it for six counts before slowly releasing it through my mouth.

Are you ready to tell me?

"Can I trust you?"

I can't win with that question. If I say yes, you won't believe me.

"Well, is the answer yes?"

Yes.

"Of course you'd say yes."

You've made my point for me. Why not allow me to demonstrate that I'm trustworthy? Tell me about Maddie.

"How do you know her name?" I demand.

I heard you call it out.

"Give me just a minute of privacy, please." I flip on the lamp and grab my deck of tarot cards. I love my cards; they belonged to my mama. One of the few items of hers that I have. I hold them to my heart. Should I let Damion help me with Maddie's case? An upright card means yes. A reversed card means no. I give my cards a shuffle and then flip over the Devil upright. So my cards decided to get all literal in that answer. Ask the devil for help, got it.

"Damion?"

Yes?

"My best friend was murdered a year ago. I want to find out who killed her." It's ironic that I told Debbie to wait and let the police do their job in finding her missing daughter, Charlotte. That's exactly what I did with Maddie. I waited on the police to do their job, and my best friend's body was fished out of the Mississippi River.

Tell me about your friend.

"Madison Williams, Maddie for short, moved from Arkansas to Memphis my freshman year of high school and we became instant best friends. She was like the sister I never had. We graduated high school and she went on to college here at the University of Memphis. She wanted to be a teacher. We stayed close, even though she was in school and I wasn't."

Why didn't you go to college?

"I'm practical, always have been. I'm a witch who runs my family's magic shop. A degree would have been wasted ink and paper. Anyway, about a month before Maddie died, she started distancing herself from me."

Why?

"Honestly, I thought it was because she didn't like my boyfriend at the time, and that may have been true, but there was more to it. I found out from the detective working the case that Maddie had been messaging back and forth with someone for about a month. Detective Rodriguez asked me if I knew the guy, but I didn't have a clue who he was. She kept this guy a secret from me."

Did the police trace the number?

"They couldn't. It was a burner phone. If she was seeing someone, why wouldn't she have told me? Detective Rodriguez questioned me about the phone, hinting that someone with a burner phone might be involved in illegal activity, like dealing drugs. Maddie wasn't into drugs, and I can't believe she'd be involved with a criminal."

Did investigators determine a cause of death?

"It was ruled a homicide. Her body was found in the Mississippi River, but they believe she was killed before she went in the water," I say as the bile rises in my throat. "Detective Rodriguez wouldn't tell me more because I'm not family."

What about Maddie's family?

"It was just Maddie and her mama, Leigh."

Where is her mother now?

"I'm not sure. Leigh took off after the memorial. I haven't heard from her since." No surprise there.

Would she know more about this mystery guy?

"Doubtful. Maddie and her mama were estranged at the time."

Why?

I sigh. "Because Leigh's a junkie, and Maddie finally had enough."

When did all this happen?

"About a year ago." I grab my phone to check the time. It's a little after six in the morning, and then I notice today's date. "Correction, she died exactly one year ago today." I guess that explains the timing of my dreams. "Will you help me find out who killed Maddie?"

Damion remains silent for a stretch. *Alright, Veronica Mars, I'll help you. This will be my good deed for the decade. But I make no guarantees. Who's to say that we'll have better luck than the police?*

"The fact that you even know who Veronica Mars is concerns me."

So you were having nightmares about your dead friend?

"Not exactly nightmares." I explain to him my dreams. "Maybe they're messages from Maddie."

Why would you have seen her death coming? You said that she distanced herself from you and was secretly messaging with this unknown individual.

"I occasionally receive premonitions, but I didn't foresee anything about her death." The guilt that I didn't foresee my best friend's death and warn her is almost unbearable, I don't say.

Very well. First priority is getting me back into my unbelievably sexy body, and then we'll look into your friend's death.

I roll my eyes. "Your ego is ridiculous. And just so we're clear, you're going to help me, no strings attached."

There are always strings. Don't let anyone tell you otherwise.

"That's not very reassuring."

I've made you a generous offer. Take it or leave it.

"Fine, I'll take it." I hope those words don't come back to bite me.

I flip through my cards until I find the Tower card. It depicts a storybook castle that's been hit by lightning and is engulfed in flames.

This was the card in your dream?

"Yes."

What does it mean?

"The Tower card arguably has the most negative connotation of all the cards in the tarot deck. It means chaos, calamity, or violence. But it could also represent destruction leading to a positive outcome." Why was Maddie holding this card?

"Aubry, you've been a horrible hostess to our guest. Go show Damion the town," Grandma announces.

"I haven't been to Memphis in a few years. What a wonderful idea, Vivian," he replies.

"Grandma, you do realize that Damion isn't a guest, he's a trespasser?" I take back over.

"That's still no reason to be rude."

"I'm pretty sure that it is," I say smartly.

"Go on, now. I raised you better than that."

"Fine," I grumble.

I grab my purse, and we walk outside and over to the trolley stop. A disheveled woman carrying several bags who is talking to herself looks me square in the eyes and says, "Hello, Devil," and starts laughing hysterically as she continues on her way.

Did she really sense you? I ask Damion.

Maybe. There are some humans who can sense demonic energy. The problem is for most, it drives them mad.

Boy, can I ever relate. The trolley comes to a loud stop and we climb aboard. I feed money into the machine and take a seat. Here's to hoping we don't encounter any other demon seers on this little outing.

We soon reach the Beale Street stop and I exit the trolley. It's a weekday afternoon and the scene is fairly tame. Well, tame for Beale Street. Blues music pumps from every bar and the delicious smell of barbecue fills the air. We're just in time to see a group of kids clear the street and proceed to do backflips from one end of Beale to the other.

Dropping a dollar in their tip bucket, I walk a few blocks to the Peabody Hotel and enter the ornate lobby. We've missed the duck parade, but the mallards are still taking a leisurely swim in the marble fountain.

Have you ever seen the duck parade? I ask, taking a seat in a comfy wingback chair.

No.

It's actually a lot of fun to watch. The duck master rolls out the red carpet, and the five ducks exit the elevator and race to the fountain.

We'll save that for our next date.

This isn't a date.

A server appears and I order an old fashioned. I'm not a day drinker, but since I'm here on orders to entertain my "company," I'll indulge. My drink is presented a few moments later and I go ahead and settle up.

I'm sorry, how very rude of me, I tell Damion as I grab the cherry from my cocktail and pop it in my mouth. *What would you like to drink?*

Nothing for me, thank you. Since you're such a lush, one of us has to be sober enough to navigate us back to the shop. Besides, I'm too busy picturing what's happening with your tongue and that cherry.

You're terrible, I inform him with a smile. And then he takes over—my tongue performing some sort of acrobatics. He reaches my hand up and pulls from my mouth the short cherry stem, now tied into a triple knot. I can't help it, I laugh out loud. And then I wonder if he could do that with *my* tongue, just what he could do with *his* tongue? Dang it, he's a tricky demon.

I change the subject. *This is one of my all-time favorite bars. What's your favorite?*

The carousel bar inside the Hotel Monteleone in New Orleans. It's an actual antique carousel that slowly rotates around the room. I personally enjoy a classy bar. I hate having to scream over loud music to speak to my company. Speaking of company, a man takes a seat across from me, placing his beer on the table between us.

"Hello, are you here on business or pleasure?" he asks me with a friendly smile. He's a good-looking man in his early thirties. From his business casual attire, I'm guessing he's here on a business trip.

"I suppose you could say pleasure. I'm local but decided to take the afternoon off and play hooky," I tell him.

He's hitting on you.

No, he's not. We're just making polite conversation.

I learn that Mike from Chicago is in fact here on business. I give him some local restaurant recommendations for dinner, and we chitchat about the tourist spots he should visit. I finish my drink and get ready to make my exit when he leans over the table and whispers to me, "I have a room upstairs."

Ugh, Damion was right. Now I'll never hear the end of it. "How nice for you," I dryly respond.

"It is nice. Why don't you come upstairs with me and check it out?" he whispers, moving his gaze down to my breasts and back up.

The nerve of this guy. I'm not a gambler like Grandma, but I'd be willing to place big money that he has a wedding band hidden in the zippered part of his suitcase. Before I can come back with a biting retort and make a dramatic exit, I feel Damion's power take over. In a rather menacing voice, he whispers, "Don't worry, Jeffrey Smith. I'll meet you later tonight in your room. Try to sleep knowing that I'll be paying you a little visit. I'm coming to steal your soul."

As we walk away, I'm pretty sure that Jeffrey, who is *not* named Mike, just pissed his pants.

That was unnecessary. I had the situation completely under control.

Perhaps, but now Jeffrey Smith, married father of two, is unlikely to hit on another woman during this business trip, Damion informs me, and I smile.

I step outside and make the short walk to overlook the Mississippi River. I have a seat on a bench and watch a towboat push a barge of cargo. *A towboat captain is the one who spotted Maddie's body. She was all tangled in debris*, I tell Damion, a tear escaping my eye. I will myself not to break down. *I'm sorry, you'll have to inform Vivian that I'm a terrible hostess. And clearly I shouldn't day drink*, I joke, dabbing my eyes.

Aubry, your best friend was murdered. An invisible hand gives mine a squeeze. *I told you I'd help you and I meant it.*

Without strings.

I told you there's always strings. Remove the stone from underneath your pillow and let's play tonight.

I walk back to the trolley stop and pray to the Goddess that I don't get all tangled up in those strings.

CHAPTER 17

I'm lying on my stomach, basking in the sunshine on my lounge chair. "Ready for your photo shoot?" Damion whispers in my ear. I glance over to the teak table next to my chair and spot a professional camera.

"Not getting tangled up in your strings," I tell him, willing my back not to arch. Of course that's not exactly true; otherwise, I would have left the garnet under my pillow.

"Why?" he asks, playfully tugging at the strings of my bikini bottom. He leans over me and that delicious smell of his overtakes my senses. "Don't you want to get tangled up with me?" he purrs.

"At what cost?" This time, I can't help it, my back arches, my ass hitting his hard cock. "And what happened to you 'being a good boy'?" I ask in a throaty voice. I force my body to return supine against the lounge chair.

"Your wish," he says and disappears. And dang it if I'm not disappointed.

I glance at the table—the camera disappears and in its stead is a cocktail with a colorful umbrella and a cherry garnish. I sit up and grab the cherry and pop it in my mouth. My tongue gets to work, but all I can manage is a halfway decent single knot.

Aunt Callie offers to make me a cherry smoothie the next morning. I decline, not in the mood for the Universe's antics. Damion and I spend a few minutes working on the puzzle. We've filled in most of the border pieces and are now working our way toward the center. He insists we focus on putting together Leo and Aquarius, because those two signs go together, but in that order, because Leo is the king.

I check off some not so glamorous items from my to-do list. Unfortunately, the customer restroom doesn't magically clean itself. Now that's the spell we should be searching for.

I wash up and walk to the front. Elvis is hanging out on the counter. "You know I don't like you up there," I tell him.

He responds by hissing at me.

Charlotte enters the shop carrying a box of donuts and two coffees. "I knew we were destined to be friends," I tell her as I select a blueberry cake donut from the box of assorted flavors. She hands me a coffee. "Thank you. What did you think of the other night?" I ask, taking a nibble of my donut.

"It was amazing. I've never felt anything like it before. But why didn't the ritual work?"

"That's the question. What are you up to today?"

"I have a break between classes. I wanted to get a few books." She walks over to our reading nook. "What would you recommend for a novice?"

I join her and look for a moment, and then I pull *Witches 101: A Beginner's Guide to Magic.* "Try this one. Take it. A trade for the sugar and caffeine pick-me-up."

"Thank you. I can only stay for a few more minutes. I got a call this morning from the victim liaison with the District Attorney's office. Did she call you?"

"I saw I had a voicemail from an unknown number. I just haven't checked my messages."

Charlotte nods. "She warned me that Brad's defense attorney has already filed for a competency hearing."

"Meaning?"

"Meaning his lawyer is going to argue that Brad is mentally unfit to stand trial."

"Mentally unfit my behind," I complain. "So what will happen?"

"My understanding is if the judge agrees, then there will be no trial, and Brad will remain institutionalized in a secure mental health facility indefinitely."

"How do you feel about that?"

"At first I was angry—you and I both know he's *not* insane. But then I thought about having to testify at trial. I really didn't want to tell a room full of strangers the details of what happened."

"Goddess, I haven't thought that far ahead." I'm sure I'll have to testify too. Let's see, commit perjury or tell a packed courtroom I'm a witch possessed by a demon who was kidnapped by an energy vamp. Perjury it is.

She nods. "But Brad's lost his soul, and he won't be able to harm anyone else, so I'm okay with it." Phew, hopefully I'll dodge the perjury bullet.

The door chimes and in walks Gabe. I know Charlotte's thinking what I'm thinking. Yep, that's one sexy man right there.

"Aubry." He turns to Charlotte with a charming smile and reaches for her hand. "And you are?"

"Just leaving," she says, evading his reach and walking to the door. "I've got to get to class. I'll see you later, Aubry," she tosses over her shoulder. Obviously, I was way off base concerning Charlotte's thoughts about Gabe.

Damion busts out laughing. "Very smooth, Cupid."

Why is he Cupid? I mentally ask Damion.

Not because of love magic, clearly.

"Donut?" I take back over, holding the box open for Gabe.

"Thank you," he says, picking a chocolate glazed. "Damion, you're one to talk. The only way you can keep a beautiful woman's attention is to possess her. Isn't that right, Aubry?"

"Don't drag me into your pissing contest. You two can whip them out later and measure. Let's focus on the important issue." I fill Gabe in on the circle's unsuccessful ritual.

No need to measure, mine's bigger.

I thought I already told you to keep all references of your package to yourself.

I'm making reference to our offices. Mine is bigger. But I see that your mind is in the gutter. You are a dirty, dirty witch.

"I've got to run. Damion, I'm meeting with *your* client. While you're enjoying a nice little vacation, I'm having to pick up the slack at work."

That reminds me, where shall me meet for our erotic dream? Perhaps a cabin in the mountains with falling snow in the background while we make love in front of the roaring fire? Or would you prefer a private yacht sailing the Mediterranean while I move your thong out of the way and take you from behind on the sundeck? Or did my wanton witch like the private island? We could go back there, except this time, I wouldn't be a good boy.

I assume you found your seduction for dummies online? I reply smartly, and he laughs. If I'm being honest, I want to answer yes to all of the above, but hell will freeze over before I admit that to him. I cross my arms and hope that Gabe doesn't glance down, because my nipples are hard.

"Cupid, don't worry. You'll be well-compensated for your time," Damion says.

"Time and a half," Gabe corrects.

Still think he's a gentleman?

"Why not try a contract? Agree to leave Aubry's body in exchange for something," Gabe says. His phone beeps. "Excuse me." He looks at the message. "I've got to go." With a bow, he vanishes.

I glance over to see all the black hair on Elvis's back standing on end. "I agree. It's disconcerting when a supernatural pops out of existence like that."

Elvis responds by pretending he wasn't scared. He hops off the counter and meanders out of the room. "You're not fooling anyone," I call after him.

Gabe's idea is worth a shot, Damion says.

"You think after I saw you wheeling and dealing with Brad I'm going to sign a contract with you? Nope. Not going to happen. No way, no how."

I'll keep it simple. I promise. A scroll appears and I read:

I, Aubry Brooks, being of legal age and sound mind, hereby enter into a binding contract with

Damion Blackmon, whereby Aubry Brooks agrees to refer to Damion Blackmon as "king" limited to, but no less than five (5) times, in exchange for Damion Blackmon removing himself from Aubry Brooks's body, mind, spirit, and/or aura. If Aubry Brooks fails to refer to Damion Blackmon as "king" limited to, but no less than five (5) times, then Aubry Brooks owes Damion Blackmon a kiss, upon which he may call due at his choosing.

I read the contract ten times. After you see a man's mind crushed, it makes one hesitant to enter into a deal with the devil. I reach my hand out. "You do sanitize your pen between clients?"

The tip of the pen glows for a brief moment. *There. Sanitized by demonic flame.*

The pen pokes my finger. "Ouch, that really does hurt." I sign and then Damion signs with his sigil. "Damion Blackmon, you're the king. Damion Blackmon, you're the king. Damion Blackmon, you're the king. Damion Blackmon, you're the king. Damion Blackmon, you're the king." Honestly, I would have agreed to do this hopping up and down naked on one foot if it works. I hold my breath and wait.

I'm so glad you're finally ready to admit it.

"Damion Blackmon, you're a child," I inform him and get back to work.

CHAPTER 18

Damion's phone has been ringing nonstop all morning. "If you don't answer that, I will," I threaten.

He sighs, taking over and answering his phone. "Mother—"

"I wasn't sure if you remembered how to call your mother back," a woman demands by way of greeting.

"I'm sorry. I've been dealing with a case that's taking up a big chunk of my time," Damion explains.

"Nonsense. You know you shouldn't lie to me. I was worried about you, so I spoke with Gabe. He told me all about your little 'case.'"

Damion clenches my jaw. "We're working on the situation as we speak."

"We can discuss this more tomorrow evening."

"I'm sorry, Mother, but tomorrow evening—"

"*Is* my department's annual fundraiser. Damion, I reserved your seat months ago. I will *not* have an empty chair at my table," she says definitively. "Aubry, is it?"

"Yes, ma'am," I say, taking over.

"I assume you have formal wear?"

"Of course," I fib.

"Wonderful," she says, hanging up.

What just happened? I ask Damion.

You're meeting my mother tomorrow evening.

But I thought ours was a forbidden romance? I toss back at him.

The only thing forbidden is trying to get out of this dinner with my mother.

Grandma tags along on my shopping trip, even though I specifically told her she was not invited. Multiple times. "Nonsense, sugar pie. I'm here to help you pick out a showstopper, not another boring black dress."

"I think Aubry will look beautiful no matter what she wears," Damion quietly says.

You are shameless. I try my best not to smile.

Grandma holds up a short, slinky number that has to be geared toward a high schooler wanting to mortify her parents at prom.

"No."

"See what I'm dealing with here, Damion?" Grandma gripes.

The store clerk greets us, and I jump in before Grandma can open her mouth. "Hello, I'm looking for a formal dress to wear to a conservative academic fundraising dinner this evening." The clerk helps me narrow down my selection to three gowns and I head to the dressing room.

Grandma takes a seat outside my dressing room and complains that I've picked the three most conservative dresses in this place.

Damion complains that Vivian is intruding on what could be a very sexy moment. I tell them both to hush.

Later that evening, I slip on my dress and fix my hair and makeup. I opt for curls pinned back on the side, smoky eye shadow, and a neutral mauve lip color.

Damion knocks, and I let him in. *You look amazing.*

"Thank you. Do you like the dress?" It's a midnight-blue gown with a timeless bateau neckline that's fitted until it flares out at the bottom. The color of the dress really sets off my eyes. I pick up a hand mirror and turn around so he can have a view of the deep plunging back.

I love the dress. It feels like a warm finger is tracing my exposed back, and I try not to shiver.

"Behave yourself," I tell him weakly as I grab my clutch and walk downstairs.

Damion called and set it up, but I'm still excited when I see the limo parked in front of the shop. He said it was his way of apologizing in advance for what will be an incredibly boring evening.

"You look beautiful," Aunt Callie says.

"She does. You two kids have fun. Don't do anything I wouldn't do," Grandma says.

"That leaves it pretty wide open," Damion answers, winking my eye.

"Alright, alright. We're gone," I take back over. I walk outside and say hello to our driver and step into the limo.

Damion takes over, and my finger presses a button, closing the partition. *Now that we have privacy*, he purrs. My hands pop open a bottle of champagne.

Not so fast, I warn as I pour myself a glass. *I want to know more about what I'm getting into this evening*, I say, taking a sip. I'm not a huge fan of champagne, but apparently that's just because I never drank the good stuff. And this is the good stuff.

I've already told you, an excruciatingly boring evening.

Tell me more about your mother. So she's a professor of Religious Studies at Ole Miss. How did she meet your father? Unless he's a professor too, and in that case, I knew school was the devil's work.

He laughs. *No, my father isn't a professor. If we're going to play a game in the back of this limo, I can think of one much more enjoyable than 21 Questions,* he whispers, running an invisible finger up and down my arm.

"Tell me," I stand firm. Also standing firm are my nipples, which I'm going to ignore and hope he does too.

Mother was married to a human when she was younger. The marriage didn't last, as he wanted children but she couldn't conceive, or so she thought. After their divorce, she was studying in Egypt when her mentor came across an amulet a private client wanted appraised. Mother was researching the authenticity of the amulet when she discovered Zazel.

What do you mean 'discovered Zazel'?

I mean discovered. My father had been trapped inside this amulet for a century.

See, being bound with me doesn't sound quite so bad now.

Why you won't let me make it even better—

"So she discovered Zazel?" I get us back on track.

Yes. And not surprisingly, he wanted out of his prison.

So he seduced your mother into helping him? I take a wild guess.

Zazel's an incubus. It's his nature to seduce, he says matter-of-factly. *Mother doesn't like that I'm my father's son. If she had her way, I'd come over to the academic world and leave Zazel's world behind.*

Are you and your father close?

As close as one can be to an immortal Arbitrator.

Your father is the Arbitrator you and Gabe mentioned? I ask.

Yes.

And you don't want him to know about our possession problem?

Let's keep him out of it for the time being.

Why?

I have my reasons.

But—

And that concludes 21 Questions.

Fine, be that way. I set my empty champagne flute down.

More?

No, thank you. For whatever reason, I'm a little nervous about meeting Damion's mother, and more alcohol wouldn't help the situation. And I am still trying to figure out why. Not about the alcohol, but about the nervousness. Maybe it's because Damion and I are...well, I don't know what we are, but here I am, some stranger in possession of this woman's son.

We arrive on campus and the driver navigates us to the correct building. I exit the limo and follow the men in black ties and the women in evening gowns to a large banquet room.

There she is, Damion says, taking control. We make our way across the banquet room to a lovely woman in her late forties to early fifties. She's dressed in a demure black gown and has her curly blonde hair pulled back in a knot.

"Excuse me, Dr. Blackmon?" I ask.

"Yes," she says primly, her catlike green eyes assessing me. I get the feeling I wouldn't get a passing grade.

"I'm Aubry Brooks."

"Damion?" she says quietly.

"You look lovely this evening," he answers in the same hushed tone. Her eyes go wide, but she quickly composes herself. She looks around to make sure no one else is listening. "So I understand you run a magic shop?" she asks, eyeing me up and down.

"Yes, ma'am, along with my grandma and aunt."

"Interesting how a witch 'accidentally' entraps my son," she says with a sharp tone and an even sharper look.

"Mother," Damion warns her.

"Just what are your plans for my son?"

"My *plan* is to get us unbound," I answer with much less attitude than I'm wanting to use. And trust me, I'm wanting to use a whole lot.

"Really?" she asks, unconvinced. "And you haven't thought of taking advantage of the situation? Controlling Damion's powers for your own gain never crossed your mind?"

"Don't give her any ideas, Mother," Damion jokes.

"Nora, I would never try to control anyone," I take back over. "That's not the kind of witch I am, but more importantly, that's not the kind of person I am."

"I'm so glad to hear it," she says in a patronizing tone.

I'm sorry about my mother, Damion whispers.

"Damion, have you talked to your father about this *unsavory* situation?" I'm not sure if it's the *situation* she finds so unsavory, or *me*.

"I thought it best to wait until Aubry and I know more about our situation," he smoothly replies.

A woman in her mid-thirties who likely moonlights as an international swimsuit model comes gliding over. She has an exotic look of indeterminable heritage. Her midnight-black hair is pulled back in a bun, highlighting her heart-shaped face and plump red lips. She's wearing a conservative long-sleeved black gown that works wonderfully with her darker complexion.

"Aubry Brooks, I'd like you to meet Dr. Sonia Thompson. Sonia recently joined my department; isn't that wonderful news?" She turns to Sonia, not waiting on my answer. "I know Damion will think so."

You know Sonia? I try to sound casual.

She's a succubus I used to date. I take another glance at Damion's ex. Prim professor by day, succubus sex kitten by night? I don't like that thought one bit.

Sonia the succubus? Is it some kind of demonic law you must have an alliterative name?

Wicked witch, Damion retorts.

The emcee for the evening takes the stage and I take my seat. Sonia's on my right, and a rather portly bald man is on my left. Nora is on the other side of Sonia, and it's clear I'm the odd man out. It's also clear that Nora planned Damion to be seated next to Sonia, but then I had to go and trap her son and ruin the whole reunion.

Our host for the evening starts off with some bad jokes that everyone laughs at nonetheless, and then I about fall out of my chair when I hear the obscene amount of money they've raised at this five-hundred-dollar-a-plate dinner. The salads are brought out and I dig in, figuring this will probably be the most expensive meal I'll ever eat.

The portly bald gentleman to my left introduces himself to me, and we exchange pleasantries. I tell him that I'm an owner of a metaphysical shop, and that piques his interest.

"A small world, as my area of expertise is paganism and the occult," Dr. Hugh Anderson informs me.

"Do you know anything about banishing a pesky entity?" I ask the professor. Servers appear carrying large trays and present our table with tonight's meal.

What you call pesky I call persistent.

"What type of entity?" Hugh asks, genuinely interested.

"Let's say demonic," I answer, placing my napkin in my lap.

"Banishing from a home, an object, or a person?"

"Person."

"Ah, so what you're really asking is about demonic possession. A whole other ball game. I will tell you what my dear friend, the great retired exorcist Father Morth, told me. Dabble at your own peril."

Too late, already dabbled.

The chatter ceases as the emcee introduces the speaker. Digging into my meal, I'm left rather underwhelmed. Five-hundred-dollar chicken doesn't taste nearly as good as I imagined. The keynote speaker begins her speech and my eyes quickly glaze over.

Watching paint dry, Damion agrees. Our dinner plates are taken away, and a flourless chocolate cake with a raspberry compote is presented. Now we're talking. After our speaker earns a standing ovation, Dr. Anderson is pulled away to another discussion. I patiently wait for a break in the conversation, as I really want to ask him more questions about possession.

Sonia takes this opportunity to lean in and whisper to me, "I know you're the witch who trapped Damion."

"That's not exactly what happened," I whisper back in a calm and composed tone. "But what business is it of yours, anyway?" So much for calm and composed.

"Be very careful, little witch, or I may decide to make it my business."

"Perhaps you're the one who should be very careful, little succubus. You've said it yourself; I've already trapped one demon." I'm clearly writing checks that I can't cash, but she doesn't need to know that.

The evening comes to a conclusion, thank the Goddess. I tell Nora and Sonia goodbye and make a hasty exit. I've never dealt with ex-girlfriend drama. I can't say I would recommend it.

CHAPTER 19

"Sugar pie, how was your date?" Grandma asks.

"Not a date," I say, filling up my coffee mug.

"Why are you so grumpy?"

"Not grumpy." Fine, so I'm very grumpy. Damion has apologized for his mother, but I'm still out of sorts this morning.

Grandma and I work in the kitchen mixing up a batch of four thieves vinegar. It's a warding concoction we use around the doorsteps and windowsills. Grandma suggests I try soaking in the mixture. "Light a candle and imagine Damion in the tub with you. Maybe that will do the trick," she says with a wink.

I carry the jar to my bathroom and take a very fragrant bath, and by fragrant I mean stinky. I chant my spell:

Damion be gone, washed safely away.
Leave me free of possession today.

Nothing happens other than I have to spend an inordinate amount of time scrubbing in the shower to remove the vinegar stench.

Damion and I spend a few minutes working on the jigsaw puzzle, which is difficult with two minds and only one set of hands. We keep fighting for control and wind up fitting only three pieces together. *Vivian is right, this is why we need puzzle training. I'll not have you embarrass me on national television,* Damion chides.

Wouldn't wearing a clown suit while being hit in the face with a pie on national television be embarrassing in and of itself? I point out.

"See, this is why I've got you training. You have to work together as a team. You need some team building exercises. A trust fall wouldn't work since you're in one body. I'll have to do some research on that and get back to you," Grandma offers.

"Please don't."

"Oh, and you should really take up running. Aubry, I know that you're flexible which is wonderful for the boudoir, but yoga isn't going to help you on the show. You saw the clown challenge; you need to be quick on your feet."

"Quick on my feet like this?" I spin and walk away.

"You've got to be more than just the eye candy, Aubry," she calls after me.

Later that evening, Damion's cell phone chimes. He takes control and grabs his phone, letting out a sigh.

"Problem?" I don't offer to shield myself. Fine, so I want a peek at who's messaging him. I'm relieved to see it's Zazel and not a certain succubus.

> **ZAZEL:** Come to my Charleston club, we have much to discuss.

He clinches my jaw as my fingers type back a reply:

> **DAMION:** I'm unable to at the moment.

Everything goes black for a split second and then I do a double take. I'm in an elegant room with dark wood paneling and a beautiful mahogany U-shaped bar. Expensive-looking leather chairs are paired in seating groups next to a crackling fireplace. I close my eyes and open them, making sure this is real and not a vision. *What the hell just happened?*

My father teleported us.

This is your father's club?

One of many, yes.

It's not what I expected.

What did you expect?

I don't know, I heard club and demon and pictured a seedy strip club.

You watch too much TV.

An attractive blonde woman wearing a conservative black suit approaches us. "Follow me," she says in a thick European accent. She leads us to a private room, bows, and takes her leave.

An extremely sexy man is seated in a leather armchair, cigar in one hand, the other hand wrapped around a beautiful woman perched on his lap. She looks to be a few years older than me, somewhere in her late twenties. She has on a red cocktail dress that leaves little to the imagination and fuck-me heels at least six inches high.

He nuzzles her neck and then whispers something in her ear. She stares daggers at me and then turns her attention back to the man, giving him a lustful look before she reluctantly stands and walks out, closing the door behind her. The musky scent of sex hangs in the air, along with a tendril of smoke wafting from his cigar.

"Father, you wished to speak to me," Damion says.

The demon laughs, and it feels like each vertebra in my spine was just caressed by the vibration. I mentally shield my aura. Sexy or not, these demons aren't getting near my soul. "Aren't you going to introduce me to your beautiful companion?" he says in an accent that I can't quite place. "Aubry, I am Zazel. A pleasure to meet you."

How does he know my name?

There's not much my father doesn't know. Be on your guard.

I double my protection as Zazel stands to greet me. He places a kiss on both my cheeks and I try not to jerk away. I'd compare the feeling to being shocked by static electricity. I also try not to stare. Damion's father oozes sexuality, there's no two ways about it. He's around six feet three or so, with beautiful dark features and sun-kissed, flawless skin. He appears in his early forties, dressed in a tailored black suit that screams money. A watch that costs more than my car peeks out from under his left sleeve cuff. He could be a model, or he could be in the Mafia. Either way, there's a powerful undercurrent to him.

"Thank you. Nice to meet you too," I say.

He gestures to the chair across from him, and I have a seat. "My son, so the rumors are true. If I didn't know better, I would say you were trying to keep this from me," he says in a bemused tone.

"Of course not, Father," Damion smoothly answers.

A bottle of outrageously expensive whiskey appears on the table. *Wow, your father is breaking out the good stuff.*

I wouldn't have taken you as a whiskey aficionado.

I'm not, but my ex is a bartender. In fact, Todd fancied himself a mixologist. He was known as the 'Magick Mixologist.' That was a self-dubbed title. How a mixologist is different from a bartender, I still don't know.

Zazel hands me the rocks glass and I politely take a sip. I don't care how expensive it is, whiskey neat isn't my drink of choice. But good Goddess, I'm not going to tell him that. I suspect he's used to having his every command followed without question. The apple never falls far from the tree; Damion comes by it honest.

"And I hear, Aubry, that you've met Damion's mother. I bet she's worked herself up into hysterics over this little development. Pay her no mind, she's always had a stick up her ass." I make a mental note *not* to introduce Zazel to Grandma.

"Father," Damion warns.

"Aubry, have you heard the story of how I met Damion's mother?"

"No," I shake my head. I want to hear the details.

"I was trapped in an amulet for nearly a century, buried in a crypt with, ironically enough, a Christian saint," he says with laughter in his dangerous eyes.

"How did you get trapped in an amulet?" I ask.

"A witch," he says, the laughter gone, his dangerous eyes homed in on me. I take a loud gulp of whiskey.

Relax. If my father thought you intentionally trapped me, this meeting wouldn't be nearly as pleasant.

That's supposed to make me feel better?

"Graverobbers took the amulet and it wound up on the black market," Zazel continues. "It eventually made its way to Egypt where Damion's mother was studying. Nora was completely closed off from even entertaining the *possibility* of something like me existing," he says with a wry smile. "I didn't want to scare her off. You have no idea how excruciatingly tedious it is to sit with nothing but your own thoughts for one hundred years."

"I can only imagine," I say with a shudder. "So what happened?"

"I opened a book to a page detailing enchanted objects, and of course, Nora's curiosity got the better of her. It took some time before I spoke directly to her. But one day I did, and I offered her something she couldn't turn down. If she helped me escape from my prison I would give her a child. We struck our deal, Nora helped set me free, and of course I upheld my end of the bargain with Damion."

"I take it you're not together now?" I probably shouldn't pry, but I do anyway. The woman he just fucked was definitely *not* Nora.

He takes another sip of whiskey and considers. "Nora wanted more from me than I was able to give. She'll always be dear to me; she just could never accept that I'm an incubus. Tigers don't change their stripes, you see."

Is this a cautionary tale that applies to Cambions as well?

I'm the king, remember? Lions don't have stripes.

That in no way answers my question, you vain beast.

I'm not my father and there's the answer to your question.

"Tell me, Aubry, what kind of magic do you practice? Do you partake in the dark arts?"

"I practice kitchen magic that I learned from my grandma. I also draw from other Pagan and New Age practices, but I don't dabble in dark magic of any kind."

"So you don't believe in using your magic for personal gain?" he challenges.

"Personal gain is fine, as long as I'm not harming anyone in the process. That was Nora's worry, that I'd trapped Damion for my own evil plans."

"Nonsense. You're too much of an idealist to do such a thing."

"How do you know that?" I demand.

He only smiles. "Tell me what methods you've employed to exorcise Damion."

I list off the various spells and tell him about Gabe's failed reverse demon traps.

He's quiet for a moment and then says, "My son, I'm afraid I won't be of much help. I've never possessed someone. I have neither the desire nor the need. Only a demon unable to manifest a human form would want to do so in the first place. I've heard possession is a struggle, especially if the human is a strong-willed individual."

Tell me something I don't know, Damion bemoans.

I'm so sorry I've made it difficult for you to turn me into a mindless puppet.

Zazel continues, "Not to mention if more than one demon enters the same human, that has the potential to turn into a vicious turf war." The turf getting destroyed in that scenario being the poor human being.

He pauses to think, and then an ancient-looking book appears on the table. He flips to a page and then stands with a piece of chalk in hand and draws a circle on the floor.

Was that a demonic phone book?

Something like that.

Zazel motions for me, and I know the drill. I walk over and have a seat inside the protective circle. He draws another circle with elaborate designs and utters a phrase in a language I've never heard. A shimmering black cloud appears in the circle, accompanied by a noxious sulfurous smell that isn't contained in the circle. I desperately want to cover my nose but figure that would be rude.

"Arbitrator, how may I be of service?" A high-pitched voice emits from the black cloud.

"We have an unusual case of a Cambion possessing a human. The possession was unintentional, both on the part of the Cambion and the human. Thoughts on what can be done to safely exorcise the demon?"

"I've never heard of such a thing happening before." Great, just great. "For a demon to leave a human they've possessed, they simply choose to do so, unless of course they were inside a demon trap. But once outside the trap, the demon would have the power to end the possession. Perhaps some third party magic is binding the two. That's all I can think of."

"Thank you for sharing your expertise. You are free to go." The smoke vanishes and the circles disappear.

He drums his fingers on the arm of the leather chair and then a cell phone appears in his hand. He makes a call and begins speaking in a different language—I'm not sure which one. The phone disappears, and he turns his attention back to us. "I'm sending you to Gangotri to work with a Hindi sorcerer named Ram. His English isn't the best, so be forewarned."

And that's all the *forewarning* I receive, as I'm now standing on the rocky banks of a river with majestic mountains surrounding us. I rub my arms, my teeth chattering due to the jarring temperature change. An Indian man in a red robe walks up to me and bows. He turns and walks to the water and I take that as a cue to follow him.

He casts a circle with marigold flowers and motions for me to stand inside. I comply as he fills up a pot with water from the river. He lights something inside the circle. It's a familiar smell, but I can't quite put my finger on what exactly it is. He touches what looks and smells like a clove to my forehead and begins chanting in a language I don't understand. He switches over to broken English and I catch, "I depart."

He then speaks in a different sounding voice and begins chanting again. I think he must be channeling spirit. He pulls out a fish from his pot and sticks the clove in its mouth, releasing it in the river. Before I know what's about to happen, he pours the water from the pot over my head. It's absolutely freezing, and I can't help but scream.

I assume the ritual is over because he indicates for me to step out of the circle. *Damion?*

Whoever catches that fish is going to have an unusually seasoned meal.

And just like that, I'm now back inside Zazel's club, dripping water all over the pristine marble floor. A large plush towel appears and I grab it, wrapping myself. Damion helps by increasing my body temperature, and my teeth stop chattering. "Son, I'm sorry I can't be of help, but I can think of a few things that are far worse than being trapped with such a beautiful woman."

I see you got your silver tongue from your father.
Silver tongued devils, that we are.

"I will consult my scribe on this matter."

"Thank you, Father."

Zazel nods. "Aubry, it was a pleasure to meet you," he says with a seductive smile.

"Nice to meet you," I say too late, as I'm now standing inside the break room of Memphis Magic.

CHAPTER 20

It's Friday and Grandma informs me it's a good day of the week to try a spell with Saint John's wort. Damion refuses to participate in any more stinky-herbed spells. I agree with him on this one.

The door chimes and our delivery woman, Brenda, walks in carrying a small package that I sign for.

"Girl, I knew you had a devil in you," she informs me.

"He sounds like a handsome devil, for sure," Grandma says.

"Vivian, you flirt," Damion says.

Brenda's eyes go wide and then she dies laughing. "This done beat all I've ever seen."

"Brenda, do you know how we can safely exorcise Damion?" I ask.

She pauses to consider. "I've never worried too much about a demon's safety. Once a demon's transferred into a devil doll, it's burned. Don't sound like that's whatcha want."

Don't even think about it, Damion warns me.

Then devil, you'd better be on your best behavior.

We wave Brenda goodbye and I turn to Grandma. "I'm going to run some errands. You want me to pick us up some lunch?"

"No, thank you. I'm going to pop over to Tunica. Damion, do you gamble?"

"He doesn't. Good luck," I say as I grab my purse and head out.

If Grandma thinks that you're a gambler, then she'll try and drag us to Tunica, I explain.

How do you know I'm not a gambler? I'd be all in on a game of strip poker with you.

Uh-huh. I'm sure you have a stacked deck of poker cards for just such an occasion.

The house always wins.

I'll remind you that you're still in my house.

I'm well aware.

Should we be worried that your father doesn't know how to help us?

It's not a good sign. Where are we going?

I want to go meet with Detective Rodriguez. Damion promised he'd help me with Maddie's case once he's returned to his body, but who knows when that will be?

I give him directions and he drives us over to the MPD precinct. We pay the parking attendant and find a spot in the garage. I take back over, making my way to the front door. After passing through a metal detector, I walk up to the plexiglass partition. "Hello. I'm here to see Detective Rodriguez, Homicide Bureau. It's a matter concerning the Madison Williams case."

"Do you have an appointment?" an older woman with a nasally voice asks without looking up from her computer.

"No."

"Sign in and have a seat. I'll have to check to see if he's in the office," she says in a bored tone.

I do as instructed and have a seat in a very uncomfortable plastic chair. I look around at the other people in the waiting room. It's a weird vibe of desperation and fear. I envision a shield around my aura just to be safe.

After what feels like forever, the locked door to the left of the plexiglass beeps and the detective steps out. "Aubry Brooks," he calls. The detective looks to be in his early fifties. He has honey-colored skin and graying hair around his ears. My guess is being a homicide detective contributes to the graying hair.

I stand and quickly make my way to him. "Hello, Detective Rodriguez. I'm Aubry. We've spoken several times about my friend, Maddie Williams."

We shake hands. "Of course, Aubry, nice to see you again. Please follow me." The detective scans his badge and the door opens; I follow him until we reach his small office.

"Aubry, have a seat," he says, pointing to a worn faux-leather armchair. "You want to know if there's been any development in your friend's case."

"Are you psychic?" I joke.

"That would be nice in this line of work. Big milestones are hard for loved ones, and I know it's been a year since your friend's death. I wish I had something new to report. Unfortunately, I don't," he says as he pulls a file from his desk. "No tips. No leads. No witnesses have ever come forward."

I look behind his desk to see balloons and other retirement-themed party decorations. "You're retiring?"

"Yes, ma'am, at the end of the month. Been with the department twenty-five years. It's time."

"Congratulations."

"Thank you."

"So what will happen to Maddie's case?"

"Your friend's case will be reassigned to a new detective."

"Who will shove it in a file cabinet and move on to cases with higher likelihoods of solving," I say hotly, feeling my temper flare.

"Aubry, there were over two hundred homicides last year. I'm not going to lie and say that we aren't swamped. We are. But with that said, every case matters to us. Look at it this way—there will be a fresh set of eyes on your friend's case. That's never a bad thing."

Speaking of a fresh set of eyes, I say, "I'd like a copy of her file, please."

"I'm sorry, I can't do that. But the autopsy report is public record. There's an online form on the medical examiner's website you can fill out if you really want a copy. Are you sure you really want a copy?"

"I'm sure. Who will take over Maddie's case?"

"I haven't received that information yet."

"Thank you for your time," I say as I grab my purse. I see that I'm not going to get anywhere with the detective.

"Aubry, let me give you some unsolicited advice."

"My least favorite kind."

He smiles, but then that smile fades. "Knowledge isn't always power. The nitty-gritty details of your friend's death might cause you more harm than good. Something to think about, especially considering you were just the victim of a violent kidnapping."

"I'm glad my reputation precedes me, but I'm not a victim. Enjoy your retirement."

"I meant no offense."

"None taken," I say as we stand, and he walks me to the door.

He nods as he scans his badge. "Take care of yourself."

I make my way out to the parking garage. *I'll jump through the hoops to get the autopsy report, but how do I get a copy of the detective's investigation file? I want to read his notes.*

I'll have to think about it. I don't have any connections at MPD.

Well, at least all the officers here still have their souls.

I didn't say that. He takes over my body and unlocks my car and gets behind the wheel. *Aubry?*

Yes?

You're not a victim. A phantom hand squeezes mine.

CHAPTER 21

I open the shop in a funk. Yesterday's meeting with the detective was disappointing. Not to mention I filled out the online form for Maddie's autopsy report, only to learn that the estimated turnaround time is six to eight weeks. Bureaucracy is the devil's work.

But it's not just that. I'm typically a cauldron-half-full kind of witch, but I'm starting to worry. What if Damion and I are trapped together for the rest of our lives? If his immortal Arbitrator father doesn't know how to unbind us, then who does?

I shake off the brooding and focus on the task at hand, which is cleaning the customer restroom. "Feel free to take over at any time," I inform Damion as I give the toilet a scrub.

Don't you have a familiar that you can assign with this task?

I glance over at Elvis who's seated in the doorway. He gives me a "yeah, in your dreams" look.

I wash up, walking to the front of the shop. The door chimes and in walks Gabe. "Hey, Gabe."

"Hello, Aubry. Damion. Do you have some free time? I've set up an appointment with El Exorcista."

"Who is 'El Exorcista'?" I ask.

"That's the nickname for Father Perez. He's a renowned exorcist. Zazel has agreed to transport you to Nicaragua. Are you ready?"

"Sure, I can squeeze an exorcism into my morning schedule." I wonder how my life got so weird as I lock the shop door.

Gabe sends a text and then we're standing in a small stucco shack filled with various religious objects, including crucifixes, candles, flowers, and an altar in the corner. An older man wearing a white robe greets us in rapid Spanish, and Gabe smiles and returns something fluently in Spanish.

"Welcome, I am Father Perez. You have demon?" he asks me.

"Yes," I answer.

"Okay, okay. I help you. I cast out 40,000 demons in twenty-five years," he boasts.

I silently do the math. *That's 1,600 exorcisms a year, 133 a month...*

So almost five exorcisms a day, Damion finishes for me.

We sure this guy isn't a snake oil salesman? I ask.

"Diagnosis five hundred dollars. Exorcism one thousand. American dollars."

Snake oil salesman it is, Damion announces.

I give Gabe a look. "He's the best," he reassures me.

"Okay, but we don't need a diagnostic evaluation," I explain.

"I can vouch that she's possessed," Damion takes over.

Father Perez crosses himself and shoves a crucifix in my face. I recoil, not because I'm possessed, but because I don't care for something being shoved in my face. He then flings what I assume is holy water in my face. I cry out. Again, not because I'm possessed, but because he got water in my eye. He speaks in Spanish and switches over to English. "The power of Jesus Christ compels you! Tell me your name, Demon!"

"No need to *compel* anyone," Damion answers. "I'm Damion Blackmon."

"Okay, you have demon." Thanks for that. "I set up ritual. Pay first," he says.

Gabe hands him cash and I try not to wince at the price tag. Father Perez busies himself gathering his ritual supplies. He says something in Spanish and Gabe translates as we step outside. "You need to strip down to your underwear."

I cross my arms. "That's a big hell no."

"He's going to cover your body in mud as part of the ritual and then place a sheet over you,"

Gabe explains.

"I want a tank top and shorts," I demand.

Those items appear in my hands, and I walk inside the shack and change. "He's almost finished. Don't worry, Aubry. You'll be perfectly safe," Gabe reassures when I join him again outside.

I watch as Father Perez prepares the circle and then pours gasoline all around it—I know because that smell is unmistakable. "Perfectly safe?" I cry.

"If a single hair on her head is harmed, the good father and I are going to have a problem," Damion says in a rather menacing tone. "Translate."

Gabe walks over to Father Perez and does so. Father Perez nods. "You be fine. No problem. Everything ready. Come."

I take a deep breath and step inside the circle. He grabs a large paintbrush and begins covering my body with mud while chanting in Spanish. He moves the brush to my chest, and Damion takes over, grabbing Father Perez by the wrist. "Okay, we skip that part," he says nervously.

He places on my head a crown weaved out of some sort of grass and then holds the palm of his hand a few inches from my face, his other hand holding the crucifix. He thunders something, maybe in Latin, and then gives my head a shove.

"Ouch," I cry.

He looks confused. "Fall."

"Not happening."

Apparently this is not how the ritual is supposed to go, if the confused look on his face is any indication. "Okay, lie on your back."

I do as instructed, and he covers me with a white sheet. He places in my left hand a wooden cross, my right a chicken egg, and sprinkles me with flowers. Finally, he positions my arms outstretched and my ankles together, forming a T. Wrapping black ribbon around my hands, he begins chanting.

He strikes a match and tosses it. The circle quickly goes up in flames, dancing all around me. Father Perez continues his fervent chanting.

I'm not sure how long I've been lying here. All I know is it's hot, I might have a splinter in my hand from the cross, and I've accidentally cracked the egg because I'm gripping it too tightly. He thunders a phrase, which I assume is the grand finale of the ritual, because he pours a bucket of water all around the flaming circle. It goes out with a violent *hiss*.

He extends his hand and helps me to my feet. "You good now?" he asks.

"Yes, thank you. The demon is gone," I quickly answer.

He smiles and hugs me with a hard back thump. I look over to Gabe. "Ready to go, please."

He sends a message, and we're now back in the break room of the shop. "Cupid, you're not getting reimbursed for that," Damion answers for me.

Grandma and I work in the kitchen. "Oregano for happiness, basil for love, and thyme for affection," she tells me as we channel our intentions into the herbs. "I used to make your Grandpa this lasagna. A little kitchen magic plus a little bedroom magic equals a long and happy marriage." She gives the herbs a chop and tosses them in the meat sauce.

I wrap my arms around her, squeezing tight. I know she misses my grandpa. I also know that I'll regret it, but I ask anyway, "What kind of bedroom magic?"

"I'm talking sexual chemistry. Either two people have magic in the sack, or they don't. Your grandpa and I had it. Boy, did we have it."

And I knew that I'd regret it. I take a seat at the kitchen table and work on the puzzle. "We've made progress," I inform Elvis, who's sitting in the chair beside me. He doesn't look impressed. "Then you grow opposable thumbs and give us a hand."

The cat responds by hissing at me.

After dinner, we get sucked into *House Guest*. "Where's Aunt Callie?" I ask.

"Says she's out with friends. I hope to the Goddess she's not back with that no count Craig."

I grab my phone and do an inmate search. "Well, if she is back with her ex, she's seeing him through bars because he's back in prison."

Your aunt's ex?

Yes. So I admit my aunt doesn't have the best track record. At least her track record is better than her ex-boyfriend's criminal record, which is too long to fit on my phone screen.

"Sugar pie, when you and Damion are on the show next season—"

"*Not* going to be on the show next season or any season, for that matter."

Not without your bikini pics, we won't.

"You have to make a smarter alliance than Brant and Gia have made with the Whiz. They've skated by thus far, but I'm afraid the next puzzle challenge will put them in the bottom, and the Whiz will turn on them."

"Vivian, excellent point," Damion says.

Do not encourage her, I inwardly groan.

The show ends, and Grandma heads over to Brenda's house for poker. I search for the remote to turn off the television when a local commercial comes on showing New Life Spiritual Center. I remember the flyer advertising this place and Grandma going on about the good-looking guru from the trade show.

"...with over fifty acres to explore, from hiking trails, meditation gardens to our newest addition, our observation tower, you'll find the perfect place to watch the sun rise and unplug..."

Observation tower? I see Maddie holding the Tower card. *Checking out this retreat is definitely in the cards.*

Damion groans at my pun.

CHAPTER 22

"Any updates in Brad's case?" I ask Charlotte.

Why for the love of God will she not pass this car? Damion bemoans and I ignore him, as I have been doing for the past twenty minutes. He seriously is the world's worst backseat driver.

"No. But I get the impression that everything moves slowly in the legal system," she answers.

"How are things with you? How's school?"

"Weird. Everyone thinks they know what happened and so they tiptoe around me. Except for my roommate."

"Well, that's good." I glance over to see her making a face. "Not good?"

"My roommate kept hounding me to go out with her and I finally relented. I rode with her to a bar and then she ditched me so she could go home with her new guy. I walked outside at night alone trying to find a rideshare when Brad came along and…" she trails off as she lightly rubs the fading scar that runs the length of her forearm.

"Goddess, I'm so sorry."

She nods. "She pretends the whole thing never happened."

"That's really messed up."

She nods. "She's probably feeling guilty and so she's in denial. That's what my therapist thinks, anyway."

"Sounds like it. Well, don't tell Florence and Amelia. They'll offer to hex your roommate for you."

"I'm in a much better headspace now, but I'm not sure if I would have been able to turn down the offer right after it happened. So what are we looking for at the Center?"

"That's the problem, I don't exactly know. I get the feeling Maddie's guiding me here, but I'm not sure why."

We arrive at New Life Spiritual Center with plenty of time to park and mill around the visitor's center before the daily tour begins. The Center is set on a sprawling wooded campus, with multiple buildings and smaller lodges. It has a very upscale, modern summer camp look. Granted, I've never been to a summer camp, but I assume this is what one would look like, if it were for adults with large disposable incomes.

Our tour guide Kate introduces herself. She's a beautiful woman I'd guess in her early forties, with long, lustrous blonde hair and kind brown eyes. We follow her to the meditation center, a large freestanding domed building next to the visitor center and café. We pass a tranquil meditation garden and our guide points out several nature trails. Our last tour stop is one of the deluxe guest accommodations, and then we make our way back to the visitor center.

"How many people work here?" I ask Kate. Maybe Maddie's mystery man was an employee.

"We have a full-time staff of ten employees who reside on campus to ensure all our guests' needs are met," she quickly answers. Veronica Mars, my ass. I wouldn't know how to even start to go about getting that list of employees. I can't exactly go to Detective Rodriguez and say, "I dreamed about Maddie holding the Tower tarot card, and I saw a commercial about a spiritual center that has an observation tower, so you need to raid their compound." Yeah, that'd go over big.

Can you get us that list of employees?

I could if I were returned to my sex god body.

By seducing Kate into turning it over? I ask, not liking that thought one little bit.

"Where is the observation tower?" I ask Kate, not waiting on Damion's reply.

"It's actually a little hike to reach the tower, so we haven't included it in our tour," Kate informs me. She then gives us the sales pitch and encourages us to try lunch at the café.

I stop Kate before she leaves and ask her, "We'd really like to check out the observation tower. Could my friend and I maybe get a day pass so we could take a look before we leave?" Apparently no one has ever asked Kate this question. She eventually returns with two makeshift visitor badges and gives us a property map and directions to the sixty-five-foot-tall tower.

We make our way to the trail and begin our hike. "What do you think of this place?" Charlotte asks. "Getting any weird vibes?"

"Not really. I don't know, maybe I got my signs crossed? Nothing has jumped out at me so far."

Damion?

Nothing.

We walk along a meandering wooded trail. We're in West Tennessee, so there's no elevation change to speak of, which is fine by me. I didn't anticipate a hike, and while I'm wearing boots, they aren't of the hiking variety. We round a bend and I spot the tower. It's a modern steel and stone design in the shape of a helix with a round observation platform and a thin, antenna-looking architectural feature on top.

We reach the tower and ascend the spiral staircase. I mentally smack myself for not wearing more appropriate footwear as I hold on tight to the railing. Damion takes control of my limbs and we quickly reach the top of the tower.

We step out onto the large circular platform and take in the view. The Center is a huge area with several trails cut between the trees. I see a tendril of smoke on the edge of the woods in the distance. It's a chilly spring day. Someone must be using their fireplace.

I walk around to view every possible angle, but again, nothing sticks out. I walk around one more time and examine the walls and floor of the structure. I don't know what I was expecting, maybe a "Maddie was here" written somewhere on the tower itself.

"You see anything?" Charlotte asks.

I sigh. "No."

We climb down and make the trek back to the visitor center and turn in our badges. It's nearing lunchtime, so we decide to try out the café. "This is pretty good," I say between bites of my vegetarian curry. "My aunt would be all about this place."

"Where has Callie been lately?" Charlotte asks. "She's helping me shield my aura, but she canceled on me last week."

"I don't know. Probably back with her ex-boyfriend and doesn't want Vivian to know."

Finishing lunch, I grab my bottle of ginger kombucha to take with me. A good-looking man in his thirties holds the door open for us. "Ladies, did you enjoy the tour?" he asks in an unusual accent. Almost British sounding, but not quite. His dark blond hair reaches his shoulders, and he has beautiful amber-colored eyes. Around six feet tall, he has a lean, athletic build. He's wearing a white long-sleeved silk shirt, matching pants, and mala beads around his neck. The only reason I know what mala beads are is because Aunt Callie has some from India that she uses in her meditation practice.

"Yes, thank you. You didn't happen to be at the metaphysical trade show in Tunica, by chance?" I ask as we walk outside.

"Yes," he answers, a bit surprised by my question.

This is the guy Vivian was going on about? Damion snorts.

"My grandma and aunt were at the show. We own a metaphysical shop in downtown Memphis."

"What a small world. My name is Ethan. I'm one of the yoga and meditation guides here at the Center."

"A very small world. I'm Aubry and this is my friend, Charlotte."

"Hello," Charlotte says.

"Ladies, a pleasure. If you decide to come back, make sure to join me for one of my classes. That's where I'm headed right now. If you'll excuse me."

Charlotte and I walk to my car. "Grandma will be so thrilled that I ran into her good-looking man from Tunica. Speaking of a good-looking man, I'm surprised you didn't think the same about Gabe." I think back to Charlotte's cold reaction to Gabe the other day.

"He is gorgeous, but I don't know. Something about him disturbed me," she says with a shudder.

"Well, he is half angel," I inform Charlotte, and her eyes go wide. She looks like she could be knocked over with a feather. Maybe an angel's feather.

"Just don't fall for his demigod line," Damion advises.

CHAPTER 23

Pack a bag, *we're going to Jackson.*

You know, please is a polite little word us southerners still like to use. Why are we going to Jackson?

Because I need to go to my office.

I ready myself and we head downstairs. "Damion and I are going to Jackson, so I won't be able to help with the shop today and possibly tomorrow."

"Sugar pie, that's just fine. We're perfectly capable of managing without you. Besides, you two could use some privacy. Stay at a romantic bed and breakfast. See if you can find one with a heart-shaped jacuzzi tub; those are nice. Maybe get a couples massage." Grandma stops to think for a moment. "You wouldn't even need a couples massage; a single massage would do the trick. So it's really a two-for-one bargain."

"Grandma, this isn't a romantic getaway. We're trying to get ourselves unbound," I groan.

She ignores me and continues on. "Damion, it's been years since I've been to Jackson. Is there an arts district? Aubry is very artsy and into that sort of thing. I'm trying to think of what else we should add to your romantic trip itinerary. Definitely brunch. FYI, Aubry likes a mimosa, but won't touch a Bloody Mary. Girl doesn't like tomato juice. Isn't that the darnedest thing?"

"Wonderful suggestions, Vivian."

"Do not encourage her," I wrestle back control. "Goodbye, Grandma."

Grandma sighs dramatically. "Your Aunt Callie's boring sensibility, I repeat."

"Mama, I'm still in the room, I repeat," Aunt Callie retorts.

We drive to Damion's office, which is on the second floor of an old building a block from downtown Jackson. The sign on the door reads *Damion Blackmon and Gabe Jennings, Consultants.*

"I thought you and Gabe are lawyers?"

We are.

"Then what's with the sign?"

We don't want human walk-ins. We represent those who've fallen from grace, not those who've fallen in a grocery store, he haughtily replies.

We walk upstairs and are greeted by a rather robust woman with short blonde hair in her late fifties seated at the reception desk. I notice a scary looking 666 tattoo surrounded by unusual symbols on the top of her left hand. She doesn't strike me as a Satanist, but then again I don't strike most folks as a witch. The moral of that story is don't judge a book of shadows by its cover.

"Helen, it's me," Damion announces, her eyes becoming as big as saucers.

"Gabe warned me, but I still can't believe it," she says, clutching her hand to her mouth, trying not to laugh.

"Something funny, Helen? Do let me in on the joke," Damion says in a rather menacing tone.

She quickly loses her smile. "No, boss. Gabe told me you were bound with a woman, but I wasn't sure if you were just trying to take an extended vacation," she quickly covers. "He's been in a mood having to work your cases, just lettin' you know," she whispers the last part. "Luckily he's in an arbitration all day."

"Don't worry about Gabe, I'll handle him. Helen, this is Aubry."

"Hello," I take over.

"Hello, dearie. Tell me how this happened!"

"We're still sorting it out," I answer.

"I'm going to get caught up," Damion throws over my shoulder as we walk down the hall.

"You might want to prepare yourself," she calls after us. He walks us past a small conference room, and we come to the end of the hall with two offices. It does appear that Damion's office is bigger than Gabe's, and I can't help but smile.

What's with your secretary's tattoo?

It's what happens when a human tries to weasel out of a deal with a demon.

Remind me never to make another deal with a demon. We enter his office to find his desk buried under a stack of files. *Better you than me*, I inform him.

Helen had an excellent idea about the extended vacation. Why don't we lie down on my comfy couch and take a little nap? I'll meet you at the beach, he whispers seductively.

Nice try. Get to work.

He sighs as we take a seat in a large leather chair behind a beautiful mahogany desk. He opens the file on top of the stack. I can't help but notice the name *Sonia Thompson*.

I have a client meeting. I'll need you to shield yourself.

With Sonia?

Yes.

Sure, no problem, I mean to say. Instead, what pops out of my mouth is, "You mean your succubus ex-girlfriend who threatened to make our business her business? The same succubus ex-girlfriend whom your mother wants you back together with? That Sonia?" I realize I have no right to be jealous. The only logical explanation is this demon has driven me insane. I need professional help. Maybe I should start a survivors of demonic possession support group.

Are you jealous? You have nothing to worry about, he says smugly.

"Knock knock," Sonia enters the room, and unfortunately, it wasn't a fluke—she's just as stunning as I remembered. Her dark hair is down today, and she's dressed in a prim yet sexy white silk blouse that ties around the neck and a pencil skirt that hugs her curves just right.

"Damion, I can't believe you're still stuck with that little witch," she says in a pouty voice.

"Believe it," I say, taking over and giving an easy smile. "Sonia, nice to see you again."

"Aubry is going to mentally shield herself so we can discuss your case, Sonia," Damion takes back over.

Aubry, trust me.

Isn't that exactly what a tricky devil would say? I grumble. *Fine, shielding myself now.*

I create a mental wall, but then I cut a teeny-tiny peep hole. Yep, I lied. So sue me.

"Sonia, have a seat," Damion motions to a leather chair across from his desk. He proceeds to discuss the details of her short-term employment contract with Ole Miss. Okay, I'm not sure what I expected, but it wasn't something so mundane as this. "I've stricken one provision, but otherwise it's a fair agreement," he says, handing her the document.

"Damion, thank you so much. Let me repay you," she says, her eyes now glowing like they're backlit. "I've never been with a woman before, but I'd make an exception for you."

"Not necessary, but you do owe me a favor," he says with a wink.

"Whatever you want, I'm ready," she says, biting her pouty lip seductively.

"Sonia, I'm interested in Aubry," he says as we stand and usher her to the door.

"Damion, you can't be serious! Does your father know about this? This little witch has put you under a spell," she says as she touches my cheek. It's all I can do not to take over and knock her hand away. "I'm worried about you."

He removes Sonia's hand from my face and gives it a squeeze. "Thanks for the concern. Zazel is aware of the situation. Hopefully Aubry and I will be unbound soon."

"Well, unbound or not, my offer still stands. You know where to find me." She gives me a lingering kiss on both cheeks and shakes her hips out the door.

Still can't recommend ex-girlfriend drama.

Damion spends the rest of the day working. I spend the rest of the day alternating between meditating, napping, mulling over Damion's "interested in Aubry" comment, and last but not least, plotting Sonia's downfall. Not really the last one, but almost.

Aubry?

"Yes," I say, mentally stretching.

Maddie's class schedule with a list of her professors. A list of students in each of her classes. A list of all her friends and followers on social media. Emails and DMs, he goes through a thick stack of papers.

"How did you get these?" I demand.

I have all sorts of tricks in my bag.

Grabbing the folder, he walks us down the hall. "Helen, we're gone."

"Alright, boss. Damion, can I talk to Aubry alone for just a sec?"

"Sure," he says.

Shielding myself, go right ahead.

"Yes, Helen?" I ask.

"You seem like a sweet girl, and I'd be remiss if I didn't say something. Damion's a nice demon, but darlin', he's still a demon." She holds up her fist and rubs her 666 tattoo to prove it.

"What did he sell you?" I can't help but ask.

"I wanted to be a Broadway star, but I'd just about given up on my dream. Too old and all that. He promised he'd help me with my career."

"Did he?"

"I'm working a dinner show two nights a week here in town. Not exactly what I had in mind." The devil's always in the details, but I guess she had to learn that lesson the hard way. "He's seductive and charming and a hell of a salesman. You be careful, you hear me? Guard your soul."

"Thanks for the advice."

"Well then, take care."

I'm not so sure if it's my soul or my heart that I need to be worried about. Regardless, I just hope this doesn't turn out to be a lesson I have to learn the hard way.

CHAPTER 24

I sit on my bed, flipping through Maddie's University of Memphis schedule. I don't know any of her professors or most of the people in her classes, but I wouldn't have a reason to. Maddie and I really lived in two different worlds.

Next, I look through the names of her small circle of friends and followers. Like me, she didn't live her life on social media. I highlight the names I don't recognize and search them. Most appear to be Maddie's classmates.

I scan her emails and read her private messages. Nothing out of the ordinary. A group message from class. A few messages and emails from her roommate and my not-so-favorite person in the world, Lydia Smith.

I don't want to, but I send Lydia a text asking if she could meet up this evening. She surprises me by responding with an immediate yes and tells me which coffee shop.

I throw on some clothes and we're out the door. Damion drives us and we snag a spot, pay the meter, and walk inside. This just so happens to be the same coffee shop where I met Brad for our first date. He's not only ruined my favorite little black dress, but he's also ruined hot chocolate for me.

I spot Lydia tucked in the back, working on a laptop. "Hey, how's it going?" I take a seat across from her. Lydia's a year younger than I am, and much curvier, with short brown hair, brown eyes, and a look of disdain on her face that she always reserved just for me.

"Do you put people under spells?" She eyes me suspiciously as she closes her laptop.

Seriously, what's up with everyone accusing me of spell casting today?

Damion makes a *tsk tsk* sound. *So you didn't shield yourself with Sonia.*

You're telling me you shielded yourself with your secretary? I counter.

"Maddie was attached to your hip, and then my cousin," Lydia answers, snapping my attention back to the verbal conversation.

"No one was 'under my spell.' Maddie and I were best friends. I'm sorry you didn't like it, but that's not my problem. As for Todd, I'm sure you heard that we broke up months ago."

"Yeah, I heard he broke up with you," she says with a smug smile. "Smart move."

Let me take over and—

Butt out.

"Look, you were determined to hate me from the moment we met," I say. Maddie and Lydia became roommates just a few months before Maddie died. Lydia chose not to like me. I chose to be okay with that, because quite frankly, I wasn't her biggest fan, either.

"I didn't hate you. I just didn't understand you and Maddie. She was so normal and you are so"—she pauses—"not."

"Thank you." I'll choose to take that as a compliment. "Let's talk about the reason I'm here."

"It's been a little over a year since Maddie's death. I figured that's why you texted me."

"Yes. Has Detective Rodriguez been in touch?"

"Not since it happened. I get the feeling he's given up."

"He's retiring soon, and a new detective will take over. Maybe that's a good thing."

She shrugs. "Maybe, but I'm not sure much can be done. They've got nothing. Whoever did this is going to get away with it. I don't get why it had to be her," she says sadly.

"I know. I don't understand it, either," I say, twirling my bloodstone bracelet. "Let's compare notes about what happened. Maybe Detective Rodriguez missed something. What do you remember about the time leading up to her disappearance?"

"Don't tell me you're trying to play Nancy Drew?" She snorts.

"I prefer Veronica Mars."

"Who?"

And this just highlights why Lydia and I were never friends. "What do you remember about that time?"

"It was right before the week of spring break. Maddie told me she was going to stay in Memphis to work and hang out with you. I begged her to come with a group of us to Panama City, but she said she wanted to save money. I sent her a couple of pictures from the beach, but she never responded. I figured she was just busy with the kids that she nannied. That, or she was stuck up your butt."

I ignore her last comment. "She told me the opposite—that she was going with you to Panama City. I also texted her, but she didn't respond. I thought she was just busy having fun at the beach, so I didn't think much about it."

"Why did she lie to both of us?" Lydia asks.

"I don't know. Before that week, did you feel something was off with her?"

"Not really. She was always busy. We both were. We were prepping for our licensure tests and getting all our paperwork turned in for student teaching in the fall. Plus, she had started nannying, so we really didn't see as much of each other as we used to."

"Who was the family that she nannied for? I can't remember their name."

She thinks for a moment. "The mom's name was Kathrine, I think. I can't remember the last name. I'm not sure about the dad. He was some big shot business owner and traveled a lot. I believe the mom sold real estate, but don't quote me on that."

"Did you have any idea Maddie was seeing someone?"

"No. That was a shock. Did you know?" she counters.

"No. I don't understand why she'd keep it a secret, unless—"

"Unless she knew we wouldn't approve," Lydia finishes for me. "Like how the detective talked about this guy's burner phone. Maybe she got caught up with a drug dealer."

"Do you really believe that?" I ask.

"I don't know. Nothing makes sense," she says, taking a sip of her coffee.

"Was there anyone from class who gave you weird vibes? A professor who showed too much interest in her, or maybe another student?"

"No. I mean, I'm sure a lot of guys in our class were into her, but nobody sticks out in my mind as being weird about it. A professor? No, not that I ever saw."

"Who were her closest friends at school besides you?"

She opens her notebook and grabs her phone, writing down names and numbers. She tears out the piece of paper from her notebook and hands it to me. "They don't know anything, but if you want to waste your time, be my guest."

I have a smart reply on the tip of my tongue, but instead, I ask, "How are you doing?" Lydia isn't my favorite person, but she cared about Maddie too.

"I'm okay. At first it was rough, but I eventually moved and got a new roommate. I couldn't stand to be in that apartment with her empty room." She glances at her phone. "I need to get going." She gives me a hard look. "How do I know you didn't bring this down on her with all the weird devil worshipping you're into?"

"Goodbye, Lydia." I don't dignify her accusation with a response as I stand and make a dramatic exit.

So about this devil worshipping you're into...I know a devil who'd be interested.

)))◑●◐(((

I'm seated at a corner table across from Damion at the carousel bar in the Hotel Monteleone in New Orleans. The bar's empty except for the two of us, but the carousel is still making its slow rotation around the room. I can't see Damion's face, as the light above us is out.

"Why can't I see you in these dreams?" Damion's secretary's warning didn't stick, clearly.

"You'll be gifted with the perfection that is my human form when we're unbound. Patience."

"That in no way answers my question, you slippery demon lawyer," I grumble.

An old fashioned with a cherry garnish appears in front of me. "I thought my wanton witch would like a change of scenery. Your favorite drink in your favorite bar with your favorite Cambion."

"Do you ever get tired of seducing?"

"No," he says, sending a phantom touch up and down my spine.

"What happens when the chase is over?" I ask, trying not to shiver.

"My secretary is right—I am a demon."

I make a *tsk tsk* sound. "So you didn't shield yourself."

"And as a demon, I'll show you *exactly* what it means to be possessed by me," he says, that delicious scent of his filling the bar.

"You've already possessed me," I say weakly.

He disappears and then suddenly, I can feel him behind me. "I want to see you. To smell you. To taste you. To drive my cock in you so deep you scream out in such exquisite ecstasy," he whispers in my ear, and I have to clench my thighs together. "I want to brand you with my fire from the inside out and have you in every possible position," he says, fisting a hand in my hair. "And maybe a few positions you've never even thought of."

A whimper escapes my mouth. "No, I haven't possessed you, my sweet Aubry. Let me know when you're ready," he says and is gone.

CHAPTER 25

Damion's phone chimes and he takes over, grabbing it.

> **ZAZEL:** You're coming to my Chicago apartment.

> **DAMION:** Give us a minute.

"Why does your father want to see us?" I walk over and flip the closed sign and lock the shop door. Not gonna lie, his father is a little bit scary. Sexy, but scary nonetheless.

Damion doesn't have a chance to answer, as we're now standing in what I assume is his father's apartment. I've materialized now a few times, but it's still an odd experience. My guess is humans weren't meant to defy the rules of time and space.

I take in the sleek and modern living room with a wall of floor-to-ceiling windows. The view tells me we're in the penthouse of a high-rise city apartment. Zazel is seated on a black leather couch with a different woman than the one I saw at his Charleston club, but that same unmistakable scent of sex hangs heavily in the air. Well, he did warn me tigers don't lose their stripes. He whispers something in the woman's ear. She reluctantly stands and walks out, not before shooting me a death look.

Zazel is dressed down this evening, and by dressed down, I mean he's removed his suit jacket. He stands and greets me with a kiss on both cheeks. Even though I was prepared this time, I still jerk back when his lips touch my face. "And how is Aubry this evening?" he asks in that melodic, sexy voice of his.

"I'm good. Your apartment is amazing," I say, shielding my aura.

"Thank you. I don't get to spend as much time in Chicago as I'd like. It's one of my favorite cities. And my son, how are you?"

"I'm well, Father. You have good news, I hope?"

"My scribe will be here momentarily with a game plan."

The doorbell rings, and a servant scurries from the back and escorts inside a portly, bald gentleman that I've seen before. It's Dr. Hugh Anderson, the professor I was seated next to at the Ole Miss fundraiser.

You didn't tell me he was a demon!

You didn't ask.

"Aubry, a pleasure to see you again," he says.

"Hugh, thank you for your help," Damion takes over.

"Of course. Damion, what a predicament you've found yourself in," he says excitedly. Sorry, but not sharing in his excitement. "If everyone will follow me, I've prepared our ritual space."

I stand, assuming he means follow as in *walk*. I really shouldn't assume anything at this point, because now I'm standing inside a large cavern. Dripping water makes a rhythmic pitter-patter sound. The jarring temperature change has me rubbing my arms together. Damion takes over and increases my body temperature. *Thank you.*

I follow Hugh and Zazel, who are illuminating the way with flames dancing from their outstretched hands.

We walk until the opening becomes narrower and narrower. I take a deep breath. I've never thought of myself as claustrophobic, but now I'm second-guessing that stance. We reach a point where we have to walk one at a time, the damp cave walls brushing my shoulders with each step.

Damion?

It's alright. I've got you.

Thankfully, things open up, and we enter a large, cavernous space that's illuminated by glowing torches on the walls. I look down at the floor and spot an elaborate pentagram drawn in what looks to be blood. But that's not why I scream. No, I scream because there's a dead body inside the bloody pentagram.

"Perhaps I should have warned you," Hugh says. "We're going to perform an exorcism and transfer Damion to the corpse," he explains. "Damion, once you've animated the corpse, you should be free to leave and manifest your human form."

"What if we're successful in the transfer but then Damion's trapped in the corpse?" I point out.

"Then you've traded one problem for another," Hugh admits.

"If it were me, I'd much prefer the company of a beautiful woman than a dead man," Zazel weighs in.

"Let's leave this option as a last resort," Damion quickly announces.

So you're going with the devil you know, I tell him.

Damn right.

"Very well. But I hate to waste this corpse," Hugh says reluctantly.

We're now standing back inside Zazel's apartment, minus Hugh.

Where's Hugh?

I guess he decided not to waste the corpse, Damion answers. Welp, no more questions for me.

"Father, what is this?" Damion asks, pointing to a terra cotta bowl with writing etched on the inside. I'm unsure of the language, but the writing goes round and round starting from the outside of the bowl and ends in the center with a primitive drawing of an impish creature.

"Ah, this is my dear friend Phenex." Zazel motions for me to have a seat, and I do so. A dry martini appears in my hand and I take a sip. "He's trapped in this spelled terra cotta bowl. Hugh unfortunately couldn't help free the poor demon." Zazel takes a sip of his martini and considers.

"You will take the bowl and work on releasing Phenex. Perhaps inspiration will strike and help with your own situation."

"Of course, Father. We'll certainly try." I'm not sure saying no was an option, so I don't complain about Damion speaking on my behalf.

"Wonderful. You two will stay for dinner." Again, I'm not sure saying no was an option, but that's fine, as I'm not one to turn down a meal.

A man pops his head in and announces that dinner is served. We move to the über-modern dining room. Zazel takes a seat at the head of the table and motions for me to sit next to him. I notice the painting behind him, an abstract of what looks to be a nude dark angel. I quickly avert my eyes, as I'm not sure if it's a self-portrait.

Zazel's personal chef announces our dinner of poached lobster tails with a curry reduction, and yes, I said personal chef. I spot a 666 tattoo on his hand, and Damion's secretary's warning sounds in my mind.

"My son, Hugh will continue with his research into your predicament. We'll reconvene with a new game plan," Zazel announces. Hopefully without a corpse next time, I think with a shudder as I take a sip of wine.

"Thank you, Father."

Zazel nods. "How is the sex while sharing one body?" he asks, and I just about spit out my wine. "That would be the only saving grace of such a situation."

"Father," Damion warns.

"You're no fun," he says with a huff. "What shall we discuss, then?"

"Tell me about the origins of demons," I ask, taking back over. Might as well get the story straight from the source.

"What are the origins of humans?" Zazel counters.

"Well, there are different scientific theories, religious beliefs, and origin myths, but we really don't know for sure. The first human isn't around to tell us one way or the other," I answer.

"It's not so different for demons."

"But if you're immortal, then you had to have been there from the start," I point out.

"Imagine existing outside the confines of linear time. Infinity if you want to label it. Then imagine coming to a different plane of existence, one in which time is of the utmost importance. And then imagine trying to recall something that happened outside of the new linear timeline, which is now how the mind has been trained to think and process information."

"So nobody knows?" I ask.

"I didn't say that," he smiles. I suspect this demon could go round and round like an infinity symbol, answering a question without really answering a question. I've said it before, apples don't fall far from trees—like father, like son.

Tigers also don't lose their stripes, I remind myself. So many warnings, but the question is will I heed any of them?

CHAPTER 26

I grab a bowl of cereal. *Not* my aunt's cereal. Learned that lesson the hard way. Also a regular bowl, not a demonically possessed bowl. Guess I should clarify.

The Phenex bowl is currently housed in the back of my closet with a black salt protection circle around it, just to be safe. That still didn't make it any easier to sleep knowing there's a demon in my closet. Then again, there's a demon in my bed, but Damion makes it difficult to sleep in a completely different way.

"Where's Aunt Callie?" I ask Grandma.

"She texted me that she had an early yoga class. She's not fooling me. I know she stayed somewhere else last night," Grandma says with a huff. I regret bringing up the subject as I finish breakfast and get ready for the day.

I spend the morning speaking to Maddie's school friends. Lydia was right—I am wasting my time. No one knew of a guy Maddie was seeing, and all were shocked and still saddened by her death.

Frustrated, I return to the shop to find Charlotte cornered by Grandma. Poor Charlotte. "Ready to go?" I ask her.

"Charlotte, maybe you can encourage Aubry to become a runner. She really needs to work on her physical conditioning before the auditions."

"No auditions and we're going for a *walk*. We'll be back in a little while," I throw over my shoulder.

"Bye, Vivian," Charlotte calls.

We make our way down the street and over a block until we reach the Big River Crossing pedestrian bridge that spans the Mississippi River. "Running would be good for your *House Guest* endurance training," Charlotte says with a mock serious face.

"Not you too?" I groan. "Seriously though, you could run if you want and then meet back up with me," I tell her. I've never been into running and see no good reason to start. Maybe my dislike of the activity originates from high school PE class. Maddie and I used to sneak off and hide under the bleachers until Coach Carlson found us and made us join in the "fun" with a few extra punishment laps.

"No, I'm good," she says. "So I got a call from the victim liaison at the DA's office this morning. Brad's trial is on hold indefinitely. The psychologist says he's incompetent, and the judge agreed. Brad suffers from 'schizophrenia' and believes himself to be a vampire. Oh, and that he's obsessed with demons. He's terrified of a particular demon who owns his soul."

I smile, looking over to Charlotte. She's smiling too, and then we both laugh. "But seriously, are you okay with that?"

"Yes. I'm trying to move on and I don't want to dwell on it any longer. Besides, the fact that he's so scared of Damion and that he'll never leave that hospital is punishment enough."

We reach the end of the bridge and turn around. We're almost back to the shop when I stop dead in my tracks. Sometimes the Universe sends me an image like I'm looking at a photograph. Other times it's like I'm watching a television show, or if it's about me, then it's like I'm watching myself in the show. This morning, the premonition is just a message. "Wait until tomorrow to fill up your car."

"Why?"

"Don't know. Just relaying the message."

"I've got to get to class," Charlotte says when we return to the shop.

"I'll see you this evening," I say, waving goodbye.

I quickly get ready and walk downstairs to find Aunt Callie arranging the crystal section. "Morning. You've been so busy lately, I feel like it's been days since I've seen you," I say.

"I know, I've been taking an intensive meditation workshop. I think it'll be really helpful in my regression practice."

"That's what you're going with?" Grandma snorts as she joins us.

"Yes, that's what I'm going with," my aunt snaps.

I excuse myself to the back, as this little mama/daughter dispute doesn't involve me. I busy myself with paperwork.

I enter some invoices into our system and send an email to our new accountant. You better believe I found a new accounting firm. I still need to rate our former firm online. *Service was great until the accountant assigned to my account kidnapped me. One star.*

I tag out and let Damion check his email and make some work-related calls. This time I am a good girl and shield myself. *Knock knock,*" Damion says, holding up his phone.

"What am I looking at?"

Maddie's W-2. If only we had Brad here to give us an accounting tutorial.

"How did you get this?" I demand. "And don't even joke about something like that." I scan the form until I find the name of Maddie's employer. Lydia thought this woman was a realtor, so I do a quick search for "realtor Kathrine Jones."

It's a good thing I'm sitting down. "We've met Maddie's boss before. She was the tour guide at New Life Spiritual Center," I say in disbelief. "I guess she goes by Kate instead of Kathrine, but it's the same woman."

Before we jump to conclusions, it could be a coincidence, Damion warns. Maybe, but I'm becoming more and more convinced there are no coincidences.

The day passes quickly, and we close shop early to get ready for tonight's ritual. We get to work physically cleaning the shop and the apartment and then energetically cleansing the space with sage and four thieves vinegar. I take my smoking sage bundle to my room and walk around and mentally repeat the intention: *let go.*

I stop at the framed picture of me and Maddie from our high school graduation. Tears begin to run down my cheeks. *Maddie, I can't let you go, not until I know who killed you.* I dry my eyes and continue cleansing the rest of the room.

Amelia and Florence are the first to arrive. This run they have going without a feud might be the longest in recent memory. And I hope I haven't just hexed it, pun intended. "And how is that demon of yours?" Amelia asks.

"I'm well, Amelia. You're looking lovely as always," Damion answers.

"You charmer," Amelia says, flushing with pleasure. "Aubry, dear, Vivian told us all about Damion's old flame," she stage whispers. I made the colossal mistake of telling Vivian about the academic dinner. "Have you thought about hexing her? I'd be more than happy to give you a few pointers."

"Don't listen to her. You don't need to go the nuclear option when something more subtle will work just as well. How about a keep-away spell?" Florence suggests.

"Subtle like you dousing yourself with an entire bottle of Chanel No. 5 at church last Sunday?" Amelia complains. "God Lord almighty, we can smell you coming before you even get out of your car."

I interrupt before things turn ugly, "Thank you ladies, but no."

"What are we talking about?" Julia enters the shop wearing leather pants and a black T-shirt that says *Witch or Bitch—Your Choice.*

"Aubry hexing Damion's ex-girlfriend," Florence says helpfully. "Take a cue from Julia's vulgar shirt, darling. You're too good for your own good," she informs me while at the same time giving Julia a backhanded compliment. Amelia and Florence are professional backhanded complimenters. Seriously, they could put on a master class. They'll insult you, but do it in an old southern accent and with a prim smile.

"When did your life become a soap opera?" Julia asks.

"It didn't and it's not. And I'm not hexing anyone," I say defensively. "Amelia, how's your gentleman friend from Mobile?" Deflect, deflect, deflect.

"Oh, we've lost touch. Just as well," Amelia says.

Charlotte is the last to arrive, and she hugs my neck. "I saw on the news that there was a robbery at the gas station near my apartment this morning. I would have stopped to fill up my car after our walk if you hadn't warned me. Thank you."

"Welcome." A huge wave of guilt washes over me. If only I'd been able to warn Maddie.

I shake away those thoughts as we head upstairs to the rooftop. Aunt Callie and I prepared our space earlier. We cast our circle, Grandma invoking the Goddess as we chant:

> These chains of Aubry's possession we cleave.
> Damion it is now time to leave.

We each cut a black cord, symbolically cutting the energetic cord that links me to Damion, and then we burn them.

After the ritual, we pass around a tin of the crescent-shaped shortbread cookies that Grandma and I baked last night. We added just a pinch of cayenne to help drive Damion away, and cinnamon to speed up the process. "Well, Aubry?" Aunt Callie asks.

"I'm feeling lighter, so that's something," Damion answers for me.

I sigh as I take a bite, my palate regretting the decision to add cayenne to a cookie.

"Charlotte, darling, what's happening with this Brad character?" Florence asks.

"Why don't you let us take care of him for you," Amelia chimes in before Charlotte can answer.

"We'll fix him right up," Florence nods. "An eye for an eye. Aubry, we'll need some eye of newt."

"Don't be so Shakespearean. Aubry, we'll need brown mustard seed," Amelia explains to me like I *don't* run a magic shop.

"Ladies, I don't need your services, but thank you," Charlotte says.

"Too good for your own good," Amelia admonishes.

"Agreed," Florence says. "If there's to be no hexing, then we need to get going. The old crone and I have a bridge breakfast tournament tomorrow morning, and this one needs at least a solid ten hours of sleep to be a halfway decent partner."

"Please, you're the one who nodded off during our first round at the last breakfast tournament. I was terrified you were going to fall face first into your egg casserole," Amelia retorts.

"At least it would be a safe landing. That casserole was as rubbery as an old tire," Florence snorts.

"Someone should tell Pam that her egg casserole is atrocious," Amelia agrees. I'm sure these two are just the women for the job.

"Ladies, I'll walk out with you. I have an early class," Charlotte says.

We say our goodbyes, and Grandma turns to Julia. "Speaking of tonight's theme of chains, I hate to hear that your sub Amy didn't work out." Julia's sub being *submissive*. "She safe worded too much," Grandma explains to us.

"I bet you've been busting at the seams to say that line all night," I tell Grandma. "And how you keep track of everyone's love life is beyond me."

"She gets her hair cut every four weeks like a good hair client should," Julia chastises me. "Keep a regular trim schedule and you might be in the loop too."

"Julia, what hairstyle do you recommend for Aubry's upcoming television debut? She and Damion are going to Nashville to audition for *House Guest*. Do you do spray tans? She's a little pasty, and I think a nice glow will look better for her bikini pics."

"I'm not going to be on television," I try to explain.

"Callie, what crystals would you recommend for television stardom and success?"

"I'd go with a throat chakra stone for clear communication and confidence in public speaking. A blue kyanite or lapis lazuli," Aunt Callie suggests.

"You're now on her side?" I give my aunt the stink eye and cross my arms.

"I would encourage Aubry to go on a juice cleanse with you, but I don't think that would be a good idea. Aubry gets terribly cranky when she's hungry. Unless you're going for a good cop/bad cop showmance persona? In that case, you definitely should be the bad cop. You're a terrible actress, but you won't have to act when you're hangry," Grandma tells me.

"The only detox I'll even remotely consider is the avoidance of all busybodies butting their noses in my business."

Aunt Callie's phone chimes and she checks the message. "I'm meeting some friends for candlelight yoga. I'll be out late," she tells us as she waves goodbye.

"Vivian, to answer your question, I'd go with lowlights to accentuate Aubry's natural golden tone in her hair. And yes, I just sprayed a couple of college girls getting ready to head to the beach for spring break. Aubry, I'll get you all television vixened up, no problem. The only thing I ask is that you promise me you and your demon will make a better alliance than Gia and Brant have made with the Whiz. I swear, I want to strangle them for that stupid move."

"Would you use a ball gag during strangulation, or does that device come into play with some other form of sadism?" Grandma asks.

"Strangulation is too risky. It's specifically excluded in the agreement of understanding that my sub and I work out on the front end. But a ball gag can be used at any time and for whatever reason I choose. Usually it's for punishment, but sometimes it's just for the heck of it. Like one time..."

"Speaking of time, will you look at the time? I'm going to turn in," I announce.

"She's always been wound tighter than an eight-day clock. Can you believe she's possessed by a sex demon and *isn't* having sex with a sex demon?" Grandma says incredulously as I make my exit.

I'm having a hard time with that, myself.

Then up your seduction game, I taunt him.

Challenge accepted.

)))◐●◑(((

I'm leaning on the edge of an infinity pool perched high in the cliffs, overlooking the turquoise sea below. I watch the sun make its spectacular descent. "Beautiful," I say, admiring the pink-and-orange watercolor sky.

"Yes, you are," Damion says, now standing behind me.

"You just want me because you can't have me."

"Don't presume to know *what* I want or *why* I want it," he says haughtily, gripping my ponytail.

"Alright then, *what* do you want?"

"Everything," he whispers in my ear.

"You're not getting everything." I spin to face him, but he's no longer there. No matter how I turn, he's always behind me. Placing his hands on my shoulders, that delicious scent of his overtakes my senses. "Let me pleasure you," his words tickle my ear, my center clenching involuntarily.

"So you're going to pleasure me, no strings attached?" I demand. Why am I fighting against this again? Because it sounds like a hell of a good deal to me.

"I told you there are always strings," he whispers, moving his hand lower and toying with the string of my thong.

Ah yes, because he's a demon who steals souls. That's why. "Still not getting tangled up in those strings with you."

He laughs. "*Yet*," he says, pulling my thong back and letting it go, popping my ass. My vibrator appears by the pool. "You'll need this in the meantime," he announces.

"You are still a prick!" I growl, but he's already gone. "And it's a good thing my vibrator is waterproof!" I shout.

CHAPTER 27

I spend some time in our library searching for a spell to release Phenex from the bowl. When that proves fruitless, I search the Internet. I stumble upon an academic paper discussing incantation bowls of ancient Babylon. An incantation bowl, also known as a demon bowl, is basically an antique demon trap.

Look on the bright side—you could be stuck in dinnerware, I inform Damion.

Such a cauldron-half-full witch.

My cell phone rings but I don't recognize the number. "Hello?"

"Hello, this is Detective Chris Sullivan of the Memphis Police Department. May I speak to Aubry Brooks?"

"This is she."

"Ms. Brooks, I just wanted to follow up with you about Brad Cunningham's case. I'd like to meet with you today if you're available."

"I'm working, but you're more than welcome to stop by my shop. I'll be here from nine until five," I tell the detective and give him the address. I don't remember a Detective Chris Sullivan, but I was pretty physically and emotionally spent by the time the cops showed up at the warehouse.

I grab a jar of dried herbs from the pantry and brew a batch of my contraceptive tea. I spend a few minutes on the puzzle as my tea steeps. "I'm not putting together Aquarius because it goes with Leo. It just so happened to work out that way," I inform both Damion and Elvis.

If you say so.

Elvis likewise gives me an "if you say so" look.

I drink my tea and then get ready, throwing on a Memphis Magic long-sleeved T-shirt and my distressed jeans. Aunt Callie eyes my outfit when I walk downstairs. "You know you'd get bad karma if you try to sneak into my closet and throw out these jeans."

"Yes, but it might be worth it," she says.

I check the schedule. "Mrs. Vaughn's leaving the house now?"

"Yes, and it's major progress," Aunt Callie says. "There was a breakthrough during her last session. Mrs. Vaughn remembered that she was drug out of her cottage kicking and screaming during the Inquisition and burned at the stake."

"I guess I wouldn't want to leave my house, either," I say with a shudder. Mrs.Vaughn suffers from agoraphobia, or the fear of leaving her home. "But how do you know it isn't her subconscious mind making up that story?"

"If it helps her walk out the front door, does it matter?" Aunt Callie counters.

"Still not poking around in my head," I point to her.

I'm saved from the regression sales pitch, as Mrs. Vaughn arrives for her appointment.

A few minutes later, I'm ringing up a voodoo doll for a tourist when I hear the door chime. A good-looking man enters the shop wearing a nondescript gray suit and bland tie, but it's his military-style haircut and swagger that gives him away. This has got to be the detective. "Thanks for stopping by," I tell the woman as I hand her the gift bag. She watches the man out of the corner of her eye as she quickly exits the shop.

"Ms. Brooks?" he asks without a noticeable accent.

"That's me."

"Detective Chris Sullivan," he introduces himself.

I shake hands with the gorgeous man standing in front of me. I'd guess the detective to be in his early thirties. He's several inches taller than I am, and from his bulging muscles underneath his suit, it looks like he logs quite a bit of gym time. He has a square jawline, light brown hair cut short, and penetrating whiskey-colored eyes. In a partner situation, my guess is he's *always* the bad cop. "Can I get you a cup of coffee?" I ask.

"Thank you, that'd be great."

I don't like this guy.

He has literally done nothing to make you say that.

I escort the detective to the seating area and excuse myself to the back to grab coffee for him and tea for myself. Grandma brewed a pot of coffee earlier this morning, so it should be borderline drinkable. Considering the awful coffee I drank after the abduction, I don't think cops are coffee snobs.

I return with beverages in hand to find Grandma circling the fresh meat like a shark that's detected a drop of blood in the water. "And so Chris, you're single. Good to know."

"Grandma," I warn.

"Did you play sports in high school?" she asks.

"Yes, ma'am. I played football."

"Athleticism is important for the physical challenges of *House Guest*. You want to have the most advantageous showmance pairing." She turns back to Chris. "Aubry was never into sports, but she is into yoga and is extremely flexible."

I cut her off before she says something else that makes me want to curl up behind the couch and die. "Goodbye, Grandma."

She huffs at me. "Chris, stop by the shop anytime for a coffee refill." She winks and then walks out.

"I'm so sorry about that. Vivian's life's work is to embarrass me whenever possible," I say as I hand him the coffee and take a seat on the opposite end of the couch.

"Thank you. Your grandma seems skilled at it," he says as he takes a sip.

"You have no idea," I nod in agreement.

"What did she mean about *House Guest*?"

"Do you watch the show?" I ask.

"No."

"Then it would take too long to explain, and even if I did, then you'd question why I took so long to explain something so stupid."

"Fair enough. Ms. Brooks, let's discuss why I'm here."

"Sure, but please call me Aubry."

"Aubry, it's my understanding you didn't know Brad Cunningham very well prior to your abduction?"

"No. Like I told one of the detectives at the scene, I met Brad when I dropped off some documents at his accounting firm, and he asked me out. We met one time for coffee and then a separate occasion for dinner. That was the extent of our involvement until the jerk kidnapped me."

"Did he ever mention New Life Spiritual Center?"

"No. Why?" I'm on high alert. This can't be a coincidence.

"We found some odd items when we searched his house. It appeared that he was a member or somehow involved with the Center," he says as he takes a sip of coffee.

"What kind of 'odd items' did you find at his house?"

"It's an ongoing investigation. I'm not at liberty to say. I also wanted to let you know I'll be taking over the Madison Williams investigation. It's my understanding that you were friends with Ms. Williams?"

"Yes, Maddie was my best friend." I decide to lay my cards on the table. "Look, I believe that someone at New Life Spiritual Center is connected to her murder."

"What makes you think that?" he asks without inflection.

"Kathrine Jones is involved with the Center. Maddie was the nanny to Kathrine's children. Maybe Maddie got hooked up with someone at the Center through her boss." He gives me a dubious look. "Okay, so I don't have *proof*. It's just my gut feeling."

"Your gut feeling," he repeats.

Alright then, maybe it's not best to lay *all* my cards on the table, not the Tower card anyway. He's already looking at me like I'm a few tarot cards short of the deck. "Is there a way we can get a list of the Center's employees?" I press on. "Maybe that's where we should start."

"Not we. Me. I will conduct the investigation. You will stay out of it. Do you understand?"

Great, just what I need, another bossy man in my life.

Told you I didn't like this guy.

"How can we get a copy of Maddie's file?" I ask Damion when the detective leaves.

178

Memphis PD is warded, so even if I were back in my body, I can't retrieve the file using my powers.

"Why would the police department be warded?"

Most government buildings are. Perhaps Sonia could help get us a copy.

"But you just said the building is warded." I pause for a moment. "You mean *seduce* Detective Sullivan to turn over a copy?" I'm not sure I like that idea, although if she's going to be using her succubus charm on someone, I'd rather it be on the detective instead of a certain Cambion. "Okay, but would she help us?"

She owes me a favor, so yes.

Great, more of Damion's ex-girlfriend. That was sarcasm, by the way.

He takes over and grabs his phone:

> **DAMION:** Sonia, I need a favor.

> **SONIA:** Anything.

Gross.

> **DAMION:** I need Madison Williams's homicide investigation file. The detective is Chris Sullivan of MPD. Work your magic.

> **SONIA:** Consider it done. And I'd be happy to work my magic on you, even if you are stuck in the little witch.

Gross again.

After I close up shop, Julia texts me, asking if I want to go out to dinner. I've just put a homemade pizza in the oven, so instead, I text her just to come over. It's not long before Julia arrives, wearing a black T-shirt that says *Bite Me*, a black leather mini skirt, black fishnet stockings, and you guessed it, black military boots.

"You're overdressed for the occasion."

"I'm meeting a potential sub later." I'm not going to ask for details about the submissive casting call. If Grandma hears about this, she'll be mad I didn't get the scoop, but I can live with that. "I wanted you to go out with me."

"Ah, so I would have been your exit strategy if things didn't work out? I feel so used."

"Okay, you got me. I'll make it up to you by giving you a trim, on the house."

"Is my hair really in that bad of shape?" I ask as I grab a strand and inspect the ends.

Your hair is beautiful, don't cut it. The perfect length for me to fist as I'm—

Enough! I shouldn't encourage this demon, but I can't help but smile.

"What's with you? You're seeing someone. Spill, I want details."

"I'm not seeing anyone."

Technically true, but that will be remedied.

Goddess, let's hope so.

"How would that work, you being with someone while you're possessed?" she asks.

"Please don't get all Vivian on me," I groan.

"Can Damion hear us?"

"Hello, Julia," he says quietly. "Yes, I can hear you, and no, I don't share my possessions."

I snort. *Let's get one thing straight—I am not nor will I ever be one of your possessions. This is a girl's night. Please shield yourself.*

Very well.

"Hey, I get that. I never share my sub. Where's Vivian?" Julia asks as we work on the puzzle.

"Not a possession. Not a submissive. And I don't know where Vivian is," I say, probably too defensively. Just then, Grandma arrives home wearing a hot-pink Tunica T-shirt and spandex shorts and sneakers. Speak of the devil.

"Hey, Vivian. Whatcha been up to?" Julia asks.

"Hip-hop dance class with Brenda." I went to class with Vivian one time and one time only. I never want to see my grandma twerk again. Ever.

"You want to join us for dinner?" I ask.

"No thank you, I grabbed a bite earlier."

I walk over to the oven and take the pizza out and set it on the counter. I rummage through the drawer until I find the pizza cutter.

"Julia, has Aubry told you the big news? She has a new admirer," Grandma announces.

"Oh my Goddess, I do not! Detective Sullivan was nothing but professional," I groan. I cut the pizza into triangles and grab the salad from the fridge. Making a salad is a whole lot of trouble in my opinion, but luckily for me, Aunt Callie's already done the veggie prep work.

We fix our plates and then have a seat at the island. "So tell me about this new guy," Julia says as she pours ranch over her salad and passes me the bottle.

"Aubry's admirer—"

"Still not my admirer," I cut Grandma off.

181

"Boy, is he one sexy detective," Grandma whistles. "I love a good love triangle, don't you? Speaking of love triangles, the new season of *Bermuda Love Triangle* starts next month. Maybe we'll have a viewing party here. That way Aubry, Damion, and Chris can watch together."

"I'm personally not into threesomes. I've always found them way overhyped. And don't get me started on the pitfalls of a polyamorous relationship. But hey, Aubry, whatever floats your boat. I'm guessing this detective is an alpha male."

"Oh, most definitely," Grandma answers. I roll my eyes.

"And it sounds like Damion is as well. So then the best bet would be a polyamorous V with you, Aubry, at the point. Realistically though, alphas don't share. This is really good," Julia says between bites of her pizza.

"I don't even know what you're talking about, and it's probably best we keep it that way. And thank you. I added extra crushed red pepper and fennel seeds for protection. Obviously it doesn't protect me from boundary-challenged family members."

"Let's just keep it simple and start with a threesome. I wonder if there's ever been a threesome with a witch, a demon, and a detective?" Grandma muses. "Aubry, you might be making history! I'll come up with a sexy menu. Maybe oysters and chocolate-dipped strawberries. And I'll make everyone a themed cocktail. Aubry, my guess is you'll need the booze to loosen up."

"Arrg! I'm not into threesomes or Vs or any other letter in the alphabet, and for the last time, there is no love triangle!"

"Whatever you say, sugar pie," she winks at me. "Julia, I'll hook you up with the deets at my next haircut."

"Please don't say 'hook you up with the deets' ever again," I call after her.

CHAPTER 28

Unable to find a spell for Phenex, I decide to create my own. I walk upstairs to the patio, cradling the incantation bowl like it's a newborn baby, lest I drop it. I want to remain on Zazel's good side.

I cast my circle and light seven red candles, red representing the cleansing power of fire. I place the bowl in the center of a smaller circle that's beside the one I'm in. I don't want to actually release Phenex and run the risk that he possesses me. No turf war inside me, thanks. One demon's all I can handle. Well, this particular demon is probably more than I can handle, but I'll never tell him that.

I clear my mind and center my energy as I walk around to each candle and hold a sage bundle in each flame. As I do so, I chant:

Cleansing smoke break the spell.
Release Phenex from this prison cell.
Cleansing smoke break Damion and my bond.
With smoke and this magic wand.

Yes, I'm also holding a birch wand in my other hand, and yes, I feel a little silly doing so. I blow the smoke toward the bowl as I pass the bundle through each flame. Making my way over to the seventh candle, I repeat the process. Nothing. Okay, so maybe a spell with dual goals was too ambitious. I try again, this time only focusing on Phenex. And nothing happens. Again.

Sage is still stinky.

If the devil horns fit.

I sigh as I close my circle and clean up the spell remnants. Depositing the bowl in my closet and encircling it with salt, I walk downstairs. I'm surprised to see the detective.

"Chris, how nice to see you again so soon. Can I get you a cup of coffee?" Grandma asks, falling all over herself.

"Thank you, Vivian, that would be great." She heads to the break room with a wink at me.

"Chris, has something new happened in Maddie's case?" I realize I've accidentally called him by his first name, but amazingly enough, he doesn't correct me.

"Yes, Aubry. You could say that." He gives me a hard look. "A woman tried to get my case file. You wouldn't happen to be friends with Sonia, would you?"

"No." That's definitely not a lie.

"What kind of witch are you," he poses the question as a statement.

We play stare out, but it's not long before I fold like a cheap suit. "Who says I am a witch?" He gives me another hard look. "Let's say hypothetically that I am a witch. I'd be the kind of witch that doesn't take too kindly to threats from bossy detectives." Antagonizing him is probably not in my best interest, but it's too late to turn back now. "What happened with Sonia?"

"She didn't get the file. That's all you need to know," he says with crossed arms.

I try a different tactic. "Look, you and I are on the same side here. I want Maddie's killer brought to justice. We can work together, or I will work behind your back. Either way, I'm not going to give up. Tell me the odd items you found at Brad's house."

"*My* investigation, still not *our* investigation." He walks toward the door. "If you happen to have a friend named Sonia, tell her she's going to have to do better than that," he calls over his shoulder.

Damion calls Sonia on speakerphone. "Sonia, this is Damion with Aubry. What happened with the detective?"

"I don't know," she hisses. "But I'll not be bested by some holier-than-thou choirboy. I'll get you that file," she says with determination and hangs up.

I'm sitting on a plush white rug in front of a crackling wood-burning fireplace. At least a foot of freshly fallen snow glimmers outside the window in the moonlight. Damion has a seat behind me. I find myself leaning back against his hard chest and taking a deep breath. Trying to catch a whiff of that delicious scent of his, I'm disappointed that I don't smell it.

"You've met my parents. Tell me about yours," he says.

"Is this a new strategy?" I ask with suspicion.

"Maybe I just want to get to know you better."

"Uh-huh."

"Tell me. I'm interested."

Alright, I'll play along. "I don't know who my daddy is. Grandma says that Mama wouldn't tell her. From what Grandma has told me, Mama was a very powerful witch. She was a member of a coven in New Orleans and then moved back home and gave birth to me. I wish that I could remember something about her, but I was just a baby when she died." I take a sip of champagne that's magically in my hand now. "This is a depressing topic. Tell me something about you. Where did you grow up? You don't have a thick enough accent to be from round these parts," I stretch out the last words "round these parts," really laying on the southern.

He laughs. "You are correct. Mother was a professor at Yale. We lived in Connecticut until she transferred to Ole Miss when I was eight."

"Was Zazel around when you were a kid?"

"We didn't throw a baseball in the backyard, but he taught me many things about my heritage and how to use my talents." The absurd image of Zazel and Damion playing catch in their backyard with a little white picket fence makes me smile.

"How did you become a lawyer? Did you go to a regular law school?"

"I'm well-versed in human law, but no, I did not go to a traditional law school. When I turned eighteen, I apprenticed with a demon lawyer."

"Aren't all lawyers demons?" I ask sweetly.

"One could certainly make that argument," he answers, running his hand through my hair. It feels so nice.

"Why do you think we're still bound?"

"I don't know," he sighs.

I finish my champagne, and Damion floats the empty flute over to the table. "Don't go," I say before I can stop myself.

"Your wish."

"You're not getting my soul," I inform him.

A contract appears, hovering in the air. I grab it and stand, moving next to the fireplace so I can get a better look.

> I, Aubry Brooks, being of legal age and sound mind, hereby enter into a binding contract with Damion Blackmon ("the Demon"), whereby Aubry Brooks agrees to go on a romantic date with the Demon within seven (7) days of the Demon being exorcised from Aubry Brooks in exchange for the Demon not stealing her soul. Said date shall be a dinner prepared by Aubry Brooks, which shall include the following: steak cooked medium, baked potato with butter and sour cream, salad is optional. Dessert shall include a French apple tart with vanilla ice cream. If Aubry Brooks does not prepare the aforementioned meal within seven (7) days of the Demon being exorcised, then Aubry Brooks will owe the Demon not only the aforementioned meal, but also a kiss, the kiss to be called due at the Demon's choosing.

"Not so fast. I want a clause in here that forbids you from thwarting the date. I also want another clause that says in the event of an emergency or sickness, I have a time extension."

"God, I've never been more turned on in my life," Damion groans, his delicious scent filling the room. I lick my lips as his quill pen appears in my hand.

Does a deal with the devil count if it's made in the astral plane? Guess I'll find out.

CHAPTER 29

Damion drives me to the Wolf River Bend Mental Health Institute. No, this isn't for a meeting of my survivors of demonic possession support group. I probably should go to one though, seeing as I keep making deals with the devil. But today's visit isn't about me. Damion and I are going to have a friendly little chat with a certain energy vampire. If Sonia can't get Maddie's file from Chris, then we'll get our information straight from the horse's mouth. Or horse's ass, because it is Brad we're dealing with.

We enter the hospital and pass through security and sign in. Having time to kill, I walk over to the vending machine and buy a cup of coffee. I try a sip and then toss it in the trash. And I thought crime scene coffee was bad.

Some time later, we're escorted to the visiting room by an older male nurse. We find Brad dressed in a white T-shirt and white scrub pants, seated on a seventies-style couch, eyes glued to a mounted wall TV. "Brad, you have visitors," the man announces and walks out.

Brad is still fixated on the show, unaware we have entered the room. I feel Damion's power amp up, like an electric current coursing throughout my body.

Brad snaps his head over to us. His eyes become as big as saucers.

"Hello, Brad. You of course remember Aubry." Brad cries out and starts rocking back and forth.

"You seriously tried to tap into my energy again?" This guy is unreal.

Damion takes over and makes a *tsk tsk* sound. "Brad, I thought you learned your lesson. Do I need to teach you another one?" he asks as we have a seat across from Brad.

"No," Brad mumbles as he continues rocking.

"No, what?" Damion says with a hand held up to my ear.

"No, your lordship." No wonder this demon's ego is so big.

"Then that's settled. Let's move on to the business at hand. I'm calling due what's mine." Brad stops rocking and looks at me with a look of abject terror. "Relax. I'm not here to take your soul. Well, *maybe* not. That's assuming you tell me the things I want to hear. Tell me about the New Life Spiritual Center," Damion commands.

The look of terror is gone, replaced by the look of the smug energy vampire who kidnapped me. "Go ahead and take my soul. Today, tomorrow, ten years from now. What difference does it make? You already own it, so I have no incentive to cooperate."

Suddenly, Brad grabs his throat with both his hands and gasps for breath. It takes me a few seconds to realize that Damion is choking Brad without lifting a finger. *Damion, stop!* He releases his phantom grip, and Brad gulps down air with a wheezing sound.

"I was just demonstrating that Brad does in fact have an incentive to cooperate." A scroll appears in my hands. "Brad Cunningham, as you may recall, you and I entered into an eternally binding contract in which I not only have the option to call your soul due at any time, but you also owe me a favor. I'm calling in that favor today. You will tell me everything you know about the New Life Spiritual Center, no detail too small. You may proceed." The clause in the contract glows and then the document rolls shut and disappears.

Brad begins spitting out the words like he has a case of verbal diarrhea. "New Life Spiritual Center is a client of mine. Well, was a client until this bitch got me fired." He jerks his head at me. The next time Damion strangles this little shit, I'm not going to stop him.

"I'm losing patience, Brad," Damion says.

"I really pushed for the Center to apply for their tax-exempt religious organization status. Granted, not all of their income would be tax exempt, such as the income from the café and the gift shop."

Brad is still the most vanilla man in the world, Damion informs me.

"Kate Jones was the Center's contact person. She runs the business side of the operation. She invited me to visit the campus, and I took her up on it. I liked the feel of her energy."

"Still waiting to hear something useful," Damion says in a bored tone.

"She gave me a tour and I tasted a bit of her energy, and then I went home. That's it."

"Bullshit. Brad, there are some things far worse than death, although trust me, I have envisioned killing you on more than one occasion. Don't make me break out my demon. It will not work out well for you, that I promise," he says in a rather menacing tone. And here's the demon Helen warned me about. Instead of being concerned, I'm a little bit turned on, and I'm not sure what that says about me.

"I'm telling the truth! I didn't go back because Kate's energy wasn't worth the effort of driving out there again. Although I did bill my time and gas mileage as a business expense."

"Brad, how have you been sleeping? Not having nightmares, I hope," Damion asks in a mock innocent tone. Brad begins rocking again. You know what, I'm not even going to ask. "Brad, things are going to get much, much worse for you unless you tell me everything you know about New Life Spiritual Center."

"I've told you everything I know! I helped set up the Center's corporate structure and then met Kate for a visit on campus. That's it."

"Have you ever seen this woman?" I hold up my phone and show Brad a picture of Maddie.

"No."

"What are the odd things you had at your house?" I try.

"I'm not sure what you mean," Brad answers. The problem is, neither do I. Chris wouldn't tell me what those "odd" items were. "I have a coin collection from childhood. Mint condition. Even at a young age, I realized it was a smart move to diversify my wealth portfolio."

Fine, Brad is the most vanilla man in the world, I tell Damion.

"Did you have anything *illegal* at your house?" Damion clarifies.

"No."

A different male nurse appears in the doorway. "Excuse me, visiting time is over."

I say goodbye to Brad with a discreetly placed middle finger. We follow the nurse and sign out. I wait until we're back in my car, and then I say, "That was disappointing."

We can go back in there and I can choke him again, if that'd make you feel better.

"That's so thoughtful."

A phantom hand takes mine and gives it a squeeze. *I know it's disappointing. It would have been nice and tidy if Brad were connected to Maddie.*

"How can you be sure Brad was being honest?" I point out.

Contract magic. He owed me a favor and I called it due.

Yep, deals with devils.

Later that evening, I grab my cards. The Tower card is important. I got that. Universe, give me a few more clues in the cards before and after the Tower. I hold my cards to my heart and then give them a shuffle. I spread them out face up in one long line on my dresser until I find the Tower. The card before it is the Moon. The card of illusion. The card after it is the Hierophant. The high priest.

I examine the Hierophant closer. This card also represents a paternal figure, such as a teacher. Looks like it's time to visit Maddie's professors.

CHAPTER 30

We make the short drive to the Education Department at the University of Memphis. I spot Charlotte waiting for me on a bench outside. "Thanks for meeting me," I tell her.

"It's no problem. I had a break between classes," she says, shifting her backpack.

We work our way down the list of Maddie's former professors. Everyone tells a similar story—Maddie was an excellent student until about a month before she died. She started missing class and not turning in her assignments. No one knew of a boyfriend, but just assumed she'd fallen in with the wrong guy.

We take a seat in Dr. Fuller's office, the last professor on the list. His door opens, and I'm surprised when Lydia walks out of his office. She stops short. "What are *you* doing here?" Maddie's old roommate asks me with a frown.

"Nice to see you too. Lydia Smith, this is my friend, Charlotte Patel." Just because Lydia doesn't have manners isn't an excuse for me to forget mine.

"Hey, how's it going? You do know that she's a *witch*," Lydia quietly informs Charlotte.

"Good thing, because so am I," Charlotte tells her with a sweet smile. I have the strong urge to hug my friend's neck.

"Bye, Lydia," I say.

We wait several minutes until the office door opens. An elderly man with a cane sticks out his head and we're called back. "I am very sorry about your friend," he says. "A detective came to see me, first when Maddie went missing, and then after," he trails off. After her body was pulled out of the Mississippi River, he doesn't finish. "But I haven't heard anything else about her case since."

"Thank you. That's why we're looking into it," I say. "Tell us what you can remember about Maddie."

"Some young people you just know will make great teachers. Maddie was one of them. She was a wonderful student. Always prepared. Always upbeat. Never missed class. That changed about a month before she went missing."

"What else did you notice about Maddie during the month before her disappearance?" I ask.

"She started skipping more classes and not being quite as prepared as she once was. I figured she had a new boyfriend and had lost some of her focus. It happens. I was also aware Maddie got a new roommate. This particular student doesn't have the best academic or attendance record in my class. Her bad academic habits could have rubbed off on Maddie. We are the company we keep."

We thank the professor for his time and make our way outside. Charlotte heads to class, and I have a seat on the bench. *If we're the company we keep, what does that make me? Half demon?*

One hundred percent demon when you finally admit you're ready for me.

I smile, but that smile quickly fades. "Even if Maddie fell for the wrong guy, that doesn't mean she deserved to die."

No, it doesn't.

Maddie only had one male professor, and I seriously doubt the elderly Dr. Fuller was her mystery guy, I point out. I really thought the Hierophant was pointing me in this direction.

Damion's phone chimes. He takes over and grabs it from my purse. We scroll through some sort of legal document. It's a list of New Life Spiritual Center's Board of Directors. And the presiding officer and director is none other than Kathrine Jones.

Damion and I are on our way to look at a house. Before anyone gets concerned things have moved too fast, relax. We're meeting Kate Jones, and this was the easiest way to get her alone so we could ask her questions about Maddie.

This is such a short drive, I'm afraid we won't have time for 21 Questions, he teases.

"Ha ha. But that does remind me of a question I've been meaning to ask. Why is your home in Jackson? I mean, with your teleporting trick, you could live anywhere, right?"

That is technically two questions.

"Fine, so I have two questions."

My house is close enough to Mother's to keep her happy without being so close as to keep me unhappy. Boy, does that ever make sense. *Also, Gabe and I were mentored by the same demonic lawyer. Gabe's from Jackson and wanted to return there to open our practice. Most of our clients can teleport, so where our office is located doesn't make much of a difference.*

"Location doesn't matter? Don't tell that to the real estate agent we're about to meet. Her head might explode."

My GPS guides us to the house, and we pull into the driveway behind a shiny luxury car that must belong to Kate.

We walk to the front door and ring the bell. Kate answers with a smile. "Hello there, I'm Kate. You must be Aubry."

"Hello," I say, following her inside. "We've met before."

"Oh?" she asks with a smile.

"You recently led a tour of New Life Spiritual Center."

"Ah, I thought you looked familiar."

"How did you get involved with the Center?"

"It's a nonprofit that's near and dear to my heart. I got the idea when I visited a meditation center in Costa Rica. I thought, why not have something like that here?"

"That's great," I say, following her into an amazing chef's kitchen. "We also have another connection."

"How's that?" she says, now looking at me dubiously, wondering if she's wasting her time on this house showing.

"Maddie Williams was my best friend."

She holds her hand to her heart. "I'm so sorry. Maddie was such a sweet young lady. My girls were so upset when she stopped coming around."

"Did the police talk to you?"

"Yes. That's how I found out she was dead. Maddie didn't show up to work, and I knew something was off. I couldn't get hold of her for days, and then a detective showed up at my house." She sighs. "I didn't have the heart to tell my girls. They're too young to really understand, so I just told them Maddie moved."

"Did Maddie have a boyfriend?"

"Not that she mentioned."

"Did she ever go with you to New Life Spiritual Center?" I try. "Maybe took your kids there?"

"No. The girls have never been to the Center. It's an adults-only property. Maddie watched the girls at my house."

"What about your husband? Where was he around the time Maddie went missing?"

"You're not insinuating that Greg had something to do with this?" she asks, offended.

"No, of course not. I'm just asking the same questions the police would have asked."

"Greg never met Maddie. He was too busy with work and his mistress in New York to concern himself with me and the kids," she says matter-of-factly. "If you're not here to see the house, then I'll be on my way."

"Sure. Thanks for taking the time to talk with me."

Well? I ask Damion.

Let's check out the husband and see if his story matches Kate's.

We return to the apartment and I quickly smudge myself. *That still stinks.*

Of course you'd think so, demon.

I grab my cards and give them a shuffle. I go with a horseshoe spread, thinking that more cards will mean more answers. And I would be wrong, as every single card is reversed.

What does this mean?

"Things are blocked," I sigh.

I walk downstairs to find Grandma running the shop solo. "Whatcha been up to, sugar pie?"

"Just running some errands," I fib. I haven't told Grandma about looking into Maddie's case. I know what she'll say—I will never get closure until I accept Maddie's death. It's what she told me after our final unsuccessful attempt to channel Maddie. Grandma said some things are just not meant for us to know and we have to be okay with that. Well, I'm *not* okay with that. I'll have closure when I know who killed Maddie.

The door chimes and in walks Aunt Callie's appointment. I escort him to the regression room and quickly walk back out front. "Have you talked to Aunt Callie today?" I ask Grandma.

"No. She's probably tangled up in the sheets with some no-count man."

I call my aunt. "Michael's here for his session," I remind her.

"Oh no, I completely forgot! I'm sorry, but I need to reschedule. Tell him that his next session is on the house."

I hang up and look at Grandma. "Maybe she was immersed in her studies again."

Grandma snorts and I admit it sounded dumb as soon as it came out of my mouth.

CHAPTER 31

"Morning, sweetie. Don't lower your vibration by eating that." Aunt Callie eyes the cheese danish in my hand. "Especially when we're about to do energy work."

"Fine." I put down the pastry with every intention of eating it *after* energy work, but she doesn't need to know that.

She hands me a shot glass of ginger and lemon juice. "Drink this to enhance the protection work we're about to do."

I knock back the shot and it burns my throat going down. "A spoonful of sugar makes the medicine go down," I inform her as I make a face.

"And then you've defeated the purpose by lowering your vibration."

"Alright, alright. High vibes here. Let's do it."

Aunt Callie leads me through a guided meditation where I envision my aura and look to see if there are any holes or weaknesses. I patch a few weak spots with glowing light and feel much better after the exercise. Aunt Callie's spent some time researching the subject of auras, being that she was married to an energy vampire with husband number two. Cult leaders, abusive jerks, politicians—the chances are high that they're all energy vampires. Add psychotic accountants to that list.

"Where have you been lately? It feels like I haven't seen you in forever," I tell Aunt Callie as we walk to the front of the shop.

"I've just been so busy with my continuing education for my regression practice."

"You know if you're back with your ex, you can just say so. Grandma will bitch and moan, but ultimately it's your life," I tell her.

"Why on earth would anyone think I'm back with Craig?"

"Well, because you've been MIA."

"I am *not* back with Craig."

"Okay, okay." I hold up my hands.

Around midday, I sneak to the break room and call Chris. Busybody Vivian doesn't need to be a part of this conversation. Unfortunately, there is no conversation as it goes to his voicemail. Again. I've already left three messages that have gone unanswered.

"Hey, I'm going to run an errand," I walk to the front of the shop and tell Grandma and Aunt Callie.

"Take these cookies to Chris." Grandma reaches behind the counter and hands me a Tupperware container.

"How do you know that I'm going to see Chris?" I demand. I thought I made that phone call in private. "And why are you baking him cookies?"

"I didn't know you were going to see him, but now I do," she says with a wink.

Grrrr. I make the drive to the station and go through the hubbub of security all for naught, as Chris isn't in the office. I walk back to my car and open the container. *What are you doing?*

"Teaching Chris a lesson for not calling me back," I say as I eat one cookie and go for a second. Okay, so it probably won't teach Chris anything, but I do thoroughly enjoy his delicious chocolate chip cookies.

Later that evening, I try my hand at water scrying. It feels like things are blocked on all fronts, but here's to hoping for a little divination inspiration. I gather my supplies and cast a circle. I anoint my white candle and set my intention to see the face of whoever killed Maddie. I hold my hands over the water and chant:

> Power of water give me a peek.
> Maddie's killer is whom I seek.

I settle my mind and gaze into the small bowl of water. I'm not sure how long I sit there, but eventually a blurry image begins to take form, but then that image quickly fades before I can make out anything useful. I take a deep breath and try to relax. I continue to gaze, but all I see is a bowl of water.

"Maddie, I haven't given up on you. I promise. But a little guidance would be greatly appreciated," I say with a sigh as I close my circle.

The next morning, Damion and I do a little digging into Kate's husband. We learn that he's the CEO of a small cyber security firm. And that he was the keynote speaker at a cyber security conference last year in New York, the same time Maddie went missing. *Looks like we can mark him off the quickly dwindling list of suspects*, I sigh.

I finish ringing up a customer when I receive a premonition that I need to look in the mirror. I immediately walk to the bathroom and take a look, but I don't get whatever it is I'm supposed to see. Maybe it's a symbolic mirror and not an actual mirror? I join Grandma and Elvis and tell them about my strange vision.

"Maybe it means you need to mirror gaze." Grandma walks back to the library and returns with a book *Through the Looking Glass: the Power of Mirror Magic*. She flips to a page that shows a picture of the mirror setup. "Try mirror gazing this evening around twilight. I'll make sure Callie and I are quiet as to not disturb you. I've never tried this method of divination, so I'm excited to hear about your experience."

I flip through Grandma's book. It describes a mirror technique that was adapted from the ancient Greek practice of contacting the spirits in a Necromanteion, a type of ziggurat temple.

Twilight nears as I pull the blackout curtains closed and place a rolled up towel under my door to block out any noise. I move the full-length mirror from my bathroom and prop it up against my bedroom wall, positioning my yoga mat to the side to where I can sit and look into the mirror without seeing my own reflection.

I light one candle on the other side of the room and turn out the lights. Taking a seat and relaxing my mind, I gaze into the mirror. I don't know how long I sit there, but I eventually enter a trance.

I step through the mirror. Suddenly, I'm Maddie and I'm running through the dark woods. I'm wearing a white billowing dress that's covered in blood, and I'm barefoot but I can't stop; I've got to get away! I run face first into a tree, and I try not to cry out. My nose gushes blood, but I keep going. I'm running and I trip over a root. Footsteps behind me are getting closer; I've got to get up! I'm back on my feet, but now I'm limping. Oh my God, he's going to make me go back! I won't go back!

I cry out and look around my room, disoriented. *Aubry! What happened?* Damion demands.

My heart races as I get up to turn on the overhead light. I stand in front of the mirror, but all I see is my own reflection. My nose is bleeding.

CHAPTER 32

"Little witch, you're calling about the file."

"Yes. Did you have any luck?"

Sonia huffs. "No, that man infuriates me to no end. But I'm not giving up. He messed with the wrong she-demon," she says, hanging up.

I take matters into my own hands and call Chris. It goes to his voicemail. "Detective, this is Aubry Brooks. If you don't call me back, I'm going to file a formal complaint." A formal complaint with whom, I don't know, but it sounded good. I leave him my number even though I know he has it.

Grandma walks into the kitchen. "Morning, sugar pie. Calling that sexy detective, I like your strategy. Damion, you'd best be on your toes."

"Always, Vivian," he replies.

I ignore them both and work on the puzzle. "How was your mirror-gazing experience last night?" Grandma asks.

"I'm not ready to talk about it." I don't want her to worry.

I'm worried enough for the both of us. For once in her life, she doesn't pry.

I let Grandma handle the shop this morning and I go to yoga. I'm too much in my head right now and I need to ground my energy. *So hot yoga is just yoga with heaters?*

Pretty much.

I bet you can bend yourself into all sorts of interesting positions when you're warmed up like this. Mmmm, I'm getting ideas.

You are a dirty, dirty demon.

Class ends and I walk back to the shop. I stop short, surprised to see Chris. He's wearing another bland detective suit along with a look of pure annoyance. He directs that look at me. Back at him.

"Sugar pie, there you are. Chris is here to see you." Grandma turns to Chris. "You'll have to excuse Aubry's appearance. She's into yoga and she's extremely flexible. Why, she can work her body into a pretzel."

As I suspected.

"Bye, Grandma." She winks at me and heads to the back.

I walk behind the counter and deposit my purse. "Morning. I need to run upstairs real quick. Do you mind giving me just a few minutes?"

"You wanted to talk. So talk." Apparently Chris is a man that doesn't waste time with pleasantries. Or waiting on a sweaty woman to change out of her yoga clothes. Or being polite in general.

Remember when I said I didn't like this guy?

"Okay, then. Let's just lay all our cards on the table. My dead best friend, Maddie, sent me a dream of her holding a Tower tarot card on a wooded path. New Life Spiritual Center has an observation tower that you reach via a wooded path."

"And?" he asks in a bored tone.

"*And* I received a vision last night of Maddie trying to escape from someone chasing her in the woods."

"You received a *vision*."

He looks at me like I'm crazy, but I press on. "She was terrified and running for her life," I say as I take a deep breath and continue. "I think someone killed her at the Center and then dumped her body in the Mississippi River. Look, I told you that I'm not going to give up, and I meant it. I just want to see the file. Please?"

Chris pauses for a moment. "What do you hope to learn from the file? If we knew who killed her, we'd have already made an arrest," he points out.

"Then where's the harm in letting me see it?" I counter.

"It's against policy."

Policy, along with bureaucracy, is the devil's work. "I won't tell if you don't."

"Why should I trust you?" He gives me a hard look.

And then as if to highlight Chris's concern, Sonia walks through the door. "Hello, little witch." She turns to Chris. "And hello to you, Detective," she says with a seductive smile.

Her eyes glow as she gives him a smoldering look. Yep, there's the sex kitten I was worried about. "Don't waste your time," he says in a bored tone. "You're not getting my file."

"Are you gay?" she asks hopefully. I guess her succubus ego is taking a hit.

He snorts. "Not gay. Also not an idiot."

"Sonia, thank you, but I have the situation under control," I tell her.

She looks at a loss for what to do next, but quickly recovers. "Very well, little witch. See you around, choirboy," she says with a smoldering look as she shakes her curvy hips out the door.

I turn to Chris. "Look, I'm sorry if Sonia's been persistent."

"Persistent? You sic the femme fatale on me like an attack dog, and you're sorry if she's been persistent?" he says in a mocking tone.

"Fine, I asked Sonia to get me a copy of your file. Wouldn't it be so much easier if you just gave it to me? I'll stay out of your hair. Please?"

He surprises me by reaching into his messenger bag, pulling out two file folders. "Your friend Madison's file as well as your ex-boyfriend's. Share them with anyone and you'll regret it, I promise you." He turns to leave.

"For the last time, Brad was not my boyfriend," I call after him.

I walk upstairs to my room and have a seat on my bed. A part of me dreads opening Maddie's file, so I start with Brad's first. I read my statement, and then I see Chris's handwritten note saying he thinks I'm not being one hundred percent forthcoming. Dang, he's good.

I then turn to Charlotte's statement, and on the next page are the results from a sexual assault forensic exam. I decide I won't read any of her information, as it feels like too much of a privacy violation. She's never told me the details of her captivity before I joined her in that basement, and I haven't pried. I figure she'll tell me if and when she's ready.

I flip through various legal filings in the case and tab those for Damion to read through later. And then I come to the photographs. I look through the crime scene pictures and photos of the bloody pallet Charlotte was lying on. Next are photos of the hunting knife found at the scene. There's a ruler beside the blade that measures six inches. Six inches of steel that scarred Charlotte's arm, not to mention the emotional scars left behind.

I have to put the file down and walk away for a few moments. My heart hurts for my friend.

I make myself some chamomile tea to help soothe my nerves and then I resume flipping through the photographs. I stop when I come upon a picture of a black robe. It looks like a typical ritual robe that a wannabe sorcerer would wear. "Fantasy role-playing with the racquetball crew?"

Perhaps, but I would say too much imagination for a man as vanilla as Brad.

Next is a hunting knife with strange symbols. "Maybe these are the odd things Chris was talking about?"

Very well could be.

I keep flipping and come to Brad's financials. Highlighted is a $50,000 donation to the Center. My mouth falls open, and I have to double check those zeros. "Brad doesn't strike me as a spiritual seeker or a generous giver, for that matter."

Unless there was some kind of tax write-off? Damion points out. Now that sounds more like Brad.

I finish with his psychological evaluation, which just pisses me off. Schizophrenia my ass.

The last document has a sticky note from Chris that says, *Stay away from New Life Spiritual Center. That's not a suggestion. Don't try me.*

Grabbing the note, I wad it up and toss it across the room. I review the Center's list of ten employees along with photos and background checks. I about fall off my bed when I see a familiar face.

What?

The Center's housekeeper is Maddie's mama. Leigh's a classic junkie who would promise to get her act together and never follow through. Maddie stayed with us a couple of months our senior year of high school when Leigh got picked up for violating her

POSSESSION

probation. There's no love lost between me and Maddie's mama. In fact, I haven't seen Leigh since the memorial. Time to remedy that. I take a closer look at her photos. Her mug shot versus her current photo is a night to day transformation. Maybe she has cleaned herself up, and that pisses me off. Why couldn't she have done that when Maddie was alive?

I make some notes about things I want to follow up on, and then I grab Maddie's file.

I start through the phone records. Highlighted is a Memphis area code number that appears around a month before her death. This must be the guy with the burner phone. I read through the highlighted text messages. All of them from this guy simply say, *Meet at our spot*. "Couldn't he have spelled it out? Like a name, an address, GPS coordinates, something?"

I get to the autopsy report and take a deep breath and steel my nerves. Maddie's body was found in the Mississippi River, and I absolutely dread seeing the autopsy pictures. It's one thing to know how she was found. It's another to come face-to-face with that image. Leigh cremated her daughter because of how bad of a shape Maddie's body was found. Well, Leigh made the decision, but Grandma paid for it. Grandma doesn't know I overheard that phone conversation. I may complain about Vivian's meddling nature, but the woman has a heart of gold.

Flipping through the report, I notice the autopsy photos are missing. Maybe Chris does have a kind bone in his body after all. Who knew?

I read through the report and tab the toxicology findings. *No traces of drugs or alcohol.* I knew Detective Rodriguez was barking up the wrong tree. He saw the burner phone and Maddie's family history and just assumed she'd gotten caught up in the drug world.

I turn to the autopsy's last page summary. *This examiner concludes that the cause of death is manual strangulation. Death is ruled a homicide.*

I don't want to, but I go back and read about Maddie's various injuries, including evidence that she had been choked and that her body suffered overall contusions and bruising. Both wrists had ligature marks encircling them. I have to skip over the detailed evidence of sexual assault. I tab the page for Damion to look through later without me, as I just can't handle it. Turning to the last page: *No foreign DNA evidence detected.* Whatever evidence that might have been on her was washed away by the mighty · Mississippi.

I walk out of my room to find Grandma in the kitchen. Whatever she's cooking smells amazing, but I don't have an appetite. "Pork chops, fried apples, and green beans with ham hock," she announces.

"No, thanks. I'm not hungry," I say as I fill up my water bottle.

"You alright, sugar pie?"

"Just tired. Good night," I say as I walk back to my room and close the door.

Just in time, as the floodgates open and I start sobbing. Damion takes over and lays me down and sends a soothing touch up and down my spine.

"Why is everything so fucked up?" I ask when I've finally cried myself out.

I don't catch his answer as I drift off to sleep.

CHAPTER 33

Chris told me not to try him, so of course I'm going to try him. I have to pick my jaw up off the floor at the price tag of a room at New Life Spiritual Center. Inner peace is outrageously expensive.

"Here's the plan," I say after filling Charlotte and Gabe in on what I've learned from Maddie's file. "Let's go back to the observation tower. Maybe we missed something. Then, let's speak to all the employees to see if they remember Maddie."

"And so Maddie's mother works at the Center?" Charlotte asks, closing the file and handing it to Gabe, whose large frame practically takes up my entire back seat.

"Yes."

"Could be a coincidence," Gabe warns.

Just as I said.

Too big of a coincidence, if you ask me. And Gabe better be here as a friend and not as a lawyer. No way in hell am I paying him his absurd hourly rate for tagging along.

I'd be happy to negotiate on your behalf, in exchange for—

Never mind.

We arrive at the Center and check in at the reception desk. A hippie-looking woman around my age with dreadlocks gives us our room key, a property map, and a list of activities.

"Meditation tonight is at seven and nine. Candlelight yoga is at ten." She marks out with a pen tomorrow's morning sunrise meditation. "Unfortunately, a lightning strike did some damage to our property. The observation tower is temporarily closed." Dang it. There goes my whole plan.

I hold up a picture of Maddie on my phone. "Have you ever seen this woman?"

"No, I'm sorry, I don't believe so. Why do you ask?"

"She's a friend. I was just wondering if she's ever stayed here," I hedge.

We make our way to our private lodge, use our key, and step inside the small two-room suite.

Charlotte looks nervous, but Gabe quickly says, "Ladies, I'll take the pullout couch in the living room. You two can have the bedroom." He uses his power and begins sliding furniture around the room.

"Watch your jaw on the floor, it's gonna get hit by a flying table," I tell her. "What are you doing?" I ask Gabe.

"Looking for runes or other symbols. Just being cautious."

"Where are your wings?" Charlotte eyes him suspiciously.

"I only break those out on special occasions," he says with a charming smile, and Damion snorts.

"Let's go ahead and walk to the tower and take a look around," I suggest.

We follow the trail signs and begin our hike. This time I am dressed appropriately in a pullover, yoga pants, and hiking boots.

We make it to the tower and sure enough, it's closed. There's obvious fire damage and it looks extremely unstable, hence the barricade.

"Okay then, let's check the meditation hall," I announce. "Maybe there's a basement or a trap door."

"Trap door?" Damion snorts. "She watches too much TV."

I take back over. "I don't hear you coming up with a better plan," I say probably a bit too defensively. And fine, I do watch too much TV, but that's neither here nor there.

"I'm going to take a look around. I'll meet you ladies back in our room," Gabe announces and then disappears.

"You get used to supernaturals popping in and out of existence," I inform Charlotte, whose mouth is agape.

The sun sets as we begin our return hike. *It's alright*, Damion reassures, sending a comforting touch up and down my spine. He must be able to feel I'm on edge, the memory of Maddie running for her life in the dark woods fresh in my mind.

We reach the meditation hall and quietly step inside, as there are several people seated cross-legged on the floor. Charlotte and I take a seat in the back. Everyone's got their eyes closed, so I take my time, surveying the room. It's a large domed structure with a stage up front. I spot the guy Charlotte and I met when we were here the first time. He's solo on stage with a serene look on his face and eyes closed. "It's Ethan, I think that's his name. The meditation guide," I whisper to Charlotte and she nods.

There wasn't anything in the file about an Ethan.

Unless he hasn't worked here very long, Damion points out.

Class ends with a chant and Ethan playing a Tibetan singing bowl. The crowd slowly disburses and we make our way to the front. "Hi there, I'm Aubry and this is Charlotte," I say.

"Ladies, a pleasure. Did you enjoy the meditation?"

"Yes," I fib. "Where are you from? You have an unusual accent," I comment.

He gives me a charming smile. "I am a citizen of the world."

Damion snorts. *Don't get me started on this guy.*

"How long have you been at the Center?" I ask.

"Just a few months. It has such an amazing vibe, no?"

"Amazing," we agree.

"Where was home before the Center?" Charlotte asks.

"Costa Rica."

"Did you meet Kate at a meditation center there?" I guess.

"Yes," he says, sounding surprised. "She told me of her dream to create a meditation retreat in Tennessee. I had to be a part of it when I saw her dream come to fruition."

I grab my phone from my back pocket, probably a big no-no in the meditation hall. "Have you ever seen this woman here at the Center?" I realize a futile question since he wasn't here a year ago, but I've got nothing else.

He looks at the picture. "No, I can't say that I have. Your sister, perhaps? You're both beauties," he says with a smile.

Damion snorts.

"Yes," I answer. Maddie was my sister in every way except blood.

"Excuse me," I hear a familiar voice. I turn around and have to pick my jaw up off the floor.

"Aunt Callie, what are you doing here?"

"Hey, sweetie. Hey, Charlotte. I told you I'm taking a meditation workshop," she says. "Ethan, will we need any props this evening?"

"Just a bolster," he says.

"Well, enjoy your class," I say as I take Charlotte's hand and lead her out.

"What's wrong?" Charlotte asks.

"I'm not sure. I guess I just wasn't expecting to see my aunt. I knew she was taking a workshop, she just never told me it was here."

We pass a woman carrying some yoga mats. "What a nice evening for a walk," the older woman comments with a smile.

"So nice. Have you seen my friend around here?" I ask, holding up my phone.

"No, I don't think so."

"Have a good evening," I say, and we walk on.

"Let's head to the café," I suggest.

"To speak to the kitchen staff?" Charlotte asks.

Sure, that's my reasoning. Grandma was right; I do get cranky when I get hungry.

Unfortunately, we reach an empty café. Charlotte and I grab fruit-and-soy yogurt cups from the refrigerated display and leave money in the honor jar. Not my first pick, but the kitchen is already closed. It's this or green juice. Soy yogurt it is.

We return to our room and quickly learn that unsweetened soy yogurt is disgusting. Gabe returns. "Anything?" I ask.

"No."

I sigh in frustration, grabbing the hotel phone and dialing the front desk. "Yes, our bathroom wasn't clean on our arrival."

The front desk clerk apologizes and promises to send house-keeping over immediately.

"I want to talk to Maddie's mama," I explain when Charlotte and Gabe both give me quizzical looks.

Several minutes later, Gabe answers the door. Leigh walks in with a basket of cleaning supplies. "Let me start off by apologizing. I'll get right to w—" She stops dead in her tracks.

"Hello, Leigh," I say. Seeing Leigh is like seeing a ghost, as Maddie looked so much like her mama. Leigh is in her early forties with long raven-black hair and expressive brown eyes. She has a pretty face. It shows some wear from her past drug use, but those telltale signs of current use are no longer there. She's even had her teeth fixed. "You wanted to start off by apologizing, go right ahead. Maddie's not here, but I'll listen on her behalf."

"I was a terrible mother. My sweet girl deserved so much better. I'll be the first to admit it. And I'm sorry that I stole from your shop. And from your purse. And from your car. And from your—"

"Okay, I get the picture." I knew about the shop; that's why Leigh got herself a lifetime ban. I cross my arms. "So I'm supposed to believe you've changed your ways?"

"This time is different. I was in rehab for the third time—this one wasn't court ordered, it was my decision. Maddie's death was the breaking point for me," she says in tears.

I cross my arms, unconvinced. "How did you wind up at the Center?"

"I met a friend in rehab who'd heard of this place. I came with her after we got out. Kate Jones has such a kind heart. She hired us despite our baggage."

"Did Maddie ever come to the Center to see you?" I ask.

"No. Maddie and I weren't talking at that point, so she didn't even know I was working here. She cut me out, blocked my number. I don't blame her for that." She takes a deep breath and continues, "I could have showed up at school and waited until I ran into her, but I thought it was best to respect her wishes. Now I just wish I could have seen her one last time," she says, tears streaming down her face.

Charlotte walks to the bathroom, returning with a tissue box. She offers it to Leigh. "Any idea who killed Maddie?" I ask.

"No, I wish I did," she says, dabbing her eyes.

"Do you think she got caught up with a drug dealer?"

"No," she says firmly. "Not Maddie."

"No, not Maddie," I agree.

I open the shop this bright and sunny morning in a glum mood. Our weekend investigation plans turned out to be an epic fail. Every time I think we have a lead, it turns out to be a dead end.

"I thought you were having a romantic weekend with Damion. Don't tell me there's trouble in paradise already," Grandma says, joining me.

"I'm not sure where you got that idea, but wouldn't it be hell instead of paradise since he's a demon?" I point out.

"Was it a hellish weekend or a hell of a weekend? Big difference there."

"Where's Aunt Callie?" I change the subject.

"She claims she's at a continuing education seminar on past life regression."

Before Grandma can say more, the door chimes. In swaggers Chris, wearing a black Henley that clings to his muscles, black jeans, and black boots. Good, his outfit matches my mood.

"Who's up for watching the new season of *Bermuda Love Triangle*? Maybe we'll have a themed menu. I'll whip us up some

Bahama Mamas, although that's the Bahamas, not Bermuda. I'll have to look online to see if Bermuda has a cocktail. I'm not sure about that," Grandma says.

I know I'll regret it, but I say, "The drink you're thinking of is 'dark and stormy.' It's a Bermuda cocktail made of dark rum and ginger beer. And now, if you'll excuse us."

"Alright sugar pie, I can take a hint. You need privacy." She winks at Chris and walks out.

"Why is the Center part of your investigation?" I demand by way of greeting.

"Not your concern."

"Was Maddie involved with the Center or not? If you say not your concern again…" I don't finish my threat, as I have nothing to back it up with.

"You just have to trust me."

"So I'm supposed to trust you because you say so?" I snort.

"I've shared information with you, but that's not good enough. You defied me, and last night you came close to jeopardizing my case," he growls, pointing a finger at me.

"What do you mean?" I play dumb.

How in the hell does he know I was at the Center?

It could be under surveillance.

But why?

That's the question.

"I will haul your ass to jail for interfering with a police investigation if you don't *stay the fuck out of it*!" he thunders. He gives me an icy look that could freeze boiling water and then spins on his heel and marches out.

"The chocolate chip cookies were delicious," I call after him.

CHAPTER 34

I finish reading The *Divine Magic of the Moon* and place the book on the shelf in our library. Other than some new ideas for full moon rituals, it was pretty useless as far as the possession problem. I take another look at the sigil I found in the book. Still not knowing what it means, I tuck it away.

"I'm going to play poker at Brenda's. Maybe I'll finally get lucky," Grandma says as she hugs me goodbye. I don't want to know the context of that statement.

What's for dinner? Damion asks.

Why, what are you in the mood for? I tease.

A contract appears. *A steak, prepared medium. Baked potato with butter and sour cream. Salad is optional.*

And a French apple tart with vanilla ice cream, I finish for him. So a deal with the devil in the astral plane counts. Good to know.

For the time being, shall I cook you dinner?

Yes, please.

The contract disappears as he takes over and opens the fridge. *What is this green sludge in the jar?*

I think that's Aunt Callie's leftover smoothie.

This is pitiful. If you don't go to the grocery store, I'm taking over your body and going myself.

"Been a little busy, in case you haven't noticed."

I tell him where to find the frying pan, and he turns on the stove eye. *What the hell is that?* He points to the crone poppet displayed on our kitchen altar above the stove.

Our kitchen witch. Grandma's had this poppet for as long as I can remember. As a child, I learned our kitchen witch was not a toy; she is something to be respected, as she protects our kitchen and aids in our magic.

God, that's creepy.

I snort. *Says the demon.*

He proceeds to make a fried ham sandwich, but burns the bread. "Shouldn't have disrespected our kitchen witch. Tell her you're sorry."

You can't be serious.

"I am serious. I don't want you burning through the entire loaf of bread."

"I'm sorry," he says to the poppet.

Wiping the pan clean, he starts again, this time presenting me with a nicely toasted sandwich. "A croque monsieur. It's the best I could do given the circumstances. Seriously, we're going to the grocery store tomorrow. How you've survived this long without me taking care of you is a mystery."

I take back control and give a derisive snort. "Your ego is absurd, but thank you for dinner. This is perfect."

I quickly eat and wash up the few dishes. I walk to my room and change into my lounge pants and Memphis Magic sweatshirt.

Get ready, we're going out, he commands.

No, we're not. I've taken my bra off and have no intention of putting it back on.

We're going to visit a suspect we've overlooked.

Who?

Your ex-boyfriend. You said that Maddie distanced herself and you thought it was because she didn't like this guy. Maybe there's more to the story.

Look, Todd is beyond self-centered, but he's not a killer. There's no way he's involved with Maddie's murder.

What's the harm in talking to him?

Fine, but I'm not putting my bra back on.

Saves me a step later.

In your dreams.

In your dreams, assuming you play your cards right.

I ignore that little comment as I walk to my closet and debate what to wear. My go-to black cocktail dress will forever be tainted by psycho Brad. Time to donate it. I grab an empty bag and shove the dress inside. I ask Damion for privacy, throwing on a cropped white sweater and my distressed jeans.

I walk to the bathroom and decide on leaving my hair down. I touch up my makeup and apply red lip gloss. "I'm ready," I say, giving myself a once-over in the mirror and screwing the cap back on my lip gloss.

Damion surprises me when he takes control of my hand and tucks a strand of hair behind my ear. *For what, Aubry?* he asks in that unbelievably sexy voice of his. *Tell me what you're ready for,* he purrs. He takes my finger and traces the exposed skin of my stomach, leaving goose bumps in its wake. It feels like warm hands position themselves on my hips.

I look back at us in the mirror. "To go," I say in a breathier tone than I intended. I turn and walk out of the bathroom and pretend that he didn't notice my hard nipples. I grab my purse and phone and walk out the door.

Damion takes over behind the wheel. We're both quiet. The sexual tension is so thick you could cut it with a knife. Luckily for me, the eighties song "Devil Inside" by INXS plays on the radio. I laugh out loud. I'm glad to see the Universe has found its sense of humor.

I give Damion directions and he parks my car. I walk past several darkened buildings until I reach an alley that dead-ends.

Are you sure this is the right place?

I push the hidden button. A man on the intercom answers. "Yes?"

"The password is magic," I announce.

"How is that spelled?"

"M-a-g-i-c-k."

You can't be serious.

The door buzzes open, and I step inside the 1920s-themed speakeasy. "Good evening," a guy dressed in a white shirt, black suspenders, and bow tie says. "Reservation?" He looks me up and down. "And this establishment has a dress code."

"I'm here to see Todd," I announce, marching past him.

"Of all the gin joints in the world, she walks into mine," Todd says, leaning over the white marble bar, clasping his hands together. My ex is extremely good-looking, but the problem is he knows it. He's wearing the same uniform as the guy at the door, except Todd has the sleeves of his white shirt rolled up, showing off his muscular forearms.

He stands his six-foot, one-inch frame upright and gives me a smirk. At least I think he does? Maybe it's his lips, but it always looks like he has a permanent smirk on his pretty face. He's wearing glasses that I'm fairly certain are just for show. His brown hair has grown out and he has it pulled back in a man bun, which I find about as pretentious as him calling himself a chaote and spelling magick with a "k." Speaking of magick, he has a new tattoo on his left forearm—it's a skull with "m-a-g-i-c-k" spelled as the teeth. He's also sporting a perfectly manicured beard. Goddess, I can only imagine how long it now takes him to get ready with the added beard maintenance.

Damion snorts. *If you're opening with a cheesy line, at least have the decency to get the line right.*

"Pretty sure this isn't your gin joint," I tell my ex as I take a seat.

I grab a drink menu and spot the guy from the door bounding over. "It's alright," Todd tells the gatekeeper. The guy nods and returns to his podium.

"Don't bother," Todd says, snatching the menu from my hands. "I've got your drink coming up." He makes a show of mixing this and that. He gives it a good shake before holding the shaker above his head and dramatically pouring the concoction into the glass.

Is this supposed to impress you?

He thinks so.

"May I present you with the Lazy Witch."

I take it back. Todd's not trying to *impress* me, but *enrage* me. I give him a saccharine smile as I take a sip. "Delicious." It actually is good. It's a play on an old fashioned, my favorite cocktail, except it tastes like he's added brown sugar and something else, maybe bacon?

"I'm surprised you think so. Your palate was always a little more PBR." Pabst Blue Ribbon, also known as PBR, is a favorite among broke college students. Maddie and I used to drink PBR together, and Todd always used to make fun of us for it.

Let me take over and make this little boy piss his pants.

Stay out of this.

"Oh, and you're wrong. This is my bar. I bought it a few months back."

"Congrats. Did you get the manifest spell from my book of shadows that you *stole*?" There wasn't anything in my book of shadows that I would consider groundbreaking. I'd mostly just written down my notes and thoughts about tarot card readings. But that's not the point. The point is I'm certain Todd stole it. That was the last straw and I dumped him.

"For the last time, I didn't steal your precious 'magic' diary." He uses air quotes.

I have to bite my tongue so hard it bleeds. Not really, but almost. "I'm not here to argue."

"Then why are you here? To beg me to take you back?" he says with a smirk as he wipes down the bar. Well, I say smirk, but again, it's hard to tell, as that's just his typical look.

I'm taking over—

Butt out. I mean it.

"Shouldn't you be the one begging me, seeing that I broke up with you?" I snort. Okay, I said I'm not here to argue. I take a deep breath and focus. "Look, I'm here because it's been a year since Maddie's death. I'm wondering if you've heard anything about her case."

"Nope."

"Where were you when she went missing?"

"You can't be serious." I give him a look. "You're serious. Aubry, you know that I was either working my ass off here at the bar or with you. You don't want to hear it, but it sounds like Maddie got caught up in some shit. You said so yourself—it's been over a year. Don't you think it's time to let it go?"

"I can't."

"Whatever. It's your life."

"Why didn't Maddie like you?"

I could come up with a laundry list of reasons and I just met the guy.

"You're the clairvoyant, shouldn't you know?" He smiles, going for my jugular.

"Humor me," I say, sipping my drink, pretending his shot didn't hit the mark.

"She was jealous of me. You two were conjoined twins and then I came into the picture." He grabs a bar rag and dries a glass; I can't help but notice the flashy new Rolex on his wrist.

"Wow, chaos 'magick' really must be paying off," I throw air quotes back at him.

What do you mean?

Todd's a chaote. As I sip my wine, something is trying to work its way to the surface of my mind. Chaos magick. The Tower card of *chaos.* Connected somehow? I don't know. It feels like I'm trying to put together Grandma's jigsaw puzzle, but the puzzle box is missing and I have no clue what the finished puzzle is supposed to look like. And then someone mixed in a few puzzle pieces from a completely different puzzle for shits and giggles.

"You have no idea," Todd says with a wink and then turns to help a customer seated at the other end of the bar.

Ready to take me home? I ask Damion as I throw down some bills.

Yes, but first I need to make a stop at the gas station.

We return home, and I laugh as I pop open a PBR tall boy.

CHAPTER 35

I'm awakened to the screeching sound of my aunt's blender reverberating in my skull. I put my pillow over my head and groan. *Good morning,* Damion says in an extra chipper tone. I toss the pillow aside and see I made it as far as taking off my boots last night.

Please take over my body and go throw the blender out the window, I beg.

On second thought, I have a better idea. I slowly get up and walk to my door and stick my head out. "Aunt Callie, I'm hungover. Will you please make me a ginger smoothie?"

"Of course, sweetie." She brings me a glass of water. "Drink this first and go take a shower."

I chug the water and turn around to go back in my room when I hear Grandma say, "Sugar pie, did you hook up with someone? Looks like you had a wild night. Would it be considered a threesome since Damion was there?"

I told you I don't share my possessions.

I don't dignify either comment with a response as I slam my door. And then I immediately regret slamming my door.

I wind up back in bed and wake some time later with Aunt Callie holding a cold glass to my cheek. "Ginger, banana, and coconut water."

"Bless you," I say as I drink, feeling less queasy.

"Go take a shower, and then have a few sips of coffee. The caffeine will help with the headache." She hands me a bar of *Hell No Hangover* spelled soap that Grandma and I make and sell downstairs in the tourist section. Looks like I'll be performing quality control this morning.

Will you carry me to the shower? I ask Damion.

Of course. I'm here for you in your time of need. I'd be happy to help you with your shower. I'm quite skilled with a loofah.

Aren't you the reason I'm in this time of need in the first place? I point out as I ignore his loofah comment. Although now I'm wondering just how skilled.

Temptation is a demon's calling.

I feel somewhat human again after my solo shower. No, I didn't take him up on his loofah offer, but I'd be lying if I said I wasn't tempted. I don't bother with drying my hair. Instead, I braid the wet strands into a loose side braid. I throw on a comfy sweater, leggings, and a pair of sneakers.

Damion takes over, and I mentally fall back asleep. I wake to the delicious smell of butter frying in the pan, and soon I'm presented with scrambled eggs and toast. It hits the spot.

Grab a bag, we're going back to Jackson.

Please is still the magic word, I grumble.

"Aunt Callie," I say, sticking my head in her room. "Damion and I are going to Jackson. Tell Grandma we'll be back tomorrow."

"Sure thing, sweetie."

"Where are you off to?" I ask. My aunt is dressed in yoga pants and a halter tank.

"I'm going to New Life Spiritual Center. I still have eight classroom hours left on my meditation course."

"How do you like the Center?" I ask.

"I love it. Everyone there is so amazing. And the meditation workshop is going to be so helpful in my regression practice."

"You don't get any weird vibes from that place?"

"No. Why?"

"I don't know. Just be careful when you're there."

"Mama's right, you fret too much."

"Yeah, yeah. Bye."

Have you considered the possibility that the Center has nothing to do with Maddie?

I'm not sure what to think anymore.

I nap on the car ride and wake to find us walking up the steps to Damion's office.

"Helen," Damion says. "You remember Aubry."

"Hi, Helen. Nice to see you again," I say.

"Nice to see you too," Damion's secretary tells me.

He takes back over. "I need Beltzar's file," he commands as we walk to his office.

Why do you need Beltzar's file? Who is Beltzar?

I recently represented the demon Beltzar in a contract dispute with a sorcerer. Care to guess who that sorcerer was?

"Please don't say Todd."

See, you're not just the eye candy of this showmance. I knew I had met Todd before last night, but it took me a moment to place him.

"Maybe it was the hipster glasses and beard that threw you off," I say. "Did that case involve a soul contract like the one Brad signed?"

No, it was a commercial real estate deal gone bad. Care to guess what real estate?

"The bar."

Yes. This was one of those cases that should have settled, but Todd was an arrogant prick and was dumb enough to represent himself. Anyone who represents himself has a fool for a client. Of course, my client won, and Todd wasn't too happy about it. But I had no reason to give it a second thought.

"And you think Todd is somehow behind our binding?"

I'm not ruling anything out.

"Let's assume for the sake of argument that Todd placed some kind of hex or used chaos magick against you. That still doesn't explain why he'd entrap you inside me. Yes, it's an awfully big coincidence that I'm Todd's ex, we broke up on bad terms, you bested Todd, and now you're stuck in me. But we're still missing pieces to connect all those dots."

True. But that's why we're here, trying to connect those dots.

"Knock, knock. Here's the file. Should I ask why you're still with Aubry?"

"We're working on it," he says. She gives me a concerned look, but walks off.

We flip through the file. *Ah, here is Todd's signature, his sorcerer's sigil.* We hold up the document and then we walk over to my purse and take out the sigil we found inside Grandma's book.

Look familiar? Damion stuck the paper in my purse earlier and now I understand why. It's the same symbol.

I rack my brain trying to get at the answer. I think back to Maddie holding the Tower card in my dream. The card of chaos. "Todd is a chaos magick practitioner," I think out loud. "He's obviously gained some mastery over the magick between when we broke up until now. He used to draw sigils all the time, and maybe he left this one in the book to intentionally forget it."

What do you mean? I know little about chaos magick.

"The chaote focuses his intent in a sigil by drawing it out of the letters of the desired outcome, kind of like a magical monogram. He then charges the sigil to give it energy and power, and then he alters his consciousness to intentionally forget the sigil by leaving it in a safe place." I continue thinking out loud. "So maybe Todd put the same desire into two sigils, but because he forgot about the first one he left in the book, when he went to charge the second sigil, it charged both?"

That still doesn't explain why we're bound together.

"True. Maybe the one we found in the book doesn't have anything to do with this. Chaos magick never made sense to me."

Let's see if Gabe is back and can meet us here. We might have enough to get a Blood Summons issued.

"What's a Blood Summons?"

An order drafted in blood by the Arbitrator. It will compel the parties to appear at the Reckoning, and the offender must either admit or refute the claims of the wronged demon.

"Hey, what about me? I've been wronged here too!"

The only thing wrong is your refusal to admit you're ready for me.

I ignore his little comment as we send Gabe a message. He quickly replies that he's stuck in an arbitration and he'll meet us tomorrow.

"I'm getting awfully close to firing Gabe," I huff.

So we are in this together. I'll remember that when the bill arrives.

Walked right into that one.

CHAPTER 36

Arriving at Damion's house, I eat takeout, and then we fuss about what to watch on TV. I click on a show and then he takes over my body and clicks on a different show. And so it goes. "Keep it up and I'll make us watch the entire past seasons of *House Guest* so we can talk about each hookup in graphic detail with Grandma."

He laughs, startling me when he takes control of my hand and caresses my cheek. *I'm going to kiss you now.*

"How do you figure—" I start, but then it feels like warm lips are lightly touching mine and I gasp. I relax and settle into the kiss, only for him to pull back. Way too soon for my liking, and I don't know how I feel about that.

"I'm going to get ready for bed," I say as I walk to the bathroom. "Privacy, please."

Of course. I'll be a good boy and wait until you're ready.

I'm pretty sure he's not talking about waiting for me to brush and floss. I look at myself in the mirror and touch my hand to my lips. They still tingle from that phantom kiss.

I grab my tarot cards from my duffle bag and give them a shuffle. I hold them to my heart and ask for guidance with one card. I pull the Lover upright. Love. Passion. Romance. This card tells me I'm at a major love crossroads. I can keep things as is, or I can throw caution to the wind and go for it. I can walk back out there, pretending that kiss didn't happen. I was just burned by Todd. Then I rebounded with milk toast Brad who turned out to be psycho Brad. Maybe it's best for me to have just a time of self-reflection that doesn't involve a guy.

I sigh as I look at my card. "Really, Universe, that's the information I needed to know at this exact moment? As if our situation needs another layer of complication, let's add sex to the mix." Yes siree, the safe thing to do would be to go about business as usual. It certainly would be the vanilla thing to do.

I take one more look at my card and place it back in the deck. Out of all his seduction moves, the sweet gesture of him buying me the cheap beer last night helps me make up my mind. He's told me more than once he'll be a good boy and wait until I'm ready. I'm as ready as I'll ever be. I take a deep breath and decide to add a few rainbow sprinkles to my vanilla scoop.

Damion?

You ready?

I look at us in the mirror. "I'm ready."

For what, Aubry? Tell me.

"For you," I whisper.

Are you sure? My body temperature increases and my breasts begin to tingle.

"Yes," I say in a breathless tone.

Good, because I wasn't sure how much longer I could wait.

"Then what are you waiting on?" I demand.

He laughs as he takes over my hands and unbraids my hair. He then moves my finger to my mouth and traces my lips. *Let me have just a little taste,* he purrs, and it feels like lips are on mine. I open for him, and a phantom tongue wraps around mine. I glance over to the mirror. It looks like I'm kissing air, but I couldn't care less. My mouth tingles just like my lips were a few minutes ago. It's the most unusual, sensual feeling.

I don't know how long I stand there, kissing him but not kissing him. *Definitely not vanilla. Let me taste more,* he commands. I'm already so turned on it's ridiculous.

I look at us in the mirror as I slowly pull my shirt over my head and let it drop to the floor. *So beautiful,* he murmurs as he takes control and looks down at my breasts, which have now become heavy, my nipples erect. I shimmy out of my jeans and give them a toss. My lacy black panties are already damp just by phantom kissing this demon. I'm clearly in over my head.

Go lie down on the bed, Aubry. My lust-hazed mind wants to comply, but then the stubborn part of me snaps out of it.

Why do you get to call the shots? We're in my body, after all.

By all means. You take the lead. I am but your humble servant.

I'm so glad you're finally ready to admit it, I say as I march over to the bed and lie down. On his side.

He laughs. I look down and begin kneading my very full breasts. I slowly trace my left nipple and then my right, and it's his turn to moan.

Can you feel how turned on I am?

Show me, he commands. I begin stroking myself gently over my panties. *Take them off,* he coaxes. I slide my panties off slowly, inch by inch. *Now show me,* he commands.

Like this? I ask, touching myself in a slow, circular motion.

Mmmm, yes, but I need more, he purrs. I comply, dipping a finger inside myself. I bring that finger up so he can see just how turned on. Very slowly, I move my finger to my mouth and give it a suck.

Aubry, you're playing a dangerous game with a dangerous demon, he growls. I swear I don't know where this wild woman is coming from. All I know is this demon makes me want to do very un-vanilla things. I laugh, that is until I feel my center's nerve endings explode like I'm on fire. I jerk off the bed and cry out.

Touch yourself while I touch you, he commands, his voice laden with desire. I begin to slowly stroke myself as I feel his phantom touch move inside me. My internal muscles tighten and contract as a bead of sweat runs down between my breasts. I whimper and writhe on the bed, feeling his demonic power increase, but I remain in control.

Just when I think I can't possibly take anymore, he commands, *Faster, Aubry. Come for me. I want to watch you come for me. Keep your eyes open so I can see.* I move my hand faster and faster until I arch up off the bed and cry out in pleasure.

A few minutes later, when I am able to form a cohesive sentence, I ask, "What the hell was that?" He wasn't kidding; it was the most intense orgasm of my life. Hell will freeze over, however, before I admit that to him. Stubborn Aquarius here.

He laughs. *You have such sweet pillow talk. That was a nice opening number, but I'm taking over for the main event.* He takes control and we get up and pull a chair closer to the bed.

"What are you doing?" I demand. We walk to his closet and drag out a full-length mirror, positioning it against the chair.

Climbing onto the bed on all fours, I look at myself in the mirror. "You are a dirty, dirty demon."

Yes, I am, and now let's see just how dirty my wanton witch can be, he purrs, guiding me up on my knees.

I watch in the mirror as Damion slowly explores my body. I'm touching myself, but it feels different this time, each caress of my own hand a surprise.

He runs my hands through my hair, grabbing a wavy piece and wrapping it around my finger, then releases it. My finger traces my lips and then I suck and gently bite down. He moves my left hand over my collarbone and gently scratches his way down my arm to my hand, then moves to the right side.

My hand lightly caresses my neck and works its way down to my breasts, and then to my nipples. It feels like his warm mouth has taken in my right nipple, and I gasp. He then uses my fingers to twist my other nipple, and I begin to gyrate my hips. Behind each touch he's leaving a wake of tingling nerves.

He gently rubs circles over my stomach and moves my hands lightly over my upper thighs. Laying me back down, he slowly splits my legs apart as far as they'll go, tracing with my fingertips where my thighs meet my pelvis. *Oh yes, don't ever neglect your yoga practice. I'm going to enjoy spreading your legs apart just like this and taking you from behind.*

A whine and a "please" escapes my lips.

There's that polite little word southerners like to use. Say it again.

"Please," I try to say with attitude, but it comes out way too breathy.

He laughs as he sits me back up on my knees. *We'll save that position for when I'm returned to my sex god body.*

"Your ego is absurd," I manage to get out. Every nerve ending in my body feels like a lit Fourth of July sparkler.

Not absurd. Just stating a fact. Damion cups my breasts as I feel his phantom touch begin to trace my clit with a warm finger. He's in control of my body, but I still jerk involuntarily. *Now you understand why it's so imperative that we return me to my body. I want my tongue right here to start,* he says, and then it feels like his tongue is working me.

I have to check the mirror to make sure I'm not levitating off the bed. Nope, but I catch a glimpse of the borderline feral-looking woman in the mirror and can hardly believe it's me. Lips swollen, cheeks flushed, eyes glazed over with desire—I've never been this turned on in my life.

Every cell in my body has gone haywire; I'm vibrating from head to toe. My hips move faster and faster, the pressure building up to the breaking point. *That's it, almost there. Eyes open,* he commands. He fists an invisible hand in my hair as I cry out with the most mind-blowing orgasm.

He chooses this moment to cede control. I tumble not so gracefully on the bed, landing on my stomach. "You are still a prick," I mutter out loud. At least, I think I do? I shake violently with aftershocks for what feels like a very long time.

Damion sends a comforting touch up and down my spine. I take it back, *that* was the most intense orgasm of my life. Holy shit, was it ever.

Have I satisfied my wanton witch?

"Meh," I say.

He takes control of my hand and moves it to feel the drenched sheets. *Liar.*

I smile, but it quickly fades. "I just wish I could see you." The picture I have of Damion in my mind is fuzzy. I only saw him for a split second before he jumped inside me. I want to look into his beautiful aquamarine eyes and touch his body. I want him to physically touch me. Good Goddess, can I even handle him physically touching me? I could barely handle what we just did, so I can only imagine the intensity of it when he's returned to his Cambion form. Vanilla ice cream, rainbow sprinkles, I think to myself as I yawn.

Hopefully soon. Now sleep.

For once I don't argue with him.

Good morning, my wanton witch.

"Morning," I say with a yawn as I sit up and stretch. No use denying it, not after last night's activities. Speaking of last night's activities, I soon realize it's cold because I'm naked as a jaybird, as Grandma likes to say.

I walk over to my bag and rummage through it to find a shirt. Damion takes over and we walk in front of the mirror. He forms my mouth into a wicked little smile as he admires my naked body.

"Excuse me, freezing over here! Didn't you see everything last night, anyway?"

He turns my body, checking out my backside. *Mmmm,* he says, moving my hand to playfully smack my butt. *Just as perfect as I thought it would be. And no, I didn't get to see nearly enough. I'm viewing everything through your eyes, so I'm getting shortchanged on the full sensory experience.*

He grabs a folded Ole Miss sweatshirt from his dresser and pulls it over my head. It's huge on me, coming down to my thighs. I try to discreetly take a big inhale. Ahh, smells good—like his sheets. "Well, I don't get to *see or touch* you, but you don't hear me complaining," I point out.

No, I most definitely did not hear you complaining. Screaming, panting, begging for more. I suspect the neighbors across the street heard you not complaining.

My cheeks heat as I look in the mirror and flip him the bird. He laughs as he brings up my hand and caresses my cheek.

After I use the bathroom in private, I announce I'm finished, and we walk to the kitchen. He takes over and cracks two eggs in the skillet and slices a bagel and places it in the toaster. He pulls the sweatshirt over my head and tosses it on the counter.

"What are you doing?" I demand.

Making you naked breakfast.

"You were the one who was supposed to be naked," I inform him.

I'm in your body, ergo if you're naked, then I'm making you naked breakfast.

Man, he's a tricky devil. A few minutes later, I bite into a delicious egg and bagel sandwich. "Thank you, this is good. But naked breakfast isn't as sexy as I imagined."

So you have imagined me naked. Good to know.

I roll my eyes. "It's not as sexy as I imagined because I'm the only one who's naked, and it's still cold in this house!"

He takes control and looks down at my peaked nipples. *I fail to see the problem*, he says, but then he uses his power and my body temperature rises.

"How do you do that?" I demand.

A magician never reveals his secrets.

"So now you're a magician?" I snort.

Last night was pretty magical if I do say so myself.

It most definitely was, but I'm not going to tell him that.

After breakfast, I walk to his bathroom and turn on the shower. "You don't have a loofah to back up that 'skilled' claim," I taunt him as I step inside.

Then I'll just have to improvise.

And let's just say that his improvisational skills with the detachable shower head are magical and leave it at that.

CHAPTER 37

"You don't have enough evidence against Todd, and you know it," Gabe informs Damion.

"What's the harm in going ahead and filing?" Damion demands.

"One, our petition is *denied*, and two, you've tipped off Todd, allowing him to preemptively cover his magical tracks," Gabe fires back.

"Then get eyes on the little prick," Damion growls, clearly frustrated.

"That's going to majorly increase your bill, my friend."

"Just fucking do it!" Damion shouts.

And on that note, we take off with a demon in a hell of a road rage kind of mood. I shield myself and pray to the Goddess we make it home in one piece.

Later that afternoon, I grab the incantation bowl. *Maybe it's like the Phoenix bird.*

What do you mean? Damion asks.

We just set the bowl on fire and Phenex will rise from the ashes.

We're likely to destroy both the bowl and the demon, and you can be the one to deliver the news to Zazel, Damion informs me.

On second thought, scratch that plan.

I place the bowl on the floor beside me and cast a protective circle. I measure a tablespoon of dried hyssop in a pot with some leftover moon water. It's true that a watched pot never boils, but I stand beside the stove and watch it anyway. It eventually boils, and I stir clockwise seven times and then counterclockwise seven times, chanting:

> From this hyssop Phenex goes.
> And the curse no longer flows.
> Break free Phenex be purified.
> The bowl's prison you no longer abide.

I turn off the heat and place a lid over the brew. After several minutes I strain it into a bowl and stir again seven times clockwise and then seven times counterclockwise, repeating my chant. I envision Phenex emerging as I sprinkle the liquid around the incantation bowl. I'm afraid to pour water on a bowl this old, lest it crumble into tiny pieces. Again, I don't want to be the one to deliver Zazel that news. I wait, but it's clear that nothing happened.

I try the spell again, this time modifying it for me and Damion. And again, nothing. I sigh as I close my circle and discard the spell ingredients.

My phone chimes and I grab it.

> **JULIA:** Offer for one free hair cut expires today! Get your ass over here, I just had a cancellation.

> **ME:** I'm walking over right now.

Better to get my hair cut than pull it out in frustration, I think as I walk out the door.

Don't you dare get your hair cut too short! I told you that I want to be able to get a good grip.

I enter Julia's salon and plop down in the chair. "Just the ends trimmed."

"What's with you?" she asks, clipping a black cape with a skull and crossbones design around me and assessing my hair.

"She's in a mood," Damion answers.

"Everybody hush," I grumble.

Julia leads me to the sink for a quick wash, and we return to her station. Sectioning off my hair, she asks, "Did you know you have a birthmark on the back of your head?"

"No, I don't."

"Yes, you do." She turns me around and gives me a hand mirror to look at the back of my head.

It's a small red spot, but I can't make out the details. "I've never noticed that before." I do have a thick head of hair, and it'd be pretty hard to find. Or it would be the perfect hiding spot *because* it would be pretty hard to find.

"Shave it," I announce.

"What?" Damion and Julia practically shout at the same time.

"Not my entire head, just around that spot. I want to make sure it's really a birthmark and not something else." What, I don't know, but I have a strange feeling it's something I *need* to know.

"Alright. But Damion, you are my witness that Aubry insisted I shave a bald spot on her head." Julia looks at my head for a moment and announces, "I'm going to cut the hair with scissors to make a small patch, and then I'll use the electric razor with the smallest attachment."

I hear Julia snipping with scissors and then the buzz of the razor. "There." She spins my chair around and gives me a mirror, but I'm too far away to make out the details.

"Take a close-up picture of it, please." I hand her my phone and she takes the picture and then returns it to me.

I open the picture and enlarge it. Son of a bitch. "We have to go," I say as I hop out of the chair and make a mad dash for the door.

"Hey, leave the cape, it's my favorite!"

"Sorry, here. Thank you." I toss the cape at her.

"Come back when your drama has died down—you desperately need your split ends trimmed," she calls after me.

CHAPTER 38

I run back to Memphis Magic as fast as my feet will take me. There, that counts as my *House Guest* running regimen. Grandma will be thrilled. Damion takes over and calls Gabe and explains the situation—that I have Todd's sigil tattooed on the back of my freakin' head!

Gabe joins us just a few minutes later. "I've submitted our Petition for Reckoning. Aubry, you'll be taken to the summoning chamber. Damion is the accuser, and since he's currently housed in your body, your attendance is necessary."

"Wait, what's a summoning chamber?" Before Gabe can answer, I'm in what I assume is the summoning chamber. I imagined it to be some type of medieval torture chamber, but it looks more like a magical courtroom. There's a kingly looking throne elevated on a black marble dais, and below it is an elaborately carved mahogany table. A smaller chair is positioned on the right side of the table.

A beautiful bowl made of some type of stone I've never seen before holds what looks to be water, and beside it sits an ancient-looking chalice. Both are adorned with menacing symbols.

What's the water used for?

It's holy water.

I thought holy water was just a prop?

For a human performing an exorcism, yes. For a demon conducting a Reckoning, no. It acts as a truth serum when drunk during our proceedings.

Tapestries with scenes of angels and demons hang from ceiling to floor. A smaller chair is positioned facing the kingly throne in the center of the room. I've watched enough legal shows to guess this is going to be Todd's seat. Flames are carved on the chair in lifelike detail.

Let's sit, Damion instructs and walks me over to the table positioned off to the side.

A small creature with ghoulish yellow skin and small horns appears holding an ancient book nearly the size of his body. He dramatically places the book down on the table with a loud thump. He produces a small bottle of red ink and a massive quill pen. The book opens by itself, and the creature dips the pen into the bottle.

The creature looks up at me and smiles. I wish he hadn't. He has glowing red eyes and a jaw full of razor-sharp teeth. "Hello, Aubry. Small world, isn't it?" He winks at me. Again, I wish he hadn't. I know that voice—it's Dr. Hugh Anderson. Really, really don't want to know what happened when he went back for the corpse.

What's Hugh's role in this?

He's the scribe, the demonic version of a court reporter.

Gabe walks over wearing a fancy three-piece suit and a look of all business. He has a seat beside me, and a file appears on the table. "Do not speak unless addressed," he quietly warns.

Zazel materializes on the kingly throne, and it's all I can do to not crawl under the table and hide.

Relax. My father's not going to harm you.

I exhale a breath I didn't even realize I was holding. I brave another look at Zazel. I can feel the power radiating from him, like I'm standing too close to a downed power line. I've never seen an archangel, but I suspect this is what a dark version of one looks like. He has huge bat-like wings that shine like polished black onyx. They're so big that they drape over his throne onto the marble floor. His skin shimmers, and his eyes glow like two lumps of coal on fire. He's wearing a blood-red robe that looks to be made of some type of fluid material. On second look, it might actually be made of blood.

I look over to Hugh's ink pot. Pretty sure that's blood, not ink. I start to ask Damion, but then decide there are some things I don't bloody well need to know.

Suddenly, Todd appears with a look of a deer caught in the headlights. He's not wearing his hipster glasses, so I'm not sure if he sees the shitstorm that's about to come his way. He has a seat on the chair of flames, and from the look of it, that was an involuntary decision. The fire comes to life and dances all around him. It doesn't appear to burn him, but I can see the sweat dripping from his brow.

A scroll appears in Zazel's hands as he booms, "Benjamin Todd Mansfield, you have been blood summoned for the Reckoning of the crime allegedly committed against our brethren *Cambion*, whom we will refer to in this proceeding as Damion Blackmon.

You are hereby charged with facilitation of the commissioning of a summoning and resulting entrapment of Damion Blackmon in a third party, the mortal Aubry Brooks, with the intent to control Damion Blackmon against his will. Let the Book of Reckoning reflect that both Damion Blackmon and Aubry Brooks are in attendance, both in Aubry Brooks's body."

"So noted," Hugh says and continues writing. I'm not sure how I feel about my name appearing in blood in something as ominous sounding as the Book of Reckoning, but I reckon I don't have much of a say in the matter. I'm glad Damion can't read my thoughts, because I reckon I come up with some terrible puns when I'm nervous.

"Mr. Mansfield, do you wish to seek representation?"

"No, I can speak for myself," he announces haughtily.

Fool for a client, Damion says.

"Very well. What say you of these most egregious charges laid against you?"

"I adamantly deny!" Todd exclaims with sweat now pouring off him. The bowl of water levitates and tips over, pouring into the chalice. An invisible hand floats it over to Todd, who struggles against it, but eventually his jaws are pried wide and he drinks. His mouth violently slams shut so hard that I hear his teeth rattle.

Zazel says, "You may begin the inquiry."

"Thank you, Arbitrator." Gabe stands and asks the preliminaries. Name, age, address, magic employed, and Todd quickly fires out responses.

"You came to know Damion Blackmon through a contract dispute with his client, the demon Beltzar?"

"Yes."

The contract appears in Gabe's hand for a brief second, and floats over to the Book of Reckoning and is absorbed into the book. That's the best way I can describe it. I guess it just became a permanent part of the record. I'm hoping I also don't become a permanent part of that record. What a terrifying thought.

"Did you know Damion Blackmon prior to this contract dispute?"

"No."

"You were angry at Damion Blackmon for besting you in this contract dispute."

"Yeah, I was angry. The Cambion really thought he was something." I can't really argue with Todd on that last point.

"And so you took revenge."

"Yes. The Cambion needed to come down a peg or two," he says with a smug smile. Then again, it could be his typical facial expression, I'm not one hundred percent sure. "I wanted to possess Damion's power, to control it for my own use."

"So what did you do?" Gabe asks.

"I modified my sigil and charged it with the intent to possess Damion's powers."

"How did you charge it?"

"I entered a trance and used sexual energy to power my desired outcome."

"What type of sexual energy?"

"I masturbated on my sigil, transferring my desired outcome to my sigil." Ugh, maybe Grandma's concern that I have my aunt's horrible judgment in men is warranted.

"When did you tattoo Aubry Brooks's head with your sigil?"

"A few months ago, before she broke up with me. She broke up with me! Can you believe that?" I try not to roll my eyes.

"Why did you tattoo your sigil on the back of her head?"

"Aubry was a lazy witch. She didn't even bother to practice her craft. She just wasted her time playing with her cards, and watching TV with her crazy grandma. Oh, and moping over her dead friend, but not doing a damn thing about it. I wanted to possess Aubry's magic. Someone should put it to use."

"And how did you tattoo her without her knowledge?"

"I roofied her." Oh my Goddess, this just keeps getting worse. I rack my brain trying to remember, but since I was roofied, I guess it makes sense that I wouldn't remember.

"How did you, as you say, charge it?" Please do not say the same method.

"I didn't think I did. Vivian came home early. I had to sneak out before I had time to charge it. Honestly, I moved on to other projects and forgot about it."

"How did you link the two sigils together?"

"I don't know. That wasn't my original intent to link the two. But since I did, that's pretty amazing!" He looks quite pleased with himself.

Gabe continues, "Damion Blackmon was summoned to Aubry Brooks when she performed a séance and unintentionally employed demon-summoning items inside a circle." Dr. Anderson looks up at me from his writing and shakes his head. "Why would Mr. Blackmon appear and take possession as opposed to another demon?"

"I wanted to possess Damion's power. That desire to possess his power was transferred to Aubry through the sigil on her head, except she literally was possessed." He stops to think for a moment. "Fascinating." I can see the wheels turning.

"Why would a spell not break the connection?" Gabe asks.

"Because of the competing desires. Even if Aubry wants to release Damion, because of the power of the sigil, she *subconsciously* wants his power. So two competing desires will always cancel each other out leaving the status quo in place."

"How do we break the link and exorcise Damion Blackmon from Aubry Brooks?" Gabe questions.

"I would think destroying Aubry's tattoo with the intent to sever the link would do it, but I'm not sure."

"Ms. Brooks and Mr. Mansfield, hold the intention to sever the link in your mind," the Arbitrator interjects. "Are you?"

"Yes."

Gabe nods at me. "Yes," I answer. The bald spot on the back of my head feels like it's been doused with gasoline and set on fire. I scream, but then the pain vanishes as quickly as it came. I rub the spot, now as smooth as a baby's behind.

Damion? I ask, holding my breath.

Still here. I just knew that would work, and from his shocked tone, so did he.

"Let the record reflect that Mr. Blackmon is still entrapped in the third party human witch Aubry Brooks. Anything else, Counselor?" Zazel asks.

"Thank you, Arbitrator. That is all," Gabe says and then has a seat beside me.

"Very well. I've heard enough. Benjamin Todd Mansfield, you are hereby found guilty of facilitating the commissioning of a summoning and resulting entrapment of Damion Blackmon with the intent to control said demon against his will. You are hereby sentenced to seven years of servitude and seven years of magical probation, to run concurrently. If this Arbitrator finds out that you even think about practicing magic in any way, shape, or form, your probation will be revoked. The Reckoning is complete and so it be done," he booms.

Todd screams in agony—a tattoo blazes on the top of his right hand. It looks similar to Damion's secretary's tattoo, with the number 666 and menacing looking symbols I can't read. Todd disappears.

Hugh thumps the Book of Reckoning closed and announces, "If everyone will excuse me, I have a lecture to get to." He vanishes with the book in tow.

What's the tattoo?

The mark of the beast. It's a symbol that lets other demons know not to associate with Todd. It also functions just like an electronic monitoring device. If Todd employs any kind of magic, Zazel will know.

Like your secretary's tattoo?

Yes.

Think Todd can go without magic for seven years? I ask.

Doubtful. He's too addicted to power.

And the seven years of servitude?

He wanted to control a demon, and now he'll find out what it means to be controlled by a demon.

What kind of things will he have to do?

I don't have any use for him, so I'll turn him over to my father. Let's just say that he won't have quite as much time to style his man bun.

And if his probation is revoked?

He'd better hope that doesn't happen.

CHAPTER 39

"Cupid, I need a sublease for my father and Todd," Damion says after we've been magically deposited inside the shop's library.

"On it," Gabe nods. "I know today's outcome was disappointing, but let's not give up hope. I will keep digging," he says with a bow and vanishes.

I walk upstairs to my room and take a seat on my bed. I think back to my tarot card reading from what seems like a lifetime ago. I grab my cards and go through them until I find the Devil, the Moon, and the Judgment cards. "The Devil represents the past, the possession. The Moon card represents the present, us stuck in a web of illusion. The Judgment card represents the future." I hold the Judgment card and examine it. "Todd used magic in a controlling way, but he's received his punishment, so the Judgment card's scales should be balanced. What we're still missing is the loophole."

I light a sage bundle and smudge myself. *That still stinks.*

Demon, I'm sure you think so.

Damion's phone chimes—it's his mother inviting us to dinner this weekend. So not in the mood for Nora. I glance at my calendar to see the full moon's fast approaching. I grab Grandma's book *The Divine Magic of the Moon* to help with some ideas for our upcoming circle, but then I glance back to my tarot cards. The Moon. *The full moon.* I grab Maddie's file and furiously flip to the autopsy report.

What?

I find the medical examiner's estimated date of death and then flip through my calendar. "Maddie died on the full moon last year." I feel like it means something, but what? I hold up the Hierophant card. If the high priest knows, he's taken a vow of silence.

The days pass quickly as we inch closer and closer to the full moon. I have a very uneasy feeling about the whole thing. I leave Chris three voicemails asking for updates. He finally replies with a text.

CHRIS: Still my case, not our case.

I text Aunt Callie to see if she wants to go to hot yoga. I need to burn off some of this anxious energy. She texts me back that she's at Mrs. Vaughn's house for another regression therapy session. I guess Mrs. Vaughn's progress might have been celebrated too soon if she's not leaving her house again.

I find Grandma in the kitchen making chicken soup. "Who's sick?" Her healing soup will help knock out a cold in no time.

"It's for you, sugar pie."

"I'm not sick."

"I didn't say you were. Come sit down."

She ladles me a big bowl of steaming goodness. I let it cool for a moment and then take a bite. I sigh, telling her what I've learned about Maddie's death from my mirror gazing, and all the goings-on that I've been keeping from her.

She hugs me, and I hold on tight. "Stop blaming yourself," she tells me as she tucks a strand of my hair behind my ear.

"Why didn't I get a premonition that my best friend was about to be murdered?" I catch a tear that's trying to escape my eye.

"It wasn't meant for you to foresee. Do you think that Maddie would want you to blame yourself? That's not who she was. I've channeled enough departed souls to know they don't want to see the people they love suffer."

"Why do you think we could never contact Maddie?" Grandma attempted to channel her three different times, but we never made a connection.

"Some spirits either can't answer the call or choose not to, and we have to respect that. I know you miss her," she says as she hugs me and kisses the top of my head. "I do too."

"Let's try to contact her again."

Grandma shakes her head no. "I think your grief is too raw to allow me to make the connection. It took me four years after your Grandpa's death before I made contact. And then I let him have it for going and dying on me."

"I'm sure you did," I smile. I let my soup cool for a moment and take another bite, feeling a rush of comfort wash over me.

"Sugar pie, I just want you to be happy. I know that Maddie does too. I don't have to channel her to know that, so stop frettin' about things you have no control over. Let Chris do his job."

I give her a noncommittal grunt in reply. "You headed out to poker?"

"How did you know I was going to play poker?"

"Not a premonition. Your shirt gave you away." She's wearing her lucky gold *Winner Winner Chicken Dinner* T-shirt.

"Did you spell the soup?" I ask, setting my spoon down. I hadn't planned on burdening her with my problems. Not to mention the sudden feeling of well-being that washed over me after I did. She just winks at me and walks out.

I finish the soup as Elvis comes over and takes a seat beside me. "I guess you heard all that. Care to weigh in?" He gives me a bored look. "Fine, be that way. Don't come crying to me when some crazy drama rocks your little kingdom." He either laughs or hisses, I'm not sure.

I wash the few dishes and do some much needed laundry. Of course, I find a load of Grandma's clean clothes in the dryer. "Mystery solving is much more glamorous on television. There's never any boring household chores between the action," I tell Elvis.

"She watches too much TV." Damion takes over, and Elvis meows in agreement.

I check my phone again for the hundredth time. Nothing from Chris. "Do you think we can trust him?" My gut says yes, but my head says that I don't have anything to back up that feeling.

I don't know.

"Not the answer I was looking for."

Aubry, listen to me. I know you feel responsible for Maddie's death, he says, a phantom hand squeezing mine. *But Vivian's right—it's Chris's job to bring in the bad guy. Let him do his job.*

I likewise give him a noncommittal grunt as I walk to my room and get ready for bed. I'm restless and can't stop thinking that there's something more I should be doing. Universe, a hint would be greatly appreciated.

I don't think I can mentally handle another mirror-gazing session, and besides, it's well past twilight. I'm not in the right headspace to consult my cards.

So instead, I ask Damion for privacy as I grab a piece of paper and pen. I write Maddie a letter, telling her how much I love and miss her. Telling her that I'm sorry for failing her. I seal the letter with my tears, light a candle, and burn the paper, the symbolic letting go of all this grief. I open my window and scatter the ashes to the wind.

And then I receive a premonition. "Alright, Universe. I don't understand, but I'll give you the benefit of the doubt." I grab my supplies and get to work.

CHAPTER 40

I still feel out of sorts, even after last night's rituals. Tonight's the full moon and I'm as nervous as a long-tailed cat in a room full of rocking chairs, as Grandma likes to say. I haven't spoken with Chris other than his rude text message. I'm not in a position to push too much, as he really might follow through with his threat and take me to jail. Orange is so *not* my color.

"Morning. How was poker last night?" I ask Grandma as I flip over the open sign.

She rubs her hands together and smiles. "Good. I'm feelin' a winning streak. I'm going to pop over to Tunica. I don't have anything on the books today." I give her a look. "I'll be back in plenty of time for tonight's circle. Don't fret your pretty little head."

I glance at the schedule. "Aunt Callie has a regression therapy session scheduled today."

Grandma snorts. "Let's see if Callie can untangle herself from the man she's been hiding from us."

"Hiding from *us* or from *you*?"

"You good here?" She ignores my point.

"I've got it covered. Good luck."

I stay fairly busy all day, but still can't shake this uneasy feeling. Four o'clock comes and goes and no sign of Aunt Callie or Mrs. Vaughn. I call my aunt but it goes straight to voicemail. I send a text and wait, but no reply. I give it a few more minutes and try again with no luck. Maybe it was a home visit and Aunt Callie is already there? I pull up Mrs. Vaughn's contact information in our system and call her. "Hello, this is Aubry with Memphis Magic. I just wanted to follow up and see if you were scheduled for a regression therapy session with Callie this afternoon at four."

"We were supposed to have an appointment, but Callie isn't here. She's been a no-show for the past three visits, so I hope I can count on her this time."

"I'm very sorry about that. I'm going to try and get in touch with her."

I call Aunt Callie, but it goes straight to voicemail again. I send another text and wait. When I can wait no longer, I call Mrs. Vaughn back. She tells me my aunt didn't show.

I hang up and look at Elvis who's lounging on the couch in the reading nook. "So Aunt Callie lied to us about doing home visits with Mrs. Vaughn. Why? As a cover to be with this guy?" Elvis replies with an unconcerned look.

I call Grandma, and it goes to voicemail. I call again, and it goes to voicemail. Third time's the charm. "Sugar pie, this better be important. I had to fold a hot hand to take this call."

"Aunt Callie didn't show up to Mrs. Vaughn's appointment and lied about going to the last three visits. Your daughter's not answering her phone. It goes straight to voicemail."

"You know how Callie jumps into a new relationship and forgets that she's an adult. Remember when she went MIA back when you were a teenager? She ran off with Jason on the back of his motorcycle and wound up broke in Atlanta. And dear old Mama had to wire her money to pay for a bus ticket home because Jason had left her high and dry *and* swiped her wallet." Okay, so I do remember that. "Now, don't call me unless it's an emergency *or* to tell me that my lottery ticket is the winner. It's on top of my dresser. Why don't you go check it now and tell me while I'm thinking about it?"

"You're thinking about a different kind of gambling *while* you're gambling?" I snort.

"Was gambling until you interrupted me," she huffs and hangs up on me.

I close up shop and walk upstairs. Grandma's not worried about my aunt, but I can't seem to shake this bad feeling. I fret a little more and decide there's only one thing left to do, and that's snoop. I hope my aunt will forgive the privacy violation, but better to seek forgiveness than ask permission. I've clearly been spending too much time around a certain demon lawyer.

I search her bedroom, looking for what, I don't know. That's when I spot her cell phone sticking out of her jacket pocket that's lying on a chair in the corner. I can't believe she forgot her phone. I try to turn it on but the battery's dead. I plug it in and wait a few minutes until it powers up. I check her messages. Last message was from a Memphis area code number sent to Aunt Callie's phone three days ago. *Meet at our spot.*

Aunt Callie didn't make this person a contact in her phone-book, so I don't have a name. I scroll up and look at the messages between them. They started about a month ago. All the messages are simply, *Meet at our spot* and a reply from Aunt Callie, *I'll be there.*

Dang it, couldn't they have been a little more specific? *Wait a second! I've read that cryptic text before. Please Goddess, tell me I'm wrong.* I have a terrible feeling in the pit of my stomach.

There's no reason to assume the worst, Damion says in a re-assuring tone. *Let's call the number from Callie's phone and see if the guy will answer.*

We do, but it goes straight to an automated voicemail. I can't leave a message because the mailbox is full.

I call Chris, and it goes to his voicemail. "Chris, this is Aubry. My aunt is missing—she's at the Center. If you don't call me back in the next five minutes, I'm going there myself!"

The doorbell rings and I run to it, hoping I'm wrong and it's my aunt. In swaggers a cop with an attitude problem from hell. Not today, Chris. Not today.

"You have to go now to the Center and get Aunt Callie," I point at him. "And how is it that you got here so fast?"

"Why do you think your aunt is at the Center?" he asks with crossed arms.

"She's been sneaking around with a new man, and now she's missing. I think she got caught up with the same man who killed Maddie!" I hand him my aunt's phone. "Look at all the messages. 'Meet at our spot.' That's what was sent to Maddie before her death."

"Is it the same phone number?" Chris asks as he hands me back the phone.

I run and grab Maddie's file and flip until I find the phone records. I compare the numbers. It's *not* the same number. "So maybe this guy has more than one burner phone," I point out.

"Alright, let's say your theory is correct. How would you suggest I get a warrant? Even if you assume your aunt is at the Center, which we have *zero* proof that she is, who's to say she's there against her will?"

"Who cares about a warrant? Let's go right now and get her!"

"The Center is over fifty acres. We have no idea of your aunt's exact location. I go in blind and I risk showing my hand. The Center has been under surveillance for some time now. I can't tell you more, other than you're going to have to trust me."

"I don't care about your secretive agenda—this is my aunt's life that you're talking about!"

Aubry, let's hear him out. We go in without a plan and we could get Callie killed, Damion points out. He's right of course, but I still don't like it.

"Aubry, listen to me. I don't need you to trust me, but I need you to trust me to do my job. Can you do that?"

"Does your *job* include saving my aunt's life?" I counter.

"I don't want anyone to die on my watch."

Not a very strong pitch, Damion comments.

"Give me just a second." I run to my bedroom.

"What are you doing?" Chris demands.

I grab my cards and give them a shuffle. Should I trust Chris and stay away from the Center? Upright means yes. Reversed means no. I hold them to my heart and pull the Tower upright. Can't get any clearer than that. "I will stay away from the Center. You have my word," I tell Chris as I walk back to the kitchen.

He looks at me intently. After a moment, he simply nods and walks out.

I didn't expect your acquiescence.

"The cards told me to stay away from the Center, so I promised Chris I would," I explain. "But I didn't promise anyone else would. Please ask Zazel for help—I don't care what kind of strings are involved," I beg.

He's quiet for a moment and then sighs. *Only for you would I even think of doing this.* He sends his father a text asking to speak to him and immediately receives an automated response. *Father is in an arbitration, so he's not going to answer his phone. I'll try again in a few minutes.*

I go to my room and pace back and forth. I'm too wired, and I need to calm down. I light a candle and sit on my meditation cushion and watch the flame.

I become sleepy, so sleepy that I can't keep my head up. I jerk awake to the sound of Aunt Callie's voice calling me from outside. I jump up from my cushion and run over to my window. I see Aunt Callie standing in our side parking lot. She motions for me to come down.

Thank the Goddess! I run downstairs and outside, but I don't see her.

Aubry, wait!

"Aunt Callie?" I call. That's when I feel a shooting pain in my head, and the lights go out. Again.

CHAPTER 41

What happened? I groan.

You have an uncanny knack for getting yourself kidnapped.

I cannot believe that I've been kidnapped a second time! It's beyond offensive. *What about Aunt Callie?*

What about her?

She was in the parking lot!

No, she wasn't.

I swear I saw her!

Dark magic, perhaps?

Who did this?

Whoever kidnapped you knocked you out and bagged your head, so I wasn't able to see anything.

I find myself tied spread eagle on a raised wooden platform. I'm wearing a long-sleeved white dress that billows from the waist down. My stomach falls as I recognize this dress—it's identical to the one Maddie was wearing in my mirror vision.

I take in my surroundings. From the single light bulb dangling from the cobweb-covered ceiling, it appears I'm a prisoner in a large, windowless basement. Ugh, I'm so over being trapped in basements. The room is empty save for the round elevated platform that I'm tied to. I spot some type of etched circle on the concrete floor. I can only see part of it, but it looks like a pentagram with unusual symbols drawn inside.

"Aubry, you're awake. So glad you could join me," a familiar voice says.

"Brad? You're seriously the bad guy?" I snort as I crane my neck. "Aren't you bad enough without adding homicidal sorcerer to the list!"

"There's that smart mouth that I love," Brad says with a smirk.

"How'd you escape from the hospital?" He's wearing a dress shirt and khakis instead of the white institutional uniform.

"Wouldn't you like to know," he says, casually strolling closer to me with his hands in his pockets.

"Let me go, and I promise to keep you safe from Damion," I lie. "I'll even negotiate on your behalf. Get you out of your contract. Right, Damion?"

He doesn't say anything.

"Right, Damion?" I say a bit more forcefully.

Magic's blocking my power, he practically growls.

"I'm not concerned about Damion," Brad says smugly. "You will both be dead, just like your little friend Maddie, and then I'll be released from my contract," he says in a sing-song voice.

"So you're the one who killed Maddie?" I demand.

"I didn't even know that you two were connected, but don't you just love the synchronicity? Man, she had good energy. Not as good as yours, but almost. And she had such a tight pussy.

I'm getting hard just thinking about it. Let's just see how yours compares," he says, rubbing himself through his khakis. "I'm not into dudes, but feeling Damion's rage while fucking you, I could get into that." He steps closer and begins unzipping his khakis.

Damion?

I'm trying.

"Brad, haven't you learned your lesson about playing with the sacrifice?" a male voice says in an unusual sort of British accent. "Run along before you get yourself into trouble." Brad ducks his head and zips his pants, and then he scurries out.

The man in the doorway smiles as he makes his way to me. He has a dark complexion, shoulder-length dark blond hair, and amber-colored eyes. "Ethan, right?" It's the Center's yoga and meditation teacher. "Whatever Brad's got you caught up in, you don't have to follow through. Please let me go."

He looks at me and laughs a melodious-sounding laugh that sends a chill down my spine. "Not Ethan. You may call me Master."

"I'm sorry, what?"

Yes, he really did say Master.

"You may call me Master," he says a bit louder. Ethan's not dressed how I expect someone who fancies himself a Master would. He's wearing a white T-shirt underneath an old leather jacket, faded jeans, and biker boots.

"I most certainly will not. So you're the guy my aunt has been sneaking around with." Figures she picked a no-count biker.

"Ah, Callie. Your aunt's life force is too old and tainted for my purposes, but I did enjoy her company in my bed."

"Let me guess. You met her in Tunica at the metaphysical trade show."

"Yes, and we had such fun together, but then she had to go and ruin our arrangement by sticking her nose in my affairs."

"Where is she?" I demand.

"I still haven't decided that naughty girl's punishment," he says with a sigh, not answering my question. "Her timing couldn't have been worse. I'm already rather upset that our temple was damaged by lightning."

"You mean the observation tower?"

"It really was the perfect location for ritualistic work," he says with a sigh. And here is my Tower card. "We had to switch to our contingency plan. So despite this unfortunate turn of events, here we are."

"Where is here?"

"Here is where you will step into your destiny. My other little pet I was grooming for tonight had the nerve to die on me, and needless to say these last-minute developments put me in a rather cross mood. But my high priest told me all about you, Aubry, and fate chose you as the lucky alternate."

"Brad's your high priest?" I snort. "Seriously?" And here's my Hierophant tarot card.

"I don't necessarily disagree with you, but Brad launders the money, so I'm willing to overlook his many shortcomings."

How was Brad able to lie to you?

I don't know. I guess this guy magically protected Brad, Damion growls.

"Did Brad kill Maddie? Or did you?"

"Who?"

"Madison Williams."

"Doesn't ring a bell," he says in a bored tone.

"Black hair. Brown eyes. Tried to escape from this place last year?"

"Ah yes. I could have killed Brad for that little snafu."

"What do you mean?"

"My high priest desecrated the sacrifice, and then the imbecile didn't have the sense to properly secure her. Madison was a clever one. That naughty girl almost slipped away. She forced me to end her life too soon. I wasn't able to use her life force to my advantage. Astrological timing is important in this sort of work, you see. But I still enjoyed watching the light go out of her terrified eyes." He smiles as if relishing the thought.

"And so as punishment, Brad had to pay a $50,000 donation?"

"And just like your friend, aren't you the clever one," he says with a wry smile.

"And you dumped Maddie's body in the Mississippi River?"

He huffs impatiently. "I'm a god. I don't concern myself with trivial housekeeping matters."

"It doesn't matter how many women you kill, you're not a god and you never will be."

"But that's where you're wrong, my pet. Your little pea brain couldn't possibly understand my ascension."

"Try me."

"I'm very close, so close that I can taste it. With your lifeblood at tonight's full moon ceremony, I'll become a god." And here's my Moon tarot card. Universe, if I make it out of this alive, I'm going to need more detailed card guidance going forward, please and thank you. "Aubry, you should be honored that you're part of this historic event. But enough talk; it's time to prepare. The show's about to begin." He walks out whistling a happy tune.

Damion snorts. *The Master watches too much TV with that cheesy parting line.*

Please tell me you have a plan.

Working on it.

I hear the door open to see Maddie's old roommate Lydia walk in holding a tray. "Lydia, I don't even care why you're here, just cut me loose and let's go!"

She laughs. "Aubry, you're not going anywhere."

"You're a part of this," I say, deflated.

"I'm the Master's best recruiter," she brags as she dips a small towel in a basin of water and squeezes it out. She proceeds to wash my feet. I try to kick her, but my legs are bound too tight to move.

"And let me guess—you recruited Maddie. How fucked up is that?"

She pours some oil in her hands and anoints my head—it's a fragrance that I've never smelled before. "I offered myself to the Master, but it wasn't my destiny," she says sadly.

"But you thought it was Maddie's?"

"The Master rewarded me well for the introduction," she says proudly. "And soon it will be time for you to step into your destiny," she says as she fans my hair around my face and then brushes it.

"The woman who was going to be tonight's sacrifice, who was she?"

"My roommate. I know what the Master likes." You hear about roommate from hell stories, but Lydia takes the cake.

"Is Maddie's mama a part of this?"

"Of course not. We need serfs for our kingdom," she says haughtily. She proceeds to do my makeup. I keep still, not because

I'm cooperating with this madness, but because I don't want to be stabbed in the eyeball with the eyeliner pencil.

"What about Kate Jones?"

"The *only* reason the Master fucks her is to keep her happy," she says with venom. "He doesn't care about her." I'm not sure if she's trying to convince me of this fact, or herself. "Kate donated the Center's real estate and gave us the cash for our temple, but the simpleton isn't *worthy* to be part of our inner circle."

She holds up a hand mirror, letting me inspect her work. "That looks awful." I guess she was going for an Egyptian cat eye, but it appears more raccoon eye.

"You were always such a bitch. It's so unfair that the Master chose you."

"If your Master's so powerful, he wouldn't need to murder women. Think about it!"

"My god requires sacrifice," she says, gathering her supplies.

Now would be a great time to seduce her into letting us go, I point out.

I still can't take control. Magic is blocking my power.

"Tell you what, I'll trade places with you! Sacrifice yourself!" I call after Lydia. I watch our one chance of escape walk out the door.

CHAPTER 42

"Universe, I refuse to die at the hands of a no-count biker, an energy vamp, and a backstabbing frenemy!" I practically shout.

What happens to you if I die? I ask Damion in a much smaller voice, the reality of the situation sinking in.

You're not dying, and that's all there is to it, he says with authority.

I take a deep breath and try to channel some of his confidence. There's not much time for me to contemplate my mortality, as the door creaks open, and the overhead light dims. One by one, I watch nine black-robed figures enter the room, each holding a single red candle.

They chant in a whisper, "The Master cometh, the Master cometh." They get progressively louder until they're shouting, "The Master cometh, the Master cometh!" I can feel the energy of the room shift—it's dense, dangerous-feeling energy that I don't like one little bit. They place their candles on a point on the star within the etched circle and kneel behind it.

Their chanting has reached a fever pitch, and in walks the Master, likewise dressed in a black hooded robe. The Master begins speaking in a language that I don't understand, but then he switches over to English. "My chosen ones, tonight I will ascend upon high. Prepare the sacrifice for your god!"

The followers reach in their robes and each pulls out a ceremonial knife. *Why didn't I let Chris take me to jail for interfering with his investigation?* I tell Damion with a loud gulp.

Let's see some of your magic, he encourages.

My magic, I say, closing my eyes, centering myself. I rub my bloodstone bracelet against the rope binding my wrist. Last night, I pricked my finger and placed a drop of my blood on my bracelet and cast a protection spell. I didn't understand why the Universe gave me the message, but I'm so glad I listened. I quietly chant:

> Bloodstone amulet infused with my power.
> Keep me safe from their blades this hour.

I chant over and over, envisioning my body surrounded by a protective shield of light that no knife can penetrate. I chant faster and faster as I feel the power of my magic humming through my body.

The Master stands before one of the hooded robe members. "My high priest! Rise! Go forth, my child, and prepare the lamb!" Brad steps up to the altar and holds his knife over my right thigh. I don't dare stop my chanting. He raises his knife up, but it doesn't come down.

"My high priest, I command you to prepare the sacrifice!" the Master says with more force. It's dark, but I can barely make out

Brad's face. He looks downright perplexed as to why his knife is suspended over my body and he hasn't cut me.

"Did I make a mistake in deeming you fools worthy of witnessing my ascension? Must I do everything myself?"

Suddenly, I hear the door creak open; I'm momentarily blinded by the glaring overhead light. It takes my eyes a second to adjust. "No! Charlotte, run!" I scream as I see my friend standing in the doorway.

"What's this? Another sacrifice? It's a sign, my children. Tonight *is* the night of my ascension!" The Master marches over to Charlotte and grabs her by the neck.

And then I wouldn't have believed it if I hadn't seen it with my own eyes. Chris appears, and all the hairs on my body stand on end. He has huge, white feathery wings that glow so brightly that it's difficult to look directly at them. He's wearing a white robe that shows off his sculpted chest, and in his right hand, he's brandishing a large flaming sword that would eat all these puny ritual knives for breakfast.

Chris is an angel? I silently ask, mouth agape.

It appears so, Damion responds in a tone as shocked as mine.

I hear a few gasps and look over to see Lydia crying. Excuse me if I don't have much sympathy for the woman. The Master's followers fall to their knees. I'm sure they're confused about whom they should worship. Chris certainly has more flash than the Master. He silently raises his sword, and the Master's hands are bound by glowing light.

He looks over to me, and I try not to tremble. Now I know the secret to his stare out prowess. The magic circle disappears, and I'm now unbound.

We cut that awfully close.

That's a terrible pun, Damion groans.

"Angel Eiael, posing as the human Ethan," Chris's voice booms with the sound of a thousand angels. Well, I don't really know what a thousand angels sound like, but you get the idea. "You were gifted dominion over occult knowledge. You abused this gift for your own personal gain, and are hereby called to the Throne on High to account for your sins in the Book of Truth."

Chris and Eiael disappear.

CHAPTER 43

Chris and Eiael are angels!?! Huh. I would have expected a showdown between two angels to be, I don't know, a little less anticlimactic. A sky fight with lightning bolts being hurled back and forth. Something.

Or maybe Damion is right, I watch too much TV. I don't catch his response, as I no longer feel his presence inside me. *Damion?*

I'm standing in what can only be described as an ethereal study. I turn around in awe of the wall-to-wall books. Looking up, I can't see the ceiling, because the bookshelves seem to go on forever. I look down at my feet standing on the firm yet translucent floor. It's adorned with unusual geometric patterns. A fireplace glows with a flame that looks too otherworldly to describe. The most beautiful music I've ever heard plays softly in the background.

"Aubry Rose Brooks, have a seat." A being rises from behind a golden desk. He's a towering figure—I'd put him at least six feet six—with fiery long red hair, red eyes, and luminous skin. He's wearing a long white robe and a look on his face that tells me he's already annoyed with me and we haven't even started yet. Started what, I don't know.

"Who are you and what is this place?"

"I am Metratron and this is my office. Sit," he barks.

I have a feeling I've been called to the principal's office. "My cat ate my homework?" I try as I walk over and take a seat in a chair as soft as a cloud. Metratron's eyes glow like hot embers. Okay, so best to shelve my comedy routine. "Why am I here?" I glance at his desk and see a jar of what looks to be glowing eyeballs. Really wish I hadn't seen that. I touch my bloodstone bracelet and envision a protective shield around my eyes. Hell will freeze over before my eyes get added to that jar, you see. I'm sorry, you'd think I'd see that all these puns during moments of crisis are not looked kindly upon. Look, I should really stop.

"I need your statement for the record. Eiael interfered with my scribe duties," he says as he takes a seat at his desk.

"Where is Eiael?"

"Ms. Brooks, please detail the events of the last twenty-four hours of your mortal life," he commands, ignoring my question. He dips his white quill in some kind of glowing white ink as a large gold book appears.

"Do you have all day?"

"I have eternity," he says, opening the book.

"Right. So the angel Eiael kidnapped me and was going to kill me, but my friend Charlotte Patel showed up and then Chris Sullivan used his magic sword and now I'm here." I give this angel as few details as possible, omitting my demonic ties. I've chosen sides—I'm team demon all the way.

He closes his book with a loud thump and stands. "That is all, Ms. Brooks."

"Wait!"

"Yes?"

"Did you also take the statement from Madison Rene Williams?" I ask.

"Yes."

"Can I read it?"

"No."

"Then let me see her before I go. She was my best friend and she was murdered by Eiael." It looks like a *no* is on the tip of his tongue, but I cut him off. "Otherwise, I'll have to file a grievance on her behalf, as the unauthorized angelic killing of mortals is frowned upon." Okay, so I pulled that one from my behind, but when you've got no cards, you bluff, or so Grandma says.

"Let me make a call and see what I can do." I assume he means a phone call, but he just sits down and is motionless for a moment. Creepy. He stands and escorts me to what looks like a conference room. "You have five minutes," he announces. A large hourglass floats in the air.

"If we're in the eternal realm, then why the time limit?" I call after him, but he's already gone.

And then my sweet friend Maddie stands before me. She looks exactly the way I remember her—several inches shorter than me with long black hair, big brown eyes, and a smile that's contagious. I look down at my white dress and over to her white dress. "I wore it better."

She laughs. "No way. White works better with my hair and skin tone."

I grab her and hold on tight as we both cry. "I'm so sorry," I tell her. "I've played it over and over in my mind, of how I could have prevented it. Why I didn't see it coming."

She pulls back and looks at me. "No more guilt, or I'll have to come back as a ghost and haunt you until you stop."

"Only if you promise," I joke, and she smiles. "Forgive me?"

"Only if you forgive me for being such a bitch and pushing you away. I went man crazy, well, angel crazy, and look what happened."

"Forgiven," we both say at the same time. "Pinch, poke, you owe me a Coke," we say simultaneously and laugh.

"Except next time, a little less cryptic with the messages," I inform her.

"Hey, I did the best I could. I think Eiael was magically blocking me. I had to get creative."

"You did good," I tell her. "So Lydia betrayed you."

"Yep. Talk about a roommate from hell," Maddie says.

I smile. "And that is why we were soul sisters, because I thought the same thing."

"We *are* soul sisters," she corrects me. "Always," she links her fingers through mine.

"Your mama looks like she's turned her life around. I thought you'd want to know."

"Don't hate her on my account. Life's too short," she trails off.

I nod. "What's the afterlife like?"

"I don't know. I've been wrapped up in all this angelic drama; I don't think I've gotten that far yet."

"I hope it's amazing," I tell her as I squeeze her hand.

"Me too."

I look over and see there's only a few grains of sand left. I grab Maddie and hold her tight. "Love you."

"Back at you," she says, and then she's gone.

CHAPTER 44

I thought I was going to have to call in a hellhound to track you down, Damion growls.

It takes me a second to orient myself. *Please don't. You know I'm a cat person.*

What happened? he demands. *I had control of your body, but you were gone.*

"I think I was in the angelic principal's office."

"Ah, Metratron's office," Gabe says, now standing beside me.

Charlotte comes bounding over, and I hug her neck. "Don't ever do something like that again," I tell her.

"Don't get yourself kidnapped by a lunatic angel and I won't have to," she retorts.

"*How* did you do something like that, by the way?"

"Chris was watching the Center and knew you'd been brought here. He needed bait to lure Eiael out of his magic circle, and I volunteered."

"How about this—we both try our best not to get kidnapped by any lunatic, whether it be angel, human, or demon for at least the next six months?" I suggest.

"Deal," she says.

A contract hovers in the air. "I didn't mean that literally," I tell Damion.

Eiael's followers are huddled in the corner on the opposite wall. "If everyone will excuse me, I have business to attend to," Damion announces in a rather menacing voice. Eight contracts float in the air. Looks like he'll be making eight deals with eight idiots. Good. Since he already owns Brad's soul, I hope he calls that fucker due. Or strangles him. Dealer's choice. Screw Helen's warning—I'm so glad he's a demon.

"Charlotte, may I accompany you outside? We'll leave Damion to his work," Gabe says, extending his arm. She nods at me, tentatively locking arms with Gabe as they exit.

My lips curve into a wicked smile as I walk over to the followers. "Brad Cunningham, you're a dead man," Damion announces and Brad grabs his throat.

Please don't kill him.

Why not?

Why not? Good question. *Because I asked you not to.*

Very well, but you owe me a favor.

Of course I do.

"As for the rest of you, hello. I'm here to make all your dreams come true."

We exit the basement and step outside, Damion pleased as punch. I asked him during one of our 21 Questions road trip games what he does with all those souls, and in typical lawyer fashion his response was, "It depends."

It's a cloudless night, and the full moon is out in all her glory. Chris suddenly appears in his human form, along with Aunt Callie. "What happened to Eiael?" I demand.

"Still my case, not our case," Chris says, crossing his arms and giving me an icy look.

How did angels become synonymous with peace and serenity? Aunt Callie takes my hand, likely saving me from throttling an angel. I don't know what happens when you get called to the principal's office a second time. I'd rather not find out.

"Aubry, I'm so sorry," she cries, but I cut her off and hug her neck.

"Grandma is right, you have absolutely horrible judgment when it comes to men," I say, and then she laughs while she cries.

"I need to secure the scene. Everyone leave now!" Chris thunders.

"Alright, alright. No need to get your wings in a twist," I grumble. We leave Chris to deal with Eiael's followers and handle all the red tape. I'm not sure how he's going to explain what just happened, but he's an angel cop posing as a human cop, so I'm sure he'll figure it out.

Gabe leads us down a wooded path to a small house with Aunt Callie's car parked next to it. Naturally, Damion takes over and gets behind the wheel. I rest my eyes for just a minute or two.

The next thing I know, Damion walks me inside and Grandma fusses over us. I might fall asleep where I stand, but Grandma won't let me go to bed until she hears the whole tale.

POSSESSION

I wake to find Damion tucking me into bed. *Meet me tonight and don't be a good boy*, I tell him as I drift back to sleep.

Your wish.

CHAPTER 45

I wake with a smile on my face. Damion still wouldn't let me see his face last night, but since I was riding his *face*, he didn't get to see much of me, either. I'd call that a fair deal.

I make my way to the kitchen to find a plate of sausage and biscuits warming in the oven and a note from Grandma. *Don't even think about working today.*

It does seem odd me going back to my day-to-day life after everything that's happened. I eat breakfast, even though it's late afternoon.

I take a solo shower, throw on some clothes, and then light a candle. Taking a seat on my meditation pillow, I hold the Judgment card. Universe, help us out here. What is this loophole we're missing? I set my intention and focus on the card.

Something appears out of the corner of my eye, and I startle out of my meditative trance. Standing, I walk over and grab a file folder on my nightstand. "What is this?" I ask.

Damion takes over and opens the folder. *The servitude sublease agreement giving my father the rights to Todd's service.*

"Why don't you just put him to work instead of your father?"

Because I would want to kill Todd every time I saw him. I'm saving myself from the temptation.

I'm not sure if Damion is joking, but I decide not to ask. He takes control and opens the file. Good thing he is in control, as I would have likely passed out seeing Gabe's legal bill.

Still think Gabe's a gentleman? Damion asks as he flips to the sublease document. His sigil appears in my hand, and we stamp on the dotted line. He texts Gabe, and the document disappears.

I take back over and closely examine Damion's sigil. It reminds me of a smaller version of a chess piece. It appears to be made of gold and has tiny symbols etched into it that I can't quite make out. And then I snort. The round top portion of the sigil looks to have an etching of a crown. Of course it does.

I start to flip it over to see the actual stamp side, but Damion takes control. *Mind if I have my sigil back?* he asks dryly, his sigil vanishing.

An epiphany hits me like the lightning bolt depicted on my Tower card. "No, because I want you to give me your sigil!"

I'm sorry, I don't follow.

"Todd's sigil bound us. Your sigil can unbind us," I say excitedly.

Damion considers, and then a big smile spreads over my face. *I'll brand you with my sigil and give you my true name. You'll possess the ability to summon me. And in order to summon something, that something has to be away from you in the first place. I have to be somewhere else for you to call me to you.*

"A technical technicality."

Sounds like a loophole to me. First, let's go do some trim work.

"I am not adding another bald spot to my head," I inform him.

Not your head. A demon trap is a real threat to me. It needs to be in a hidden area.

It takes me a moment to realize where he's headed with this. As in headed down south with this. "You want me to go Brazilian down there? You are a dirty, dirty demon."

Yes, I do and yes, I am.

Okay, but first, do you have a spoon handy?

Why?

Because I'm eating crow. I've always said it's trashy for a woman to get a tattoo of a man's name.

It's not like we're in Tijuana drunk on spring break and you tattoo my name on your ass with a dolphin and little hearts. It's my demonic sigil," he says haughtily.

"Alright, alright. Let's do it." I walk to the bathroom, turn on the shower, and strip. The water heats up, and I step inside.

Damion takes over my body and picks up my razor. *Let me.* I'm hesitant, but he insists. It's strangely erotic to watch my hand move the razor so close to my delicate flesh without me being in control. Damion apparently feels the same way, as my entire body thrums with his energy. By the time we're finished, I'm not completely bare, but almost.

He's still in control as I step out of the shower and look at myself in the mirror. He grabs a towel with my hands and gently dries my body while I watch. I ignore my hard nipples and the wet between my legs that I can't blame on the shower.

He walks me into the bedroom and lights a candle on my nightstand.

First, the contract, he says, his words laced with desire.

"I would expect nothing less," I reply in a huskier tone than I intended. A scroll opens containing one short paragraph in large, legible type:

> I, Aubry Brooks, being of legal age and sound mind, hereby enter a binding agreement with Damion Blackmon ("the Demon"), in exchange for Aubry Brooks wearing the sigil of the Demon on Aubry Brooks's body, the location to be chosen by the Demon. Upon execution of this agreement and the subsequent sharing of the Demon's true name and the placing of the sigil on Aubry Brooks's body, the Demon agrees and shall immediately exit Aubry Brooks's body, mind, spirit and/or auric field.

I read the short contract multiple times. Again, call me suspicious, but a deal with a devil makes me nervous, even if he is my devil. And I just admitted to myself that I consider Damion mine.

He pokes my finger with his quill pen. "Ouch. That still hurts," I say. He quickly moves my finger to my mouth and gives it a gentle kiss. I sign in my blood, and then he signs with his sigil. The scroll glows red, snapping shut and disappearing.

Now, for my true name. He whispers in my mind his demonic name, a name that I don't think I can pronounce. It feels like this strange sound is burrowing in my mind. It's an odd, poking feeling. It's not painful, but it's not exactly comfortable, either.

He then reaches my hand over to the candle and heats his sigil in the flame. *And finally, my sigil.* I nod and take a deep breath.

He uses his power, and my bare skin is now all nice and tingly. *Slight discomfort now*, he says as he quickly moves his sigil down.

I cry out and try to jerk away, but Damion has my body locked down. "Slight discomfort, my ass!" It feels like my skin is melting off, but the pain quickly subsides. I look down at his work. "Your sigil is beautiful." It is beautiful in a harsh sort of way. It's a blood-red design of two snakes intertwined like the DNA Double Helix, encased in a pentagram and flames with symbols I can't read.

"Damion?" No reply. Oh my Goddess, did it really work? "Damion, don't mess with me. Are you still here?" Nothing. I take a deep breath as I pull his name from my mind. It feels like his name is some kind of living creature that's attached to my brain and doesn't want to let go, but then my mouth gets warm and tingly, and the odd sound of his demonic name comes sounding out.

And then those beautiful aquamarine eyes are looking back at me.

CHAPTER 46

"Of course my sigil is beautiful. It symbolizes me. I am a beautiful creature, hence I have a beautiful symbol."

I can't argue with him. Damion stands several inches taller than me, six feet two or so. He has broad shoulders, curly blond hair that's grown out just a teensy bit in the back, a chiseled jaw, full lips, beautiful sun-kissed skin, and killer dimples. He's wearing an obviously expensive tailored black suit with a white collared shirt and blood-red tie. But I still can't get over his eyes. I'm not sure how long we stand there, staring at each other. Until he moves his gaze down, and I realize that I am naked and he is not.

He gives me a naughty smile as he takes a seat on my bed and pulls me to his lap. "Are we really unbound? If this is a dream, please don't pinch me," I say with a smile, wrapping my arms around his neck and lightly stroking the ends of his curly blond hair. It's incredibly soft. He smells divine, a woodsy smell mixed with some kind of exotic spice I'm not familiar with. It's the same smell that was on his sheets, only amplified.

"So glad I could make your dreams come true," he purrs, tucking a wet strand of hair behind my ear.

"Please," I say with attitude and an eye roll.

He laughs, gently pressing his lips to mine. I get that same tingly feeling from the first time he phantom kissed me, except this time is sooooo much better in person. I open for him, and he continues the kiss, so slow and deep that it makes my toes curl. His tongue wraps around mine, and I try to stifle a moan, but it comes out against his lips anyway. We start slow and sensual, but the kiss quickly evolves into desperate and frenzied. Or maybe that's just me, as I discreetly try to rub my thighs together.

He pulls back, and I try not to whimper. With a rather cocky smile, he stands me back up and devours my naked body with his beautiful eyes. "Wait," I say a bit breathlessly.

"Haven't I been a good boy long enough?" He growls, running a hand through his hair in frustration. "Part of me is a demon. *No* part of me is a saint." He caresses the side of my breast with his knuckles. That sinfully delicious scent of his envelops me, and I feel the desire run down my thigh. He takes his finger and traces circles with it and then smiles wickedly as he licks his finger.

It takes all of my willpower to shake myself out of the lust trance and focus. "That's just it. A part of you is a demon. I need to hear that if we're together, then it's just me. No other women." I realize me standing here naked and turned on, I'm not in the strongest bargaining position, but Zazel's comment about tigers not changing their stripes stuck in my head.

"I told you that I'm a lion, not a tiger," he says, leaning forward and capturing my hard nipple in his mouth. He lightly sucks and then gently uses his teeth.

"Are you sure you can't read my mind?" I moan.

He moves over to my other nipple and then looks up at me. "You're thinking, when is it going to be my turn to worship this sexy devil?"

I have a smart reply on the tip of my tongue, but then he kisses a trail of tingles down my stomach and I forget what I was going to say. He keeps going until he reaches his sigil, which is approximately one inch from where I desperately want him to be, namely between my legs.

He traces his sigil with his finger and my skin warms to the touch. "Mmmm," he says, leaning down to kiss the spot. "The best deal I've ever made. I like knowing my name is where no one will see it but me." He rubs his stubble back and forth over his brand, so agonizingly close to my center. "No one will touch this but me." He blows a hot breath on his sigil. "Tell me," he demands as he kisses it. "Tell me this is mine." He nips my skin with his teeth.

I jerk his head up by his hair so he'll look at me. "If you ever want to see or touch any of *this* again, then stop teasing me! And you *tell me* why I'm the only one who's naked?"

He makes a *tsk tsk* sound. "So impatient, my wanton witch." We lock eyes as he strokes his sigil with his warm fingers. He moves his head down, grazing my clit with his tongue. I moan, but he quickly moves his head away. "Are you on fire for me?" he asks, tracing the outline of his sigil. "Tell me." He strokes me again, alternating between touching his sigil and tasting my center. "Do you burn for me?" He sends a warm touch to my nipples, and my body temperature rises. I feel a bead of sweat run down between my breasts; I can't help it, I rub my thighs together.

He looks up at me with lust-laden eyes as he traces his sigil with his finger and then licks my center. Again. And again. And again.

I intend to punish him with my tongue as I jerk his head up and kiss him. That plan backfires as he takes over the kiss—dominating my mouth—and now I'm moaning and tingling all over, and I might orgasm standing right here before we make it any further.

I have to break apart from him and catch my breath. "Yes, you infuriating demon, I burn for you," I practically shout, my chest heaving.

He smiles wickedly as he makes his way back down my body. Finally, he's where I need him to be. A sigh escapes my lips as he rhythmically begins working my center with his tongue. I hold on to his head and grind my hips toward him, silently begging for more when he suddenly jerks his head away, grabs my clit with his fingers, and pinches.

"I said not to pinch me!" I half cry, half moan, pleasure mingling with pain.

He laughs, sucking my clit back into his mouth and entering me with a warm finger. He pumps and adds a second finger while he mercilessly works me with his tongue. He looks up at me, a naughty glint in his eyes as he adds a third finger, hitting my G-spot at just the right angle. My legs begin to shake, and it's difficult to remain standing, but he holds me firmly in place by my hips. "Damion," I cry, pulling his head closer as I explode in release.

My limbs give out as I crumple onto his lap. I'm still shaking as his clothes disappear. He scoops me up and lays me down, joining me on the bed. Kneeling in front of me, he grabs his cock and gives it a pump. Fine, so the Cambion does have a pretty big reason to be so cocky.

He nudges my legs apart and tosses one over his shoulder. Before I have time to worry if his huge cock is even going to fit, he slides in to the hilt. I orgasm again, or maybe it's a continuation of the first orgasm. Who the hell cares.

He groans but remains perfectly still inside me. I finally stop shaking as he begins to thrust in and out, so excruciatingly slow. In and out. In and out. In and out.

"So many ways I want to take you," he says, pulling out and then moving his cock back and forth between my slick folds. Back and forth. Toying with me. Torturing me.

"Dealer's choice—just take me already!"

"Your wish," he smiles, positioning both my legs over his shoulders as he slams into me, filling me completely. We both cry out. "So much better than I dreamed," he groans.

"I'm so glad that I could make your dreams come true, and I'm not even going to pinch you," I say primly, and he laughs. He begins to thrust faster and faster, and the pressure builds in me again, but suddenly he pulls out. In one smooth motion, he flips us and now I'm on top.

Finally, he's at my mercy. I grab his hard cock, slick with our combined desire. He wasn't lying—it is a double-fisted job. Wrapping both hands around his length, I give him a few pumps. I smile, leaning down and licking him from base to tip. "Ah, now it's your turn to tease," he says with a cocky smile.

I relax my jaw and take him in my mouth, inch by inch, as I gently massage his balls with my hand. A garbled noise escapes his lips, and I keep going, taking him in as deep as I can. We lock eyes as I slowly release him, scraping his head with my teeth. Suddenly the Cambion isn't so cocky.

I take my time exploring his body. Kissing his handsome face and those sexy dimples. Using my teeth against the stubble of his jaw. Lightly scratching the muscles of his chest. Gently biting his nipples. Licking the hard lines of his stomach and kissing his thighs. "Aubry, baby, please," he moans.

"You finally learned that polite little southern word," I say sweetly. I'm getting some perverse pleasure out of making this half-incubus beg, and I'm not sure what that says about me.

I work my way back up his body and mount him hard. Damion jerks up but I push him back down. Keeping my body perfectly still, I begin the rhythmic squeezing of his cock with my internal muscles. "Are you on fire for me?" I toss back at him. Remaining perfectly still, I squeeze down on his cock like a vise grip and don't let go. "Tell me."

"Fuck," he grits, his eyes rolling back in his head.

"Do you burn for me?" As I reach down and trace his sigil, his eyes begin to glow. I don't mean that in a lusty sort of way, I mean that his eyes literally begin to glow like they're backlit.

He flips us, pinning my arms over my head. "From the moment I saw you," he growls, his voice sounding more demonic than human. I should probably be scared, but I'm more turned on than anything, and again, I'm not sure what that says about me.

That delicious smell of his fills the room as he sets a punishing pace, demonstrating just what it means to be possessed by a demon. I wrap my legs around his waist, taking everything he's giving me, demanding more. It's not long before we both cry out in pleasure.

Damion wakes me with a nudge from behind. "Give me another taste," he whispers in my ear.

I smile, shifting my legs to grant him access. I've lost track of how many "tastes" he's had, not that I'm complaining. He kisses the back of my neck and spoons me close as he reaches around and palms my breast while he rocks inside of me. "I thought *you* were the one who was going to let me taste another flavor," I tease in a husky voice.

"Excellent point." He pulls out and positions me face down on the bed. A candle on my nightstand flickers to life as he slowly spreads my legs apart as far as they'll go. "How does my wanton witch like this flavor?" He rises on his knees behind me and brings me up to meet him, holding my legs apart as he takes me from behind, just as he promised.

I let my cries of pleasure answer for me. My body temperature rises, and I'm now tingling from head to toe. The demon doesn't play fair—sending a pulsating feeling to just the right internal spot. He picks up the pace, thrusting with such force that all I can do is grip the sheets for dear life. It's almost too much, but then he commands in that demonic tone, "Come for me, my possession," and damn if my body doesn't comply. I violently orgasm as he growls out his pleasure.

"Still *not* your possession," I manage after we disentangle.

"Keep telling yourself that," he laughs, wrapping his arms around me.

I wake the next morning equally exhausted, sore, and utterly blissed-out. I start to get up when Damion grabs me, tucking me in tightly against his body. Turning around, I rest my cheek on his warm chest. We drift back to sleep, but are soon awakened by the sound of a screeching blender.

"She doesn't turn that off in the next five seconds, I'm stealing her soul," Damion growls.

"Come on," I say, pulling him up and to the bathroom, saving my aunt. We take a nice, steamy shower. He's even better with a loofah in person, and that's all I'm going to say.

"Good morning, Vivian. Callie," Damion says as we emerge from my bedroom.

Grandma does a double take and whistles. "I knew a sexy demon matched that sexy voice."

"Morning, Damion," my aunt says. "Nice to officially meet you."

"Likewise," he says with a charming smile.

"Come on, Mama. We've got some errands to run."

"What errands?" Grandma demands.

Aunt Callie gives her a look and Grandma huffs. "I've waited all this time to finally meet Team Daubry and you expect me to leave just when things are gettin' good? And from the goings-on last night, it sounds like things are gettin' *real* good."

"Goodbye, Grandma," I say with heated cheeks.

"Fine, we're going. But we need to schedule a Team Daubry training session. You need a new strategy now that Damion's back in his body," Grandma calls over her shoulder as they walk out the door.

"You're delusional," I call after her.

"Why would I need a new strategy when last night's strategy worked so well? Especially when I…" He whispers the rest in my ear.

I have to cross my arms to hide my hard nipples. "Get out of here, already."

He smiles as he leans in and cups my face with both his hands. "Try not to get into too much trouble while I'm gone."

"I promise."

"I want that in writing." A scroll appears, but I shake my head no and play elbow him. "I'm taking the incantation bowl to my house, lest you work more intuitive magic and trap yourself inside it."

"Hey, my intuitive magic led to us getting together, and I didn't hear you complaining about that last night."

"No, you most certainly did *not* hear me complaining. No one could hear me say anything over your cries of pleasure."

"Be gone, demon," I announce dramatically, and he laughs.

"I'll be back Friday night to collect on my dinner." He kisses me possessively and vanishes.

"Show off," I mutter, placing a hand on my tingling lips.

I grab my new book of shadows. It's a journal designed for a tween, with a cartoonish picture of a vanilla ice cream cone with rainbow sprinkles. I laughed out loud when I saw it in a shop and knew it was meant for me. Julia was with me and threatened to hex me if I even thought about buying it. I then pointed out that she'd better be careful, she was sounding an awful lot like Amelia.

I think back to Todd's lazy witch accusation. It's true I didn't explore my craft, but it wasn't because I'm lazy. It's because deep down I'm scared. What's the point of being a powerful witch? Mama was, and she still died and left me anyway.

It's time to throw some magical sprinkles onto my practice. I pen the dedication in my book of shadows and gather my supplies.

I cast my circle and charge my purple vigil candle, writing with a permanent marker on the glass *I step into my power.* I light the candle and clear my mind as I gaze at the flame and chant:

> Magic, I'm sorry I've been afraid of you.
> I release the fear, let's see what we can do.
> I claim my birthright and my power.
> And so it be this very hour.

TODD'S RECIPE FOR
A LAZY WITCH

3 ounces of good bourbon
(don't even attempt to make one of my
cocktails unless you use good bourbon)

1 tablespoon of brown sugar simple syrup

2 dashes orange bitters

candied orange slice

candied bacon strip for garnish

cocktail cherry for garnish
(the cherry should be a deep burgundy red, not
one of those bright red abominations)

Add the bourbon, brown sugar simple syrup, and orange bitters
in a shaker. Shake well and strain into a rock glass with three ice
cubes. Add the cherry, candied orange slice, and candied bacon
for garnish and serve. Await your praise.

THE END

A SNEAK PEAK OF OBSESSION
A MEMPHIS MAGIC NOVEL
Copyright © 2022 Andrea Hagan

I plug in the stringed twinkle lights and place a candle in the center of the patio table on this crisp evening. My aunt is at a meditation retreat, and my busybody grandma is in Tunica, so a certain demon and I will have the apartment to ourselves.

Per my contractual obligations, I've cooked a steak, medium. I even used a meat thermometer to make sure I got the temperature just right. I've baked two russet potatoes and have portioned out butter and sour cream in small condiment bowls. I chose to go with a light salad with a lemon herb vinaigrette, the herbs I cut from Grandma's garden. I added tarragon for its calming properties, because for whatever reason, I'm a little nervous about my date. Silly, I know, considering how intimately we already know each other. The French apple tart is cooling on the counter, and the vanilla ice cream is in the freezer.

I set the prepared plates down as Damion Blackmon materializes. I knew he would teleport, but his arrival still startles me. He's a beautiful creature, there's no two ways about it. He's six feet two with blond curly hair, a chiseled jawline, gorgeous dimples, and the most unusual shade of blue eyes I've ever seen. He's wearing a navy suit with a light blue shirt and dark blue tie that makes his aquamarine-colored eyes stand out even more. We stay where we are, smiling at each other.

The trance is broken when he floats a bottle of red wine over to the table. "I didn't know you could do Gabe's little levitation trick." Gabe Jennings is Damion's best friend and law partner who worked on our case. Our case being that a certain Cambion possessed me and wouldn't leave.

A flame appears and dances in Damion's right hand, and he flicks it in the direction of the table and lights the candle. "Or that fire trick," I say with mouth agape.

"I can't let all of my tricks out of the bag at one time." He winks at me. "You look beautiful," he says as he closes the gap between us and kisses me. My lips tingle when he pulls back.

"I had my marching orders," I mean to say tartly, but it comes out breathy. I'm wearing a new red wrap dress. The neckline is a bit daring, but vanilla ice cream with rainbow sprinkles I told myself when I bought it. Tall wedge sandals show off my new pedicure of red polish, and of course I'm wearing my bloodstone bracelet. "And you look great."

"Of course I look great. When don't I look great?"

"Ugh. Are all Cambions this vain?" He does look great. Sin on a stick as Grandma likes to say.

"I don't know all Cambions, so I can't answer that." His naughty smile makes me think of all the naughty things we did three days ago, and I try not to shiver. Okay, so I haven't actually been able to stop thinking about all the naughty things we did three days ago. That was after we finally figured out the magical loophole and were able to exorcise him.

"Hush and let's eat."

We sit down, and he opens the wine and pours us each a glass. I take a sip as he leans back in his chair and loosens his tie. "I didn't have a chance to grab lunch today, so I'm starved. This is delicious," he tells me between bites of steak.

I salt my baked potato and pass him the shaker. "How you've survived this long without me taking care of you is a mystery." He smiles at me throwing his words back at him. We play fuss back and forth and just enjoy being in each other's company as we finish dinner.

"Be right back." I walk downstairs and cut a small piece of the French apple tart and place a scoop of vanilla ice cream in the center. I grab two spoons and walk back upstairs.

I set the bowl in front of him with the flourish of my hand when he surprises me by grabbing me and pulling me to his lap. "Let me have just a little taste," he whispers in my ear. I try not to tingle at his words as I grab a spoon and scoop up an equal portion of tart and ice cream and feed him a bite.

"This fulfills my end of the bargain. You're not getting my soul." I want that out there on the record. And yes, there is a record keeper named Metratron, and he keeps a jar on his desk full of creepy eyeballs, but I see I'm getting off track, pun intended. The important thing here is that I signed a contract with Damion— he's not stealing my soul in exchange for this little date. A win/win for me, if I do say so myself.

"Not today," he says, nuzzling my neck.

"Wait a second!" He laughs as he picks up the spoon and takes another bite. "Damion, I mean it." He scoops up a bite and feeds it to me, watching my mouth intently.

"And I mean it," he retorts, kissing me sweetly. Well, it starts out sweet, but quickly evolves into tongue and teeth, and now I'm finding it hard to catch my breath.

He stands me up and looks me over with glowing eyes as that delicious scent of his envelopes me. Damion smells divine, but when he's turning on the incubus charm, it's really not fair. I will my thighs to stay still, as I desperately need to rub them together. "I love the dress. I especially love this part," he purrs, as he reaches for the bow on the side that ties the wrap in place. He slowly tugs on the ends, and my dress parts like a curtain.

And then he disappears.

ABOUT THE AUTHOR

Andrea Hagan has an accounting degree and a law degree, but she is neither an energy vampire nor a Cambion (although if she were, it would make for a much more interesting bio). She lives in the Southern United States with her husband and three children. Follow Andrea in a non-cultish way on Instagram @ andreahagan.author and on Facebook @Andrea Hagan Author. Go to andreahaganauthor.com and sign up for her newsletter for all things Memphis Magic!

ACKNOWLEDGEMENTS

So many wonderful people in my life have helped me turn this dream into a reality. Thanks to my first beta readers—my husband and my sister—and to all my awesome beta and ARC readers. Thanks to the ladies at Cover2Cover who held my hand the entire way, and to my amazing editors. Thanks to all the rockstar bookstagrammers who have helped spread the word about Memphis Magic.

And thank you for reading this book. I hope you become possessed with these characters like I have! Not literally—you know what I mean.

Made in the USA
Monee, IL
10 June 2022

97830213R00175